Fishing Hole

Hillary DeVisser

To Hunter,
XOXO –
Hillary DeVisser

hillarydevisser@gmail.com

ACKNOWLEDGMENTS

∞

Thank you to my husband and children for their encouragement to follow my heart and finally write this book. A special thanks goes out to my mother and closest friends for listening to me moan and groan about wanting to write a book without grabbing and shaking me, screaming, "Just shut up and do it already!"

A big thank you my dear friends who agreed to assist with reading and editing. Julie Natzke, Melody Ossi, and Hayley Marks, thank you for the editing help. Angie Clifton and Amy Gibbs, thank you for taking time to be critical readers for me.

One

Jesse bounced down the highway in her red Chevy Suburban, wondering just what the hell she had done. Alternating between tears and utter silence, she looked around her SUV at the faces of her sleeping sons. Behind the two in the backseat, the mound of their belongings was shoved roughly into the cargo area, partially blocking her view to the U-Haul behind her vehicle. Self-doubt had her aching to pull over and sit still for a minute. For a second, she even considered heading back in the opposite direction on the highway, backtracking the way she came. Just as she thought her mind would explode from the pressure, the song on the radio changed. Spanish Pipedream by The Avett Brothers played through her stereo, loudly enough to be heard, but not loud enough to wake her sons. As soon as the song registered, interrupting her blur of indecision, Jesse couldn't hold it in, she laughed at the irony.

She remembered back a few years when the eclectic song was released. Something about the old time vibe resonated with her, lifting her up from her doldrums if even for a few minutes, where she could let go and sing out along with the song. When it ended, she'd go back to reality. For her, the song was a little vacation, an escape of sorts. It was in that same year she decided that her marriage to Drake just wasn't going to work. It had been failing for a long while, but it was finally at the point where she couldn't prolong her decision. At that time, her boys were eight, ten, and twelve years old and quickly growing to be more and more like their dad. Jesse knew she couldn't allow that level of pomposity and hatefulness to multiply like fleas in a dirty rug. Not in her house.

It took some time for Jesse to accept her decision and put into place a plan that would allow her to provide for her boys once the divorce was final. She somehow pushed harder at work to get a promotion, and the accompanying raise that she would need to make it on her own salary. That kind of salary leap required her to gain a new certification in her field as a project manager, which took time, money and a lot more effort than she had imagined. She and Drake had dated and married young while in college. *Stupid kids*, she thought as she shook her head at the memory. Most people looked back on college as a string of wild parties, crazy experiences and overseas study programs. Jesse remembered those years as an incredible challenge, having married and had her first son the summer before her senior year. Thankfully, Michael had been a dream of a baby. He had been a good sleeper and the college had operated an on campus daycare program for students. That had been the only way she had managed to keep up with her classes and graduate during that last hectic year. Luckily for her, the late 90's hadn't been a time of great fashion. Jesse had fit right in with her oversized sweatshirts, aside the patchouli oil and flannel draped members of her business classes. She and Drake had been deeply in love at that time and Michael had been such a joy that Jesse didn't really grasp how hard that time had really been until long after. Jesse supposed that's just how things are sometimes. You keep your head down, muscle through it and feel the fallout later.

As hard as it was, as a mother of three, and being many years past college, Jesse had worked her way through the Project Management Professional program and had received her certificate and eventually, the corresponding pay raise. To get through the rigorous program, endure an unhappy marriage and manage her home, Jesse had grown a thicker layer of skin. She tackled it all and guided her boys, both tenderly and forcefully, through that cruel and crucial transition from little boys to preteen and teens. She wasn't going to allow Drake's meanness and horse-assery in general to take root and change her boys into anything but the wonderful men they could one day be.

Jesse's eyes wandered over the scenery, growing more hilly and green as the miles passed by, her mind drifted back to the day she had told Drake it was over. She had planned this talk on a night the boys all had basketball practice after school. With a feeling of dread in her stomach, she watched the clock, waiting for him to come home from work. Jesse had left the office a few hours early and fussed over her appearance. She made certain the house was immaculate, innately suspecting that Drake would explode, pointing out her flaws and her inability to keep a good house. She thought it better to be prepared.

When Drake hit the door, she greeted him as warmly as she could stomach. She gave him time to pour that ever-present glass of Scotch and settle into his chair. As he reached for the remote she took a deep breath and sat on the couch, announcing to him she needed to talk. Although this had been one of the most important conversations of her life, she couldn't remember the details of what she said. Still to this day, now that most of the fear had dissipated, she still couldn't recall how she launched into that conversation. What she did clearly remember was that, instead of the explosion she had prepared for, she found Drake to be relieved. He admitted that the marriage was dead, and had been for years. Without any of the expected bitterness, rage or ugliness she had braced herself against, Jesse found the experience eerily amicable. In preparation for the conversation and the split, she had gathered their financial records, hoping that once Drake calmed, they could work through the details of how to split assets, pay off remaining bills, and the part of the talk she dreaded most, discussing how much he would pay to help with his part of the kids' expenses. Since she wasn't greeted with the firestorm she had expected, they went ahead and mechanically worked through a first draft of what was to happen. As it was the end of the school year, they decided to tell the boys together the Saturday following the last day of school. No sense adding more stress than necessary to their little hearts. The boys were all so excited to finish school, Jesse felt a little like an executioner lurking in the shadows. She knew it had to be done, the boys deserved to be raised in a low-drama home. To keep a sense of normalcy in place, she and the boys would stay in the home until she made other plans, Drake would get an apartment.

Jesse was grateful the conversation had gone easily, but she wasn't a fool. She knew there must have been a reason Drake accepted her request for a divorce so well. It wasn't long after Drake moved out that she learned about the affair he had been having. Strangely, she couldn't even care enough to get worked up about it. After all, she had expected he was up to something. Her mom had always said, "If they aren't getting it at home, they're getting it somewhere!" Once again, her mom was right. Jesse and Drake hadn't been intimate in around two years, not by boycott or even effort. It just didn't happen. She couldn't stand for him to touch her, so it was with blessed relief that he never even tried. Jesse drew in a deep breath and let it go, trying to release the past along with that big sigh.

As for now, her SUV was packed to the brim along with the U-Haul that floated behind her Suburban. She was headed back to her hometown, refusing to go with her tail between her legs. Divorced? Yes. Defeated? No. Jesse looked again at her boys, piled in together, all gawky arms and legs, mouths slightly parted in sleep. They were her life. They would be her life until she was willing to share it. At that, she thought suddenly of Levi. When the dust had settled and she had finalized the move date, she had called her lifelong friend to see if he could help her with moving the furniture into her new house.

Levi Murray was a memory to smile over, she thought as she looked out at the passing soybean and corn fields. Once upon a time, Levi had been much more than a friend. He knew her inside and out. They had been childhood friends, but in high school, they had grown closer. He had taken her to her first homecoming dance, and a few months later, he had taken her virginity. Jesse had loved him, body and soul, back then. She still did, but things were different now. Now she felt battered and exhausted from the divorce and the emotional hardship of helping her boys adjust to this new reality. Levi had put a deep stamp on her heart, being her first true love. After their relationship had ended, she had gone her way, he had gone his. Now here they were, thrown back together in their little hometown. Thankfully, Levi had made arrangements for some friends of theirs to be at her newly purchased house, ready to help unload their belongings.

Jesse couldn't help but smile, thinking how good it would feel to see his face once she rolled into town. For her, he was a safe harbor. Though she hated the circumstances that had forced him to be alone, she was awfully glad he was around. Her smile grew when she thought about the new furniture being delivered right around the time she was scheduled to arrive. She was going to be damned if she'd sleep another night in the same bed she shared with Drake. *New house, new start,* she had thought as she shopped online for a new living room, dining room and bedroom set. The cost had been outrageous, but she was more than willing to go to the expense. She had worked really hard for her new salary and couldn't wait to set up her new home.

Jesse pulled into town, a flood of memories washing over her. She had been away from her hometown since she graduated high school and went away to college, except for visits home during weekends and holidays. Coasting through familiar streets, she felt like a kid again. It seemed just like yesterday that she was rolling through stop signs in her first car. Man, that car had been old when she got it, but she had been thrilled. It was a red little number with T-tops, faux black leather seats and a stick shift. She thought back to sitting in the driveway of her house, logging miles in her driveway with her best friend Megan by her side. She had practiced backing up and going forward, hitting the sweet spot with her gas and clutch with her Billy Joel tape blaring.

She slowed down and made the turn at her old high school, and a few doors down, she saw her house. When she stopped the SUV and cut the engine, her boys woke up, stretching and yawning loudly. Even at their scattered ages, everything they did was loud. She turned and looked at their faces, seeing not the pimply, long limbed, wild haired messes that they were, but instead, as little boys again for a fleeting second.

"We're home," she said, smiling at their uncertain faces.

Michael was the first to unfold himself from the Suburban. He walked to her side of the vehicle as she gathered her purse from the backseat. He put his hand over hers through the window and said, "This is nicer than I thought it was going to be, Mom."

At 15, he was the undeniable leader of the pack, and the one holding the most influence over how Luke, 13, and Ryan, 11, would react to their new home. She could have grabbed and kissed his face over his positive reaction, but she had learned by this time that big displays of mushy emotion were the quickest buzz kills for teenage boys. Instead, she gave him a big smile.

“Thanks, babe. I can’t wait for you boys to get inside. Let’s go take a look.” She unbuckled her seatbelt and stepped out of the Suburban, thankful that Levi and his friends hadn’t arrived yet. She had been nervous driving home, and probably went a little faster than she had expected, getting there a little early. The younger boys got out of their seats and stepped out into the driveway, stretching from their nap. How she envied their ability to sleep anywhere. She had been so plagued by anxiety for the last few years, she had a terrible time sleeping. Hopefully, that was all about to change.

She climbed the front steps and unlocked the front door, noting that the porch light was missing a light bulb. That would be first on her to-do list. She stepped aside and watched her boys walk into their new home. The house was an old one, built in 1923. It was a light gray color, two stories, and a wide front porch with a swing and room for a few chairs. Though the front was appealing, Jesse’s favorite part of the property was the backyard. It was large and fenced, with raised planting beds in a prime spot, perfect for her gardening addiction. Though her boys were bigger and getting past the point of playing for hours outside, she liked the privacy afforded by the fence. Thankfully, there was a basketball goal already up on the garage in back and room to throw baseballs and kick soccer balls. She thought for a minute with pride how her boys had inherited her athletic abilities rather than their father's lack thereof.

The boys were roaming through the downstairs, quickly racing through the rooms before thumping up the stairs. Jesse gave them a little distance so they could take it all in. Of the three of them, Ryan, the baby, had taken the separation the hardest. He didn't understand the divorce was between her and Drake, not Drake and the boys. She knew he felt abandoned by the change, and she was doing her best to comfort him. Jesse did her best to communicate that she and Drake had decided to do what was best for their family as a whole, and for them, it was best to not be married any longer. More than anything, she wanted to avoid Ryan drawing into himself and pulling away from her over this. He had been her cuddle-bug from day one, and she couldn't bear to lose that part of their relationship.

Michael, as the oldest, had accepted the change relatively easily. Many of his friends had already been through divorce, and over the years, Jesse had talked with him about how different families made it work; some easily, some not so easily. Her middle son, Luke, had been pretty quiet about the separation and divorce. Luke was her deep thinker and feeler. He required time to process change. That had been one of the main reasons Jesse had given him a few weeks to acclimate to Drake not living at home before discussing the move. Surprisingly, their house had sold within one week of listing. Jesse had taken a day off work to drive down to where they would be moving and put an offer down on her house within the same day. By the grace of God alone, she had stumbled across their new home. She loved everything about the house, from the high ceilings, to the original woodwork throughout. It was going to be costly to heat and cool with those high ceilings, but Jesse had always been drawn to this style of house. It was located by the high school, which sparked a hot debate about whether or not Michael would be getting a car to drive around town when he turned sixteen. Being a few doors down from the school, with no job to pay for gas, stacked the cards heavily in Jesse's 'No Car' favor. Michael wasn't thrilled, but she knew he'd adjust. And, she liked the idea of giving him more time, experience and hopefully maturity before turning him loose in a car.

The discussion of who got which bedroom had escalated from a gentle roar to a booming one, so Jesse ran up the stairs to help officiate. "But it's not fair! He always gets his way because he's the oldest! I didn't ask to be the middle kid and Ryan didn't ask to be the baby. It's not fair, Mom!" Not being new at wrangling the children, Jesse had the foresight to measure the rooms on her trip to buy the house. She talked the boys through how in old houses the bedrooms were generally smaller, and they were all roughly the same size. After a small battle, they had each conceded to their own rooms, and Jesse walked back downstairs as the front door flew open. Levi had arrived.

Two

As Levi stepped into the living room, Jesse practically ran into his arms.

"Levi, I'm so happy to see you!" she said, holding him tightly. "It's been such a long time," she said, pulling away but keeping her hands on his shoulders. Her eyes betrayed the horror she felt at her choice of words. Too late, she remembered that the last time she saw Levi was at his wife's funeral. She'd always shown every emotion on her face, so Levi had no trouble realizing what she was thinking. He gave her a small grin, put his hands on hers and gave her a quick squeeze.

"Hey, it's okay. I know what you meant," he said as he stepped back from her. "The place is nice, Jesse. It'll be just right for you guys."

At the sound of a male voice, the boys came running down the stairs to see what was going on. They filed to Jesse's side in an almost comical display of male guardianship.

"Hi, boys," Levi said as he extended his hand, first to the oldest son, "I'm Levi." They all seemed to thaw at the introduction, having heard their mother mention that her old friend was going to help them move. If anything, it was sheer relief that they wouldn't have to carry all the furniture and boxes while their mom gave the orders.

"The other guys are right behind me, Jess. Hank, Tony and Cole should be able to help most of the day."

Jesse visibly relaxed as the words left his lips. She loved her boys dearly, but didn't necessarily trust them to move all their things with less than a 20% breakage rate.

"Thanks so much for coordinating help, Levi," she said, looking over at the boys who had moved to the porch to admire Levi's truck. "They were really dreading today. This will go by in a flash with the guys helping out," she said, digging in her pocket for her phone. "I'll go ahead and call in an order for pizza; the very least I can do is feed you all," she said, turning to walk into the kitchen to grab a bottle of water for Levi.

He looked around as he answered, "That would be great. We'll do as much as we can to help you get this done today. I have to cut out at five o'clock; Mom and Dad have the kids and they have dinner plans tonight." Jesse turned in time to see

Levi smile and roll his eyes. His parents had a long standing dinner date every Saturday at six on the dot. Even after a lifetime of marriage, Stanley and Myrtle were one of the most ridiculously in love couples on the planet. Now in their seventies, their Saturday night dinner out was as much a part of their schedules as coffee together in the mornings.

The group filed out into the driveway as Hank and Tony pulled up together. Cole arrived right behind them, parking his motorcycle beside Hank's truck. Slaps on the back, handshakes with the boys, and hugs from Jesse were distributed as the gang was introduced. Of the men, all but Cole had been friends of Jesse's since she was a little girl. Cole had moved into town in high school and had fit like a missing piece to their group's puzzle right from the start. She hadn't seen the three of them in years and was beyond thankful that they had offered to help. That was just one more reason it was good to be home, people took care of each other. They had just opened up the U-Haul when Jesse's parents drove up.

"You made it!" her mom crowed as she moved quickly across the yard to hug Jesse and kiss the boys. As usual, Eadie was dressed in bright colors with her short blond hair styled beautifully. Wherever she went, she did it with flash and fun. Eadie had been broken hearted over her daughter's marital struggles; but in reality, she couldn't have been happier to have Jesse and the boys home. Jesse was thankful for the warm reception and knew her mother had never really taken to Drake. Eadie wasn't one to push her views on others, but she certainly didn't hold back if asked her honest opinion. Jesse supposed she had been afraid to ask Eadie's true opinion of Drake during the years she had tried to make it work, and she certainly hadn't asked once she had decided to end the marriage. She wanted to be able to say it was on her own terms. Part of her knew that what she hadn't wanted to learn Eadie never liked him and just never told Jesse. In a state of emotional upheaval, it's too easy to lay blame at someone else's feet. Jesse knew exactly who was to blame for the failure of her marriage. Drake. Cold, insensitive, and detached, he alone was the reason she had some cross between a family and high school reunion assembled on her front lawn.

Eadie had handled the announcement of Jesse's plans to divorce Drake with her usual grace, support, encouragement and sympathy. She and Walt had been married for what seemed like eons, but she knew Jesse had been so unhappy. Eadie's mantra in life had been "You only live once" for as long as Jesse could remember. Though she liked to think of herself as a fully independent woman, she couldn't remember a time in her adult life when her mother's hug had felt better. Now she really felt like she was home. Eadie went first to the boys, then fluttered through the group of men dispensing hugs to each of them and fussing over tidbits of gossip about their families. Walt, followed in her wake, and quietly said his hellos. He was, of course, more businesslike about the matter. He hugged Jesse and the boys, nodded to the men and then went to supervise the unloading of the U-Haul. Walt was a quiet man, content to be a spectator in the action since there were so many younger men about to do the heavy lifting. He had suffered a back injury years earlier that plagued him even still. Stern demeanor aside, he was an incredibly pleasant person, very calm and wise.

Jesse stood in the yard as her parents went to look through the house. She watched her sons and the men carrying furniture and boxes, and for a minute she allowed all the emotions she was trying to keep at bay rush over her. She turned her back to the guys and stared down the street at the face of the high school. She took in the big elm trees flanking the sidewalks of the brick street, and felt thankful to have trusted her gut on the house she had chosen for her family. Jesse was ready to put aside the sadness that her sixteen year marriage had failed, and was very nearly overwhelmed by thankfulness that Levi and her old friends had jumped in to help her move. She praised God that her boys were with her, healthy and safe, and felt a surge of relief to be back in her little town. Here she felt the security that only being home could bring.

Levi came around the back of the house to find Jesse standing in the front yard facing the school, looking peaceful and lost at the same time. The summer sun was shining down on her, casting a long shadow across the grass. He couldn't help but think that Jesse was every bit as beautiful as she had been years ago. She was tall and strong, maybe just a little softer than in her teens. Her long dark hair was piled into a ponytail high on her head; that much hadn't changed. That's how he pictured her in his memories over the years, something he had done often. Especially since she had called to say she was moving back home.

Thinking back on the good old days was an easy mental escape from the daily chaos of life. He and Jesse had been an item back in high school. When he and his buddies reminisced over beers about the old times, his memory of her was usually a little bittersweet. Jesse had been right in the middle of it all, right beside him. She had been as comfortable in a gaggle of girls cheering at the football games as she had been with him and his friends going mudding in the hills, or drinking beer stolen out of their dads' garage refrigerators around the camp fires.

When he went fishing, even now, he couldn't help but be overwhelmed by his memories of her. His grandpa had one of the best fishing holes in the area, way out in the boonies. Back in high school, he and Jesse used to log countless hours there, sometimes even fishing. Most of the time they made out on a blanket in the tall grass. Back then, he felt ten feet tall and immortal.

Now, Levi felt a little beaten down by life. Raising the twins was harder than he imagined. When Emma passed two years ago, he thought his world was endin. They didn't have the fire in their relationship that he and Jesse had shared, but he accounted that to maturity and hormones. His life with Emma had been comfortable, content and happy. They had been friends, almost like roommates or maybe better said, teammates after the twins had been born. The first year had been about simply surviving the twin experience, learning how to parent two tiny people at once. After that, the love making had come less frequently, but they were so exhausted they didn't really mind. They had companionship and kindness and she had been a terrific mother. The kids were six when Emma died in the car accident, and he had done his very best to be both mommy and daddy to them ever since, but he knew it wasn't the same. Life was hard, but he tried to make the most of it.

Learning Jesse was moving back home had been almost like a gift. Since he had gotten her call, he felt almost hopeful. He knew by the circles under her eyes that she was feeling a little beaten down as well, and he didn't want to rush her. He'd be her friend and give her the space she probably needed. Maybe something would come of it when she was ready. It was awfully hard not to walk over to her soaking in the sun and fold her into his arms. When she ran down the stairs and grabbed him earlier, he felt a soul-deep, happy feeling that he hadn't felt in quite some time.

Levi heard the voices of the kids and other guys coming up behind him so he made his way back to the U-Haul for more boxes. My God, three boys required a lot of stuff. Out of the corner of his eye he saw Jesse jolt back to life from her thoughts as she heard everyone approach. She grabbed a pile out of the back of her Suburban and made her way back up the stairs. It was going to be a big job making this house a comfortable home, but he had no doubt she could do it.

It took most of the day to get the U-Haul unloaded, but Levi and Cole were able to get it returned by 5:00, just in time for Levi to say his goodbyes. He and Cole pulled back into the driveway as Eadie and Walt were driving away, Walt, austere as always, Eadie waving like a madwoman. Her joy at having her daughter home again was palpable. Cole waved to Jesse from the driveway and pulled off on his motorcycle, roaring into the late afternoon light.

"He's still not much of a talker, is he?" Jesse said, wiping her hands off on a dishtowel as she crossed to Levi. He smiled back in the direction Cole had ridden and shook his head.

"Not really, but he's a good guy," Levi said. "Thank God he's strong as an ox. Did you see him nearly lift your dresser all by himself when the furniture truck got here?" he said, his laugh lighting up his face with the exception of his tired eyes.

"True!" she said. "That nearly scared me to death. I bet he'll feel that one later," Jesse said, reaching up to Levi's face. "You've got a little something right here," she said, dabbing at his temple with her towel. "Yeesh, I think it was a cobweb" she said, a shudder visible on her tired frame.

"Yuck, thanks for saving me," he said, looking back at the house. "Kids settling in?" he asked, enjoying the view as he took in her disheveled appearance. Her ponytail was off center, there was a smear of dust along her cheekbone and a rip in the knee of the jeans she'd been wearing all day.

Jesse sighed, the disguise of calmness and control nearly ready to crack. "I think they're all squared away. Mom brought some lasagna and salad over, so between that and all the pizza I ordered, we ought to at least survive until morning. It's appalling how much those three can eat," she said, grinning up at Levi. "Thanks again for the help. Hank and Tony got the last of the boxes carried up and left about ten minutes ago. I'm about half an hour from an Epsom salt bath and beer as big as my head. Care to join me?" she said, flushing red as a beet at his bark of laughter. "For the beer!" she said unnecessarily, but much to his enjoyment.

"Nah, I think I'll pass on the bath - I mean the beer," he said, raising a finger to wipe at the smudge of dust on her cheek. "You'd better go see about that bath though Jess. You're a hot mess," he said, giving her an affirmative nod.

"Oh God, I can't even imagine," she said, no hint of true dismay to be found. She always seemed so comfortable in her own skin, he thought. He was glad that hadn't changed a bit.

"I've got to go pick up the kids so Mom and Dad can go on their hot date," he said, looking down at his watch.

"Right! Levi, thank you so much. I mean it," she said, her hand reaching out to his forearm. He put his fingers on her hand for the briefest of seconds.

"Anything for you, Jess. Glad you're back home," he said, turning towards his truck. She watched him from the porch as he backed up and drove away. For a minute she just stood there on the porch, feeling slightly amazed that she had managed to pull it off. She had brought her boys home, and gotten free from her mess of a marriage. Jesse was starting to feel as if she had some control back in her life. It was a very good feeling.

Three

"Mom, there's nothing to eat in the house!" Ryan bellowed with utter dismay as Jesse made yet another trip down the stairs. They had been living on mostly left over lasagna and take-out during the first few days they had been in the house, and they were all ready for some home cooked meals.

She made her way to the foot of the stairs and yelled out, "Hey kids, meet in the living room." Raising boys didn't jive with being meek and mild. Sometimes she felt she was as noisy as the rest of them. The boys filed into the living room.

"Okay, I'm heading to the store. What do you want to eat this week?"

Funny how everyone was hungry, but nobody, when put on the spot, could name what it was they wanted her to get at the store. Jesse took down what little bones they would throw at her; meatloaf, spaghetti, hamburgers, cereal, oatmeal, lunch meat for sandwiches, and ran to the mirror for a quick check before heading out the door.

"You're all down to one or two boxes in your bedrooms. I want them all unpacked and put away by the time I'm back. Okay, guys?"

Each muttered various assents and trudged back up the stairs to their bedrooms.

The past year hadn't been easy. Jesse had been maxed out with work and her certification course, and she had been especially strict with the boys. She knew in her heart she'd be going it alone as soon as she could, so she had to be certain she was fair but consistent with them. That had been her approach to discipline with them during their entire raising. She knew she would have to be able to get them to follow directions without much trouble, not that Drake had been much help. He had been constantly away from home working late hours, and as it turned out, spending time with his piece on the side. Jesse rolled her eyes as she pulled out of the driveway, not even allowing herself to wonder how many of the late nights working were actually spent with the whore. None of it mattered now. Maybe the whore even made the divorce process easier. Drake was apparently quite content and ready to end things. Jesse wondered briefly if she should send the woman a thank you note. A snort of laughter passed through her lips as she waited patiently at one of the handful of stop lights the town possessed.

The change of pace was certainly a welcome one. Things moved slower down here. People were more of the 'handshake agreement' variety rather than the impersonal exchanges so common in the city. There, she could spend an entire day running errands and not see anyone she knew. Now that she was back home, she made sure she at least checked the mirror before heading out the door. She felt someone watching her and sure enough, she looked up from untangling her shopping cart from the others right into Levi's smiling eyes.

"Hey Jesse. Can I help you with that?" he reached across her and yanked the cart free and held it out for her.

"Thanks. The boys are ready to riot, I have to get some food in the house. They want some of mama's cooking, not fast food. I never thought they'd burn out on nuggets and burgers, but they're ready for a change." She smiled up at him and they walked into the store together. "This is kind of a weird time to shop, but look how wonderfully quiet it is in here!"

"Agreed. Hannah and James are with Mom and Dad for the morning. I do all my running on Monday mornings during the summer and just go in a little late to work. That way I can spend the weekends with them without interruption. So far it's working out well for us."

"It must help to be the boss. You can fill out your own dance card, huh?" she winked at him, then wondered where that came from. Since when had she winked at anyone in the last decade? *Old habits*, she guessed. Levi owned a body shop and towing company and had a staff of around ten men working for him. She noted his quick pace through the store, then realized the control freak in him probably hated not being at work, making sure everything was clipping along just how he liked it. She couldn't help but think of him having to transition from being a partner in a wonderful marriage, to being solely responsible for managing all the daily tasks of raising kids. As they paused in front of the produce section, Jesse drew a breath, then asked the question she had been afraid to ask for two years.

"Levi, how are the kids doing with the adjustment? My heart breaks for you every time I think about it."

Levi looked off to the side for a minute while he gathered his thoughts.

"Last year was brutal. For all of us. This year has been better. Holidays rip my guts out, but that's to be expected. The kids started sleeping better this year, thank God."

Jesse reached out and squeezed his arm, wishing she could grab and hug him. In a town like theirs, people were always watching and chomping at the bit for some good gossip. He halfheartedly smiled down at her, then continued down the aisle. He carried a shopping basket, which to her was a funny sight. Such a big, strong man in work boots and jeans carrying a prissy little basket. Levi was so at ease with himself, he probably didn't think a thing about it. They gathered their items and he stood behind her in the checkout line as they continued to talk. Conversation with him was still so very comfortable and easy.

"Levi, would you like to come to dinner this week? Do the kids like hamburgers? We could have a little BBQ, introduce the kids and just visit for a little bit?" she watched him closely, wondering if the invitation would cross any lines. His kids had been through so much, and Levi had worked like a dog for her during the move. It would feel good to do a little meal for a thank you. As a Cancer sign, mother of the zodiac, Jesse liked to show her love by cooking. Entertaining at her home and filling the bellies of people she cared about was her own personal heaven. She wished that Drake would've enjoyed having people over. They had lived in a beautiful home, perfect for entertaining, yet he always preferred for them to dine as a family in a restaurant, rather than having friends over. Jesse smiled to herself as she realized she didn't have to cater to his mood swings and preferences any longer. This was her house now; she could entertain if she damn well pleased.

"I think they'd love it. What day works best for you?" he asked as he handed his money to the cashier. They made their plans for Thursday at five. That way the kids would have time to warm up to each other. At least, Ryan would be excited to have company. Even though the twins were eight to his eleven, he was still easy going and liked having other kids around. Thankfully, the neighborhood had several families with children. Jesse envisioned lots of bike riding and playing in the tree-lined street once the kids were acclimated a little more.

Levi helped Jesse load her groceries into the Suburban and made a crack about it being a good thing she drove such a big vehicle, otherwise she'd never be able to fit the groceries inside. They laughed over how much food growing boys ate, and my God, the milk. She bought four gallons every week and by the next Saturday morning she was down to the bottom of her last gallon.

Jesse drove home excited about planning the little BBQ on Thursday and made a mental list of the things she'd need to do before then. There were Texas potatoes that could be made in advance, as well as a strawberry pie or two, as long as she hid them from her boys in the meantime. She would have to circle back to the store later in the week to grab ice cream. The boys had a radar detector for ice cream; it would never last if she brought it in the house before Thursday.

Four

Jesse was truly thankful that she had hoarded her vacation time throughout the year in preparation for the move. She had taken three weeks off from work and had enjoyed the mental break of not being tied to her email and phone over that time. Her boss was aware of her divorce and long distance move, and had been very accommodating in her request to take off such a large amount of time. He assisted her in transitioning her existing projects to the other project managers, and promised not to assign her anything new until her first week back. That gave her the freedom to completely ignore her work email inbox and focus on setting up a home. She couldn't remember the last time she had three full weeks with her boys.

Drake had agreed to give her a while to settle in before they started the visitation schedule. He would get the boys for the weekend every two weeks. Drake would pick them up on Fridays;

Jesse would pick them up on Sundays. Jesse had been so excited that he didn't fight for more time, she didn't mind picking them up on Sundays even though she would bet there would be more times than not that they hadn't finished their homework like they were supposed to. She couldn't imagine what she was going to do with herself during the span of Friday evening through Sunday evening without the boys, but this was the price she'd have to pay for escaping the marriage. She was secretly thrilled the boys wouldn't be with Drake more, leaving the bulk of their raising to her. That was how she preferred it.

Of all her boys, she had been most worried about how Michael would fight the move. Being fifteen, she had expected more resistance from him about moving to a new school for his sophomore year. Ever cunning, Michael had researched the class sizes of the new school and decided he'd have a better chance of starting in football and basketball in a smaller school. The bigger school he had attended in the city allowed him to get lost in the shuffle, competing against such a large pool of kids. He was now getting ready to turn sixteen, which gave him an enormous ego. Now, with a chance of getting more playing time, he was going to be nearly unbearable. Jesse smiled as she thought about how Michael had jumped right into small town life, riding his bike down to the football field to participate in the unofficial practices. From the stories around the dinner table, there was a lot of running, puking, passing, and formation practicing going on. He usually came home around noon absolutely drenched in sweat and reeking to high heaven. He loved it; he was keeping busy, healthy and out of trouble, so Jesse didn't mind one bit. At least he was getting out of the house and making friends. Jesse's eyes got a little wet and her nose a little tingly when she envisioned Michael in a football jersey in her hometown colors. A lot of her years had been spent cheering at that same stadium, watching those boys in purple and white take the field. Ruined marriage aside, being back home was a dream come.

Jesse walked upstairs and knocked on Luke's ever-closed bedroom door. "Hey honey, can I come in?" she asked before even touching the door knob. Raising three boys had taught her well not to barge into rooms with closed doors. There were some things a mom never wanted to see, and all of her boys were at a rather gross age when it came to privacy.

"Yeah, come in." Luke was sitting on his bed, video game controller in his hand. She sat beside him on the bed and ruffled his curly brown hair.

"We're going to need to get you in for a trim soon, Luke. Do you want to go to a barber or the salon in town?"

"Barber's fine, Mom." She looked at his little face as he maintained polite conversation despite being in the middle of a game. She waited for his game to pause before trying to talk more to him. He must have figured that's what she was waiting on, because he put the controller down. "Okay, what's up, Mom?"

"Nothing really, you seem to be holed up in here a lot, and I wanted to just be with you for a little bit. Would you like to go see some local sights?" At this question, Luke gave a derisive snort.

"What sights? There's hardly anything here but the movie theater and Wal-Mart, Mom." Okay, he had her there. Compared to life in a large city, there was very little to do here. No museums, no Apple or Lego stores, no big malls within sixty miles. She did have a few tricks up her sleeve though.

"How about a hike? I haven't been out to the national park in a hundred years, but I used to love going there. You can bring your sketch pad. There are some rock formations that might blow you away," she said, secretly thrilled at his surprised expression. "If you're interested, I'll go change and grab my camera."

"A hike?" Luke's excited voice betrayed his attempt at disinterest and usual nonchalant attitude. She smiled down at her Little Deep Thinker and rose from the bed.

"I'll grab Ryan and meet you at the front door in ten minutes." She walked out of his room and closed his door, thanking God that she found a way to drag him out of his sourpuss mood for a little while. He loved to be outdoors, but was at an awkward stage at 13. He was getting too big to really play outside with Ryan and, without being in an organized sport, he was sort of left to his own devices, which translated to him playing a lot of video games. Jesse was going to have to check into some local camping or horse riding options, even though it was hotter than blue blazes outside. Better outside sweating than inside stewing, she figured.

Jesse gathered Ryan and her camera and decided she'd do the rest of the food prep for the BBQ after dinner. She couldn't help but be excited to have Levi coming over to the house. She looked forward to showing him what she'd managed to do to make the house homier in a relatively short amount of time. She also couldn't wait to get her hands on his kids. She wanted to hug them into oblivion to make some of the hurt go away. God, losing their mother so young was just heartbreaking. Emma had been lovely. So lovely and kind in fact, that past history with Levi aside, Jesse couldn't help but like her. They met for the first time at Levi and Emma's engagement party.

Jesse and Levi had parted as friends, as amicably as possible once they had ended the romantic portion of their relationship. They had practically grown up together and shared so much that it seemed petty and foolish to dissolve the friendship just because it seemed their romance had run its course. She still remembered feeling a sharp pang when she opened the invitation to the engagement party. Jesse knew Drake would have a wise-ass remark or two about her wanting to attend, but she had made up her mind she was going to go. She even bought a new dress to wear. She was of course pregnant, as it seemed she was for years at that time, but she wanted to look pretty when she saw Levi again.

Thankfully, Drake had little interest in going, so he stayed home with Michael while Jesse made the trip alone with only minimal complaints from Drake. He didn't understand why she'd want to drive all that way to attend a party for an ex. Drake always seemed to find a poisonous barb to insert anytime Levi's name randomly came up in conversation. Jesse knew he was jealous of her and Levi's friendship. Drake certainly hadn't been able to maintain any sort of relationship with any of his former girlfriends.

Jesse had been thankful to carry pregnancy well, her frame had been tall and lean before she was pregnant and she had been fortunate to only gain around 25 pounds per pregnancy. Her belly was round and tight like a basketball, but the rest of her stayed pretty much the same. She later took quite a bit of teasing from girlfriends who had children later in life but seemed to get pregnant all over. Jesse thought back to how she felt when she stepped into the banquet hall to see Levi standing proudly next to a little blond angel. He crossed the room once their eyes met and enveloped her in his arms for a tight hug.

"Jesse, you look beautiful. My God, you're glowing. I didn't imagine I'd ever think a pregnant woman would look pretty," he said as he smartly ducked away from what would have been a hard pinch on the arm. Then Emma walked up and smiled up at her.

"You must be Jesse. I've heard so much about you!" As Emma beamed up at her with a genuine smile, Jesse knew Levi had found The One. She hugged Emma and congratulated them on their engagement. Jesse explained unnecessarily that Drake was home with their toddler, but was sorry he'd missed the party. She didn't miss the eye roll Levi gave her over the top of Emma's head. He'd always been able to tell when Jesse was full of it. After introductions were made, Levi led Jesse to the table where she had been assigned a seat. She was surrounded by friends from high school and had what could only be described as a mini high school reunion while the happy couple moved around making small talk with their guests. Jesse had expected to feel a pinch of sadness seeing Levi move on, despite her own marriage and family. After seeing the sweetness in Emma's face, she could only feel happiness for her old flame. They contrasted in appearance, him big and dark, her petite and so fair, but they seemed to belong together.

As she gathered her boys into the car for a trip to the state park, she tried to shake free from the hold of the old memory. But before she could let go completely, she let herself wish for a minute that she had stayed with Levi, that her boys were his, and that they had been one big happy family. With a melancholy sigh she wondered if they would have ended up back in their hometown in a big old house they could share. The place would be packed to the brim with kids and chaos, but my word, it would be heaven.

Five

The house was clean, the Tiki torches were lit in the backyard, and the house smelled like a dream come true when Levi and his kids were set to arrive. Ryan was excited to have people over, while Luke and Michael were less interested in the kids and more interested in the food. Jesse had kicked herself into high gear to get everything in order before the party. She peeked out the window and saw Levi walking up to the house, pausing to look at the bright red geraniums that she had sat out on the porch. Hannah and James were following close behind him, whispering to each other. During a previous conversation, Levi had shared that his twins sort of 'moved as a unit' when they were anxious, that they had started holding hands again a lot. He had said that when they were younger they were always touching in some way, but they had grown out of it until Emma passed. Just six at the time, the kids had reverted back to being constantly connected in some way. Jesse's heart broke for them all over again when she thought of how much those kids had suffered. She remembered sucking in a breath when Levi said out loud that if one of them had to go, he wished it had been him. She saw the haunted look in his eye as he told her that he felt kids belong with their mothers when their mother was that wonderful.

Levi had told Jesse that Emma had been perfectly suited to motherhood. They had been married for several years before trying to start a family. She had been in the middle of a graduate school program when they married; he wanted to give her plenty of time to focus on that. It was enough that she worked full time while attending school; he wasn't going to force a family on her. Many nights they had stayed up late, wrapped in each other's arms as he talked her into waiting a bit longer. Emma had wanted to be a mother since she was a little girl. Much to Jesse's amusement, she remembered Levi telling her that he couldn't believe the societal pressure for women. They were expected to rival their men in careers and paychecks, keep a perfect house, all while raising a family.

"Where are women supposed to find the time or the energy?" he had said, eyebrows raised to the ceiling. Levi had been able to talk Emma into waiting to try and start a family until graduation from her program. When they did finally start trying for a baby, they had the miraculous luck of getting pregnant the first month they tried. As a matter of fact, they liked to joke that they had the twins because they had made love two nights in a row. As he told that story to Jesse, she had had to turn her head to wipe her eyes. There was a part of her that greatly envied the joy he had experienced in his marriage. She tried to picture Drake retelling a story about their life together with happiness in his eyes, and she just couldn't see it.

Jesse moved to the door and swung it open as Levi had his hand out, ready to ring the doorbell. Ryan ran over and got right in front of her, perfectly oblivious that he was blocking the door. He was more than a little excited to have other kids over for a change, and especially happy to not be the youngest in the house for once.

"Hi guys, come on in!" Jesse grinned up at Levi over the top of Ryan's head. She gently scooted him to the side and stepped back so her guests could enter. As they filed into the house, Jesse put her arm on Levi's and said quietly, "I'm so happy you're here."

Levi looked around, his face showing his shock at the progress she had made inside the house. There were pictures of the boys, and art already hung up on the walls. The paint colors she had picked out seemed to emphasize the natural light flooding into the place, and the dark wood trim seemed to shine. Jesse had been very busy. She dropped down to one knee to be at a better height with his kids and with a smile, she pulled them both to her in a hug. Levi could do nothing but stare at how both James and Hannah allowed her, a virtual stranger, to hug them so tightly. It tugged at his heart to think they were in such need of a woman's hug. He supposed she wasn't really a virtual stranger; once he knew she and the kids were moving home, he had been talking about her and sharing different funny memories from his early years. It just seemed natural to share stories about her, as natural as it was to talk about his parents, his brother or any of the guys he grew up with. She was a part of his history and that's just all there was to it.

Jesse pulled back with a tight smile that he knew held her tears at bay. She was clearly thinking of Emma and the terrible weight her death had been for the kids, but she smiled her way right through it.

"Kids, there's a cartoon on in the living room for the next few minutes, then we'll move the party outside once we start grilling. Go on down the hall and hang a left," she said, standing. The twins looked up at Levi who nodded in assurance. "The bathroom is just off the kitchen if you need to wash up."

Hannah and James linked hands and looked around at the prettily decorated house as they went along their way to the living room. Jesse looked up at Levi and threw her arms around his neck, saying nothing, but trying in her own way to hug the sadness right out of him. It was a hard embrace, willing him to feel safe and secure. There was nothing romantic or seductive at all in it, just an 'I love you' type of hug. She broke free, turned on her heel to hide the sting of tears in her eyes and walked back to the kitchen. Levi took a ragged breath and followed her there to see if he could pitch in.

A bark of laughter escaped him once he got in the kitchen. It was clear she had the food situation very much in control. There were two strawberry pies on the island, as well as a coconut cream, if he was any judge. Next to that, he noted a giant pan of Texas potatoes, coleslaw and salad. Hamburger and hot dog buns were in a mound on a platter and there were large pitchers of iced tea and lemonade on the sidebar. She was pulling a platter of hamburger patties and hot dogs out of the fridge, pausing to cover them with foil.

"Lord, Jesse, is it just us or is the football team coming over as well?" he asked with a look of utter disbelief on his face.

"Football team, my foot, you should see how my boys eat. We'll be lucky if there are any leftovers at all!" she said as she laughed. "It's amazing how they put it away. I keep thinking that they're in a growth spurt, but it never ends. As soon as one spoons up his second serving, another asks for thirds. I can barely keep them in clothes and shoes. I think I'm growing a herd of farm hands or something." As she finished her sentence, Luke and Michael entered the room, saying hello to Levi and wandering into the living room to plop down next to Ryan. Each boy said hello to the twins and then they all sat entranced by a cartoon. Oh cartoons, the great equalizer.

Levi assumed a position at the sink, washing and drying dishes while Jesse fussed around him, setting out condiments and silverware. He couldn't help but be a bit dazzled by her. She seemed completely comfortable with extra people in her house, like a natural hostess. He figured she must have done a lot of that in her old life, but he couldn't have been more wrong. Jesse did love the excitement of entertaining, but it was all new to her. When she had lived with Drake, there was very little entertaining. They even went to restaurants when his family came to visit rather than host them in her house. She had started off their marriage suggesting they just stay home so she could cook, but he always found a way to say with a look that her cooking wasn't quite good enough for his parents. Jesse pushed aside that memory and looked at the kids piled in the living room. She knew she'd be happiest when she saw the kids were getting their tummies full. Nothing spoke contentment to her like a full house, lots of laughter and full bellies. She couldn't quite believe she had her own house and could do what she darned well liked with it.

After the cartoon wrapped up, Jesse and Levi shooed the kids outside and made their way toward the grill. She opened up a couple of beers, and took one over to him where he was lighting the grill.

"I'm surprised you even have one of these. Most women I know aren't big on grilling their own burgers."

"Well, to be honest, I don't know how to work the darned thing and was hoping to learn by secretly watching you today. The boys love grilled burgers and dogs, but Drake insisted on handling that at home. I want to be able to cook them whatever they like, but I never had the chance to learn before."

As the words left her lips Jesse made a mental note to temper what she said. She didn't want to become a negative, bitter ex-wife. She wanted to lay that all behind her, at least when around other people. Alone, she knew she'd be working through it for a long time yet to come. Jesse stayed a few feet back as if the grill might blow at any moment. Levi chuckled at her standoffish posture.

"Come here, don't be a chicken," he said as she came to stand beside him. He placed his hand on her hip to move her in front of him and felt her give a little shiver. He looked down at her face then, but saw she was looking no place but at the grill. Her face was set in a hard line and he would have given a hundred dollars to know what was on her mind right then. She relaxed in front of him as he explained the best way to stack the charcoal, what kinds of meat gets centered or positioned around the side of the flames. He even admitted to a certain cookbook that had become a bible to him as he now cooked almost all of the meals for his kids. They made friendly chit chat and he bossed her around throughout the rest of the grilling experience. The mosquitoes were getting vicious outside, so once the food was done cooking, they ushered the kids back in the house to enjoy their meal in the air conditioning.

Jesse looked around her crowded farm style table and felt a sense of contentment at seeing all the little faces, especially those of her boys. She was awfully proud of how they went out of their way to be friendly to little Hannah and James. That was a very impressive feat for Michael, who at nearly sixteen could barely be counted upon to be kind to his own brothers. At any rate, the kids were eating and she was able to sit back and enjoy feeding those that she cared about. After a while, the dinner was finished, the pies polished off, and true to her word, there was very little left on the sideboard.

The kids all cleared their plates then filed to the bathroom to wash their faces and hands. Then, they headed back into the living room while Levi helped Jesse with the dishes.

"This was really nice," Levi said as he washed off the plates, while Jesse loaded the cups into the dishwasher.

She nodded her head, "You know, it really was! I was worried a little over the age differences, but the boys really made me proud tonight. Now if I can only get them to be that sweet to each other without having to throw a major hissy fit." She shook her head, clearly thinking back to some antics from earlier in the day. "Your kiddos are very sweet, Levi. I hope we can do this again soon.

It was nice to have a full house tonight. I enjoy the chaos of it all. It feels homey when there are a lot of bodies around the table."

He put the last plate in the dishwasher, drying his hands on the towel. "Speaking of getting together again soon, Jesse, would you want to go fishing with me this Sunday after church?" Stunned, she dropped the plastic cup she had been holding and it bounced loudly across the floor.

"Fishing?" she asked with her eyes wide as saucers. Suddenly, she broke into great gales of laughter, making Levi feel more than a little idiotic. By the time the kids all rushed in, Jesse was folded in half, bent at the waist and laughing none too graciously into a dish towel. She sat down right on the kitchen floor, telling the kids that she was fine, to go back and finish up their show. Unsure of what to make of the antics, Levi sat down beside her on the floor once the kids left the room and stared at her strangely, as if she had come unhinged.

Jesse dried her eyes with the dishtowel and with her face as red as a beet, she apologized profusely.

"Levi, oh my gosh. I'm so sorry. When you said fishing, my mind went right back to 1995 with my bra hooked over the peach tree branch and us naked as jaybirds on that blanket you used to keep in your truck." His eyes bugged slightly, then a big grin spread across his face. When he looked back up at her, Levi was smiling and his ears were pink. She remembered exactly what that meant. She continued, "I didn't mean to lose it like that, but that's right where I went. Oh my word, to think of that now after all these years with a room full of kids and life between us! Mercy, it just made me laugh. I'm being silly, I just can't help it."

She couldn't help but have some feelings for this man. Despite the years, he still made her feel so happy. That little self-admission helped her make the choice. Cocking her head to the side, she reached out and put her hand on his and said, "Yes, if the invitation is still open after all that, I'd love to go fishing with you. I'll see if Mom and Dad can watch the boys." He shook his head at her and hopped up from the floor, extending a hand to help her up as well.

As he herded his kids towards the door, he looked back and said, "I'll pick you up at one. Try not to have a fit like that, you'll scare the fish." She could only close her eyes and nod her head at that, ready to croak after losing control like that. God, it had been years since she had laughed like that. She realized how much tension she had been holding for so long and let the embarrassment go. Life was too short to hold in laughter like that.

Jesse waved goodbye to Levi and the kids as they pulled out of the driveway and made the rounds to be sure the doors were locked. She hugged and kissed each boy and reminded them of their lights-out curfew. She grabbed a big glass of water and made her way upstairs to take a nice, long soak. She had been on her feet for most of the day with the preparations for the party and she felt exhausted. She needed to get some rest and focus on the next important decision: what to wear for her fishing date with Levi.

Six

The red pickup rumbled along the gravel road, stirring up dust while the air breezed through the cab, tossing Jesse's hair around. She couldn't help but smile to herself, enjoying the scenery and the butterflies in her stomach. She wasn't embarrassed by her fit of hysterical laughter any longer, though Levi had already ribbed her about it once she got in the truck. They had been driving for half an hour and the ride had been filled with conversation and comfortable silences. Levi snuck glances over at her, and she enjoyed each one that she caught.

She knew without even asking that they were going back to the same pond they used to fish at as teenagers. They were young, hot blooded and in love back then, barely able to keep their hands off each other long enough to get to the property. Back then, they called the large pond the Fishing Hole, getting a kick out of how comfortably rural it sounded. Thinking back on it, she knew they were making fun of themselves a little. At that point in their lives, they had grown up in the sticks but had big city ambitions. They had good-naturedly mocked their humble upbringings and kept a sharp eye towards the future, never dreaming they'd end up on different paths. They had especially never dreamed they'd end up driving out to the Fishing Hole together after so many years, even if it was just as friends.

Memories and different paths aside, here they were, pulling onto the familiar dirt drive. Jesse noticed that it hadn't changed much over the years. The same barbed wire fence and rusted red gate guarded the property, but the trees had thickened along both sides of the lane. With a quick smile, Levi pulled into the gravel drive and stopped the truck. He got out and unlocked the big gate blocking the Fishing Hole from other fishermen. The gate really didn't provide much in the way of security. Around the area, most country boys would just park the truck and hop the fence, but at least it made Levi's dad feel secure, now that he had inherited the land. Jesse couldn't help but admire Levi as he fiddled with the lock. In jeans and an old t-shirt, he didn't look much different than he did twenty years ago. A few fine lines had been added around the eyes, his shoulders were bigger, and a smattering of gray had grown in at his temples. The subtle changes only enhanced his handsomeness. There were some more obvious changes, though. There was a sadness in Levi's eyes that hadn't been there before. A little bit of a hardness as well. Losing a wife would do that to a person, Jesse figured. She hoped over time that hardness would subside, but she had a lot to learn about her old friend and who he was as a man and a father now, versus who he was as a teenager so long ago. She knew only time would tell if he would let softness and love back into his life. As it was, her main priority was making certain her boys were happy, that they were well provided for and that they felt loved. Anything beyond that was more than she was prepared to worry over just yet.

As Levi walked back to the truck, he saw Jesse watching him. He felt like a kid again. He felt horny, excited, and not just a little anxious. Taking Jesse back to the Fishing Hole felt like stepping back in time. He couldn't imagine how many times they'd been there together before. He had fished there over the years with his grandpa, dad and brothers, but he had never been back to that spot with a woman. Not even Emma had been invited there. That place felt a little like sacred ground. Some of the best days and nights he had ever spent were right there, curled up with her in the sunshine and then the moonlight, sipping beers and keeping themselves entertained as teenagers do. Levi stepped up into the truck and drove up the lane to the large pond. Jesse took the picnic basket, camping chairs and a blanket. Levi hauled the rods and bait. Not a word was said on the short walk from the truck, up the path to their favorite spot from years ago. Jesse knew by the way Levi kept adjusting the bill of his faded cap that he was just nervous; she found a little comfort in his old anxious habit.

Though it had felt like a lifetime ago, Jesse thought back to when they dated as teenagers. It had been hot and heavy, as most teenage love stories are, but after the summer of graduation, the relationship ended as they packed up and moved to different colleges. There had been a few emotional calls and letters sent back and forth. Jesse still had a few tucked away in her jewelry box. She had kept them hidden beneath the lining in one of the drawers for years, afraid Drake would find them, but unable to part with the letters. There was no forgetting your first love; Jesse felt that sentiment was true.

Over time, they had walked down their own separate paths, checking in together every few years. Theirs was an easy companionship, a kinship built on time and happy memories. Jesse had to stop and shake her head over the fact that they went off in different directions and both ended up back in their hometown. Jesse faced a little embarrassment over her marriage ending in divorce, but she felt certain she had made the right choice for her boys. One thing was certain, she knew she'd always remember his phone call when the accident happened. The world seemed to stop with his words. She'd never forget the emotion choking his voice as he tried to get the details out. When he realized he couldn't get it out, he simply said that he needed her. That was enough for her. She made arrangements for her mother to come up and watch the boys at her home, while she traded places and went to stay at her childhood home for a few days. Drake had been furious that she would "run off like a whore to play nurse to Levi," as he put it, but she hadn't regretted her choice for a minute. Levi was one of her best friends.

Jesse remembered when she got into town that night. She had texted Levi to let him know she was there and he had replied, asking her to come over. Jesse had barely parked the car in the driveway when she saw him running out of the house. She had enough time to get out of the car when he grabbed her so tightly she thought she'd break in two. She held him as he sobbed, petting his hair and murmuring comforting words to him as she might do to one her boys. They stood outside for a while; once he calmed they went to sit on the porch. She had stayed for probably only an hour or two that night, mostly just listening to him talk and sitting beside him when he wanted to be still. She left him that night with another fierce hug and a kiss on the cheek. She saw him during the services, but they didn't get the chance to spend time together. Nearly the whole town had turned up for the visitation and the funeral, and he of course had Emma's parents and his precious children to tend to. She was so thankful to be able to be there for him in whatever small way she could at the time. The man had had his heart ripped out and laid at his feet. There's no real way to repair that type of damage. From the outside, he had done a fine job taking care of the children, learning how to be both mother and father.

As they set up their fishing spot, Levi reached and took Jesse's hand. She let out a breath she didn't realize she'd been holding as he turned her to him and tucked her against his chest. His hands went to the back of her neck, as they had a hundred times before. When Levi's lips touched Jesse's, it was as if the years melted away. There was a tenderness, a maturity to his kiss that had been added with time. There was a banked fire beneath, but it was a different kind of need than they had known before. The scruff of his day old beard scratched against her chin, but it was a pleasant, exciting feeling. It was a reminder that he was a grown man, who no doubt knew how to please a woman. People learn things over time, and if her memory served, he was starting off from a very good place. Prickles of excitement ran through her at the thought.

There must have been a silly, dreamy look on Jesse's face because Levi chuckled a little as they separated. With a quiet smile that turned to a belly laugh, it was Levi's turn to laugh like a fool.

"Jesse, remember the time..." and he had to cut off with another deep roll of laughter. "Remember the time we were out here fishing and you slid down a slippery spot and fell in the pond?"

Jesse hooted with laughter, having forgotten about that incident. "Oh God, yes! Remember we tried to dry my clothes on the branches, but it was still as could be and no breeze to be found. I rode home in your truck in my panties and your t-shirt, and my parents were furious! They grounded me for a month and took me to the doctor to get on birth control!" They laughed till they cried and got started telling one story after another. They were too loud to attract any fish, but had a nice visit picking through memories and thinking back on some very entertaining times. While listening to Levi tell yet another story, Jesse looked at him and realized she felt as good as she had as a teenager.

Seven

The next few days flew by for Jesse and her boys in a haze of relaxation. Her plan was to squeeze as much time in together as she could before the busy school year began. By Friday, Jesse had to face the facts that her boys were growing tired of the constant togetherness and getting a little edgy. Jesse decided she couldn't put off school shopping any longer, so she put on her most comfortable tennis shoes and decided take the boys shopping and tackle it all; everything from school supplies to new shoes in one big fell swoop. Jesse and the boys walked through the crowded stores, filling their carts with school supplies. Even though she had been out of school for years, there was still a certain butterfly-in-her-stomach feeling that she got every year, buying paper, folders, pens and pencils. She loved the anticipation of something new and different, the way a new school year meant the possibilities were endless. Her boys were less excited about the end of summer and the beginning of a new routine.

There was a certain amount of anxiety that went along with starting a new school with new friends, and Jesse was doing her best to be understanding with her sons.

Michael would be walking through the same halls that she had as a teenager; thankfully, the school was just at the end of the block. At least she didn't have to worry about him driving on top of all the other worries she had. Luke and Ryan would both be at the new middle school, a sprawling new building at the edge of town. Jesse's work schedule would be flexible enough to allow her to take them both to and from school, much to their horror. They both much preferred to ride the bus than to be delivered to school by their mommy, but Jesse had made the switch to her small town and slower pace to be able to do exactly that, be as involved as much as she could in the daily routine. Both boys were in a precarious spot, coping with the rising hormone tide and adjustments from the divorce. Visits with Drake would be starting soon and she wanted as much time as she could get to prove that she was 100% available for them, should they want to talk.

As far as her own changes, Jesse was excited to be returning to work. She had set up a tidy little office in the smallest bedroom of the house. She had written down a daily schedule to help her stay on track and ease into the transition of being back in the trenches. Often her job threw her into a feeling of ADD, with each new message demanding action right away. She hadn't missed that piece of the job. The time off had been a real blessing. She'd been able to successfully settle the house, spend time with the boys, and even relax.

The time preparing for the separation, the divorce, and being quickly thrown into the move after the house sold so fast had all taken a toll on her nerves. The weeks spent off the clock had given her time to decompress and let go of some of the anger she had been keeping a tight lid on. That level of stress can do a number on a person. She noticed that she had trouble falling asleep for months, and when she was able to conk out and get some rest, she often woke up in the middle of the night. She trained herself to not look at the clock, to not count up how many hours she had before her day started. Of course, just those few minutes got her stirred up to begin worrying over her troubles and kept her awake for hours. If she did drift back to sleep, she'd wake with her jaw sore from clenching her teeth.

Now though, she was noticing she hadn't felt so anxious in the last few weeks and had even slept through the night most nights. She considered even that small little victory to be proof that she had made the right choice. Her boys seemed to be happy. Luke was still pretty quiet, but he was smiling more and spending less time in his room. Ryan was a cuddle-bug as always, happy to sit with her in her big two person chair at the end of the day to read together if the big boys weren't around to tease him. She was going to cherish and nurture that baby stage as long as she could. After all, he was her last baby, and he'd be her baby even when he grew into a big man, which he was certainly bound to do by the looks of his feet.

They made their way from the department store back into the car and headed off to the mall for the dreaded school clothes shopping. Ryan and Luke were easy. She bought them jeans,t-shirts, a new pair of tennis shoes and they were happy as can be. Michael was a little more of a challenge. He had his "image" to consider, of course. He also wanted a pair of brown leather boots to wear in addition to his new giant tennis shoes. It was hard on the purse, but all a part of the experience. Oh, and the cologne. That was the most amusing part of the shopping extravaganza. Michael took forever making his choice of what would attract the perfect female. At this stage, she had a pretty good idea what kind of girl he hoped he'd attract; most likely a busty cheerleader with a fast car and propensity to quickly jump in the backseat. She was going to have to talk with him again about maturity, morality and safe sex. Michael was quite a stylish kid, walking the line between sporty and what she used to call preppy when she was in high school. She urged him to stay pretty casual, to maybe plan on a second shopping trip a month or so in at the new school. Michael still hadn't fully grasped that he was in a very rural community. She wanted him to be himself, but to also take a little time to acclimate to the new environment.

Several hundred dollars later, Jesse treated them to dinner at a sports bar and grill, and watched them inhale chicken wings at a startling speed, while watching all the games seemingly at once. She sipped her cold, well-deserved beer and enjoyed her spicy chicken salad. She loved her boys with all her heart and truly enjoyed watching them grow. Jesse was apprehensive about the visits with Drake, but maybe he would be more fun and relaxed after having so much time off from parenting. All she could hope was that he didn't push his new hussy on the kids. She knew she had no control over that aspect of his life, no say in how he handled it; the best she could do is let the boys know that he was dating someone and get them a little prepared. She'd have to show them that she was fine with it, and in reality, she was.

She was almost thankful for that whore because she made it easier for Drake to make the transition. So what. As long as she was good to the boys, that was really all she cared about. She'd save that talk for the house, she didn't want to spring it on them in public. She also wanted to look directly in their little faces instead of the rear view mirror. They needed to see her face to really understand how she felt about it. For now, she'd just relax and enjoy them. She'd have time to tackle that discussion soon.

Eight

The weekend breezed by. Tremendous piles of laundry were folded and put away and finally, the first day of school had come and gone. At dinner, Jesse put the spaghetti and meatballs on the table as the boys finished setting it. As the boys launched into their dinners, Jesse dove into the conversation she had been dreading. “Boys, I wanted to talk to you about something. It’s not a big deal, I just wanted to make you aware before your visit with Dad this weekend. He has a new friend in his life, and I’m not sure if you’re going to meet her or not, but I wanted to let you know so you weren’t surprised.” She made a big effort to look completely calm as she took a big sip of tea.

Six eyes were fixed on hers when she looked back up and continued eating. “What do you mean ‘a friend’?” Luke asked.

“Well, honey, he’s dating a woman named Rachel, and has been for a while. I just wanted to let you know before the visit.” She went back to eating.

"Is that why you guys divorced?" Michael asked, his face getting redder by the minute.

"No, son, we divorced because we weren't happy together. We tried for a long time but it didn't seem to be getting any better. We each want to be happy, so that we can both make good homes for you all. We just couldn't feel that way together." Jesse inwardly flinched at the partial lie.

"Well, I'm not going to like her, no matter what." Ryan sulked into his spaghetti.

"It's ok, boys. You don't have to like her, or not like her. She's someone who's in Dad's life right now, so I do hope you will show her good manners and try to have a nice visit. I'm not even sure if you'll meet her this time, I just thought it would be a good thing to talk about beforehand." With that, Jesse changed the subject to asking how their first day of school went. Thankfully, Ryan had a lot to share. Between mouthfuls of spaghetti, he told her all about the details of his first day at middle school.

"...then we had to go down to the gym to listen to the principal talk about what kind of clubs there are to join, and we got to go down on the floor and visit the tables that were set up for each club. I walked around with a kid wearing a Rams jersey; we both signed up for a football club." Luke had decidedly less to say about the experience, however he did sign up for the Art and Photography clubs. At least he was choosing to get involved with something of his own volition.

Michael thankfully hid his eye rolls over Ryan's enthusiasm, deeming that level of thrill to be uncool unless of course it was Michael gushing about football practice or new drills that were being practiced. The boys cleared the dinner table then settled in their rooms to start homework, which was thankfully a small amount, being the first day of school. Jesse took a deep breath, walked to her own desk in her little office so that she'd have her calendar nearby and called Drake.

"Hello?" he answered.

"Hi Drake, do you have a few minutes to talk about the visit this weekend?" She heard the noise of pots in the background and stopped herself a little too late from wondering if his girlfriend was cooking him dinner.

"Yeah, sure, give me a minute to get to my desk." He was quiet for a minute, not bothering with small talk along the way. "Ok, shoot."

"This is the last weekend before football games start; I'll make sure Michael packs a schedule for you in his bag. Last time we talked you, said you'd be picking them up at our house on Friday by seven. Is that still the plan?" At that Jesse looked down and realized she had an iron grip on her desk. She had hoped not to feel uncomfortable during these calls. Drake was such a taciturn character, she never knew what she was going to encounter.

"Yeah, that still works. We'll have to figure out what to do on game weekends. I still want my time with them, Jesse. I want to see the games, too. I still don't understand why you had to move all the way back to that little shit-hole town. It sure would have been easier had you stayed here."

Jesse wasn't about to launch into that argument; she moved back home because it was *home*. She had parents here, the love and support and the security that comes with being in a small town. The only person it would've been easier on had they stayed, was Drake. She wasn't about to do him any favors.

Tired and anxious to get off the phone, she decided to change the subject. "The first day of school went well for all three of them. I'm sure there will be some homework to be done this weekend; hopefully, it will be a light load for the first week. I don't want to start this off by micromanaging, but there will be things I have to ask about." She heard him sigh in exasperation and said a quick prayer that he could try and not be a jerk for their first visit. "Please be sure they finish their homework during the visit."

"Yes, Jesse." At that, she could tell he had about used up his tiny stock of patience, so she ventured into friendlier territory.

"Would you like to speak to them?" she asked as she turned to walk out of the office towards the hallway.

"Yes, but I've only got a minute," he said, exasperating as usual.

"Okay, I'll start at Ryan's room, he's less likely to have gotten very far into his homework." She hit the mute button and poked her head in Ryan's room. "Hey buddy, want to talk to Dad real quick?" her heart broke as Ryan's eyes lit up. She knew that even though Drake was an asshole, his kids did love him. She knew she should be grateful for that. She took the phone off mute and asked Ryan to pass the phone on to Luke, then Michael once he was done talking. At that, she walked back down the stairs and poured a nice, big glass of Cabernet and sat down to look out the window onto her sleepy street.

After about thirty minutes Michael walked into the living room with a weird look on his face.

"Uh, Mom, you got a call while I was talking to Dad. I didn't answer it because I thought it might piss Dad off." Jesse frowned at the language and held her hand out for the phone. She got to the missed call list and found it. Missed Call: Levi

Murray. Her heart leapt a little, and she could tell that her face betrayed her attempt at masking her feelings by Michael's grossed-out expression. She grinned up at him and said, "What? Don't I get to have a friend?" He made an exaggerated disgusted face complete with finger down the throat, and she laughed at her big boy. Such a ham. He laughed and turned around to go back up the stairs.

Jesse nearly barreled up the stairs behind Michael, popping her head in each boy's room to check in with them, really assessing their eyes after their call with their father. She covered it by asking if they were making progress on their homework and to see if they liked her idea of what to cook for dinner the next evening. They all seemed nice and calm. Jesse didn't want to start off by asking one hundred questions about what was said between them and their father, but it wasn't easy. She didn't want to put the boys in an uncomfortable middleman position between her and Drake. Once she was certain they were fine, she shuffled back downstairs, pacing around the living room, buzzing from room to room putting things away. She was amazed that though they were big boys, they were still so messy.

Jesse waited about half an hour before returning Levi's call. She wanted to be sure the boys were settled into their work and unlikely to come down during her conversation. She even felt a little nervous about calling him back. She was being stupid, she told herself. She spoke to heads of companies every day with work, she could call her friend without getting butterflies in her stomach. She took a calming breath and hit the button to dial Levi, and folded her legs beneath her on the double chair.

When Levi's phone rang he nearly hurdled his couch to get to it. He grinned as he answered, seeing Jesse's name pop up as well as a picture he took of her on their trip back to the fishing hole. She was laughing and had her hand up trying to block his shot. The sun was hitting her face, throwing an almost auburn fire around that pretty dark head of hers. In a deeply exaggerated Southern drawl, he answered the call with "Fuzzy's Pool Hall, how can I help ya?" instead of hello. She clearly skipped a beat, he could just see her holding the phone away to make sure she called the right number. He heard her laugh as she said his name. He loved the sound of her laugh.

"Levi? You nut. Sorry I missed you earlier, the boys were on the phone with Drake." He didn't miss her quiet exhale. His heart went out to Jesse. She seemed to be handling the adjustment really well. He didn't know much about what happened to cause the marriage to dissolve after so many years, but he was beyond curious.

"How did the call go? You and the boys okay?" he asked, trying to keep the concern out of his voice. This was supposed to be a friendly conversation. His kids were in bed, the TV mumbled softly in the background, and all but one lamp was out in the house. He typically went to bed not too long after the kids went to sleep. There was always laundry and lunches to contend with, but after a few years he had gotten the hang of it.

She thought about his question for a minute and smiled a little to herself as she answered, "They seem fine. Drake was abrupt, but not really unkind to me on the phone, and the boys all seem fine. Of course I can't pump them for information like I'm tempted to do." At that, she heard him chuckle. Despite what he had survived with the loss of his sweet wife and being thrust into single parenthood, he still maintained his sense of humor. "We confirmed arrangements for their first visit to see him. He'll pick the boys up Friday by seven."

At this, his heart gave a tug. His own experience had been brutal; however, he knew he'd never have to share his kids, to pass them off to someone else to care for, apart from him. Away from him. Even a small amount of distance would have been unthinkable. He wasn't a perfect man, but he did his best to be a good father. A separation or divorce, he thought, would have killed him.

"You going to be okay, kid?" he asked, wishing with all his might that she would be.

Jesse answered, "I am going to try." She tried to sound upbeat and failed, even to her own ears. "It's going to be weird. I can't stop thinking, what if they want me and I'm a few hours away? I know they're big boys, but they're still my babies." At this, her voice cracked. She got up and started pacing the floor again, her go-to for self-soothing.

"Well, I won't pretend to understand. I think it would rip my guts out too." With a sigh, he stretched out on his couch. He wished he could make this easier on her, could be a strong shoulder for her. He knew what he wanted to say, but wasn't really sure how to put it. He didn't want to be awkward or forward with her, but he wanted her to know how he felt. He decided just to blurt it out.

"Jess, if you want me or need me this weekend, just let me know. I'm going to be home alone; the kids are going with Mom and Dad to see my sister for the weekend. Her son has been asking for them to come visit and you know Mom, she and Sarah can't go a few weeks without seeing each other."

“Levi, that’s so kind of you. I don’t know for sure how I’ll feel this first visit. I might bury myself under my covers and not come out till Sunday afternoon when I leave to pick them up. Thank you for the invitation, I’ll keep it in mind.” She couldn’t help but be touched by his kind words. What a good friend. What a good person.

Not one hundred percent confident in how the exchange had gone, after a few more minutes of talking about what the rest of the week held for each of them, Levi decide to go ahead and say goodnight. He had a load of laundry to put away and lunches to pack before turning in.

“Well, Jess, just remember I’m here. Time to go take care of the rest of my chores and turn in for the night.”

“Thanks, Levi. Goodnight.” Jesse hung up the phone and grabbed a tissue, hastily wiping away the tears that popped out of nowhere. Heaven forbid someone be nice to her, the tears just appeared at the most random times. She checked the locks on the doors one last time, turning off lights as she went. Jesse made her way up the stairs to tuck Ryan in and remind Luke and Michael of their bedtimes. She never went to bed before the boys on a weeknight, but she was absolutely spent from the evening. Jesse had a feeling this new life would be full of emotional ups and downs. Good thing she was a strong woman.

After saying goodnight, Levi ended the call and hopped up off the couch, ready to end the night. He put away the clothes then piddled around the kitchen, packing peanut butter and jelly sandwiches, baggies of carrots and grapes and of course a handful of Starburst candies in each lunch, just like his wife used to do when they'd pack picnics. It gave him special joy to continue that little tradition with the kids. They missed Emma so badly. They all did.

Nine

Jesse felt abnormally anxious waiting for Drake to pick up the children. It was 6:30 PM on Friday; he was due at seven. She had made sure the boys were all packed up with their bags piled near the door. After much conversation and after counting to ten about thirty times, she even had them corralled in the living room. She wanted their time before they went to their dad's for the weekend to be calm, not fretful even though she was so full of nervous energy she was practically vibrating from the strain of sitting still. Jesse wanted them leaving her house with a happy, confident feeling, at least with regard to her time with them. If they dreaded the time with Drake, she wouldn't be surprised. He was an ass, after all. In addition to not wanting to badger them for information, she had also vowed neither to badmouth their father nor pretend he was faultless to nourish their relationship. She was in charge of their well-being and took that responsibility very seriously, but she wasn't going to be fake with them.

Not surprisingly, Jesse had scoured the entire house probably out of the force of habit. She didn't want Drake to look around and see even one thing out of place because she didn't want to see that sour expression of his turn to smugness at her inability to provide well or keep a nice place of her own. She knew he liked to think he was the one with the taste in the relationship, so it gave her a special thrill that the place had turned out so nicely. Her house was decorated in light, airy shades of blue with an almost silvery, ethereal feeling to it. She had added some art to the walls with deep blues, peacock and green colors. Throw pillows on the couch were soft and fluffy and completely snuggly. Drake had never allowed her to pick out the colors in their house or furniture, and his taste was all dark leather, maroon and sage green. It was like he was trying to recreate a classic men's club without any consideration to the fact there was an entire family living in the house, not just him. Because of that, when feathering her own nest, Jesse went in the total opposite direction. Everything she chose made the mind drift to sand and sea, open cloudless skies and was soft to the touch. Even being relatively frugal, weeks after purchasing her $40 throw pillows, she didn't regret splurging for the plush, heavenly soft pillows. The minute she saw her boys hold them up to their cheeks, she knew she had made the right choice.

As they heard Drake's car pull into the driveway, the boys looked at Jesse. She gave what she hoped was a convincing smile and hopped up from her spot between Ryan and Luke on the couch. She turned to the boys before answering the knock at the door and looked each in the eye before saying, "I love you, boys. With all my heart." She drew a breath and opened the door to Drake.

Jesse wasn't exactly sure if he looked exactly as she expected he would, or if she was bewildered by the sight of him standing on her porch, polo shirt and khaki shorts, sandals with the darkest tan she'd ever seen him with in all their lives together. He had a pair of sunglasses in his hand, the arm of one in his mouth. He pulled the sunglasses away, looked her dead in the eye, and then stepped past her into her house without the faintest hint of an invitation for him to come in. There was a part of Jesse that felt a little disgusted even having him sully her house by stepping into the foyer.

The boys sensed the change in her posture and stood, picking up their bags. They mumbled a hello to their father as he held out his hand. Jesse felt her stomach turn a little at that. *Hug them, you bastard* she silently willed. She could only hope it got less tense as the weekend went on. She walked over to the door and held it open, stepping onto the porch. Drake stepped out first, looking around at the hanging baskets and potted flowers and then back at her. "You can get them Sunday at eight. No earlier."

Finding a steel inside herself that her she didn't know she had, she managed to give him a scathing look while keeping her voice pleasant. The boys were behind her and couldn't see her face. She looked him dead in the eye, "Drake, I'll pick them up at seven on Sunday as we have already agreed. The boys are to be allowed to call me *whenever* they want to call me." At that, he lifted an eyebrow and kind of laughed to himself as he turned and walked back to the car, getting in without even popping the trunk for the boys so they could put their bags in the car. She couldn't help but wish for a minute that he'd just drop off the face of the earth. She turned and stepped out of the way so the boys could exit. She hugged and kissed each of them, whispered her *I love you's* to each, and watched from the porch as Michael walked to the car and knocked on the trunk for Drake to open it. He put his bag in, then took Ryan's and Luke's. He went around to the passenger side as Luke and Ryan got in the backseat. As they backed out and drove away, she smiled and waved as Ryan looked at her through the window, no smile, no frown, the face he made when he was uncomfortable and trying to be strong. At that, Jesse woodenly walked back into the house, checked the locks and without shedding a tear, went directly up the stairs to her bed and slept in the clothes she was wearing.

Ten

When Jesse awoke the next morning, she was shocked to see it was nine o'clock. She couldn't remember the last time she had slept that late. She peeled back the covers, made the bed and took the longest, hottest shower she could ever remember taking. She knew only one place she could stand to be. Taking her time, she dressed in jeans and her favorite light pink soft V-neck t-shirt. She left her hair down for a change and put on just a little make-up, enough to hopefully lend a little color to her cheeks and make her look like her heart wasn't missing from her body.

The late Saturday morning sunlight cast a golden hue on the charming bungalow houses lining the street. Jesse parked her car in front of Levi's house and sat there, drumming her fingers nervously on the steering wheel. Checking her face for the tenth time just to be sure her make-up was spare, yet flawless, she took a deep breath and released it. On her shaky walk to his door she laughed inwardly at worrying over her make-up. Long ago, Levi had always said he preferred her low-maintenance. Here she was, perfectly groomed, smooth all over and with a hint of perfume floating up from her wrists.

He must have seen her from the window because as she stood in front of his door, taking one more big breath, Levi pulled it open before she could knock. He didn't smile or greet her. He looked deeply into her eyes like he was trying to read her thoughts before she could attempt to speak them. With that same thoughtful expression, he reached out his hand and Jesse placed hers inside. The feel of his hands had changed since they were teenagers, exploring each other's bodies at every opportunity. Their fire burned hot back then, but it was as much the freedom and excitement over seeking pleasure as it was from young love. As Jesse paused just inside the doorway, she closed her eyes and focused on the feel of his now work-calloused hands wrapped so largely, protectively around hers. He looked back to her face as he reached around and shut the door behind her. For a minute, he stood there, looking at her, trying to get a feel for how she was and what she needed from him. Before Jesse could lose her nerve, she reached up, wrapping one hand warmly around his neck, the other in his hair, a week overdue for a haircut. The silky feel of his dark hair caused her to part her lips on a sigh. He closed in on her then, his own urgency stealing away his control and his intent to take things slowly.

Her sigh and the responsive neediness in her kiss told Levi exactly what she needed. He pulled apart from her, reaching again for her hand and headed up the staircase. They didn't say a word on the walk across the upstairs hall to his bedroom. The daylight filtered through the sheers on the windows, the heavy curtains opened to greet the day. Jesse smiled at his unmade bed, thinking at least some things hadn't changed.

Up in his room, with the sun on her face, Levi smiled at how lovely Jesse was. Her hair was long and loose, set free from her eternal ponytail. Her hair was darker than it used to be, her tall body just a little changed from his memory. Levi thought she was beautiful. He placed his hands on her shoulders and slowly moved them down her arms as they hung at her side. When he made it down to her waist, he pulled the hem of Jesse's t-shirt over her head. He couldn't help but smile as he looked down at her body, filled out more so than it had been many years ago. Jesse smiled back at his appraisal, finding him appreciative of her breasts. He cupped his hands around them, feeling their weight and reflecting his thoughts with the dreamy, intense expression on his face.

She had been so nervous before this moment. Seeing him there, his hands on her body, smiling that half-grin. Jesse pulled him close and felt him hard against her middle. That gave her all the nerve she needed. She stepped back, unbuttoning her jeans and reaching next for the buttons on his shirt. Levi didn't waste any time getting down to his skin, a near growl low in his throat as he pulled her close while at the same time pulling her down on the bed.

Just before he took her mouth in a kiss, he pulled back to look at her. With his characteristic grin sexily fixed on his face he said, "It's been a long time since we did this, I wonder if we're still as good at it as we used to be."

She looked up at him, running her hands over his firm, muscled arms and said, "I don't know about you, but I'm fantastic in bed." He let go an easy laugh and bent to kiss her lips. Jesse felt her heart pound against her chest as he kissed her hard, moving his hands along her body, pressing his delicious weight against her. He was positioned between her legs, his body close, but not close enough. She could feel him pressing against her and felt herself respond greedily to his touch. She wanted him too badly to wait for foreplay, no matter how good his will or intentions. She had to have him inside. It had been so many years since they had been together, so many lonely years of rushed marital lovemaking, growing sparser as the years went on. Jesse needed this from Levi in a way that no other man could provide. There was a magnet pulling them together, no matter how she dismissed it, fought it and argued against it.

Levi could sense her urgency, though he fought against his own need to push inside her. He had wanted to make this special for her, not knowing when she would come to him. He had planned to hold out, not to rush her or make her feel pressured. When he found out she was moving back home, there was a sad spark in his heart that yearned for her. With the children, the demands of life, and the baggage they had, they both could easily have turned to stone. It was almost a dream too good to be true to hold her in his arms like this again.

He touched her body, feeling the soft skin of her shoulder down to her breasts, his lips following the path his hands had trailed. Levi heard Jesse gasp as he took the tip of her breast into his mouth, sucking the pebbled nipple while caressing her. Her legs parted in invitation and he wasn't going to deny her. His hands moved down her body as he heard her breathing grow harsher. Levi lightly touched her body, tracing around her but not quite where she wanted him most. After what felt like an eternity, Jesse smiled up at him, taking her hand down the same path, enjoying the groan he issued as he watched her. She took his hand in hers and placed it right where she wanted, right at her core.

Levi uttered, "God Jess, you're so warm and wet for me," enjoying more than he would ever say, how tight she was to his touch. He found that spot he remembered so well from their teenage years. Levi always felt a bit of pride in being able to reduce Jesse to a hot mess with the touch of his fingers. He rhythmically pressed that spot until she trembled, so very close to her release. He wanted to be inside her for that, feeling her pulsate around him. He moved his hand to hold hers above her head, pinning her writhing body beneath his. With his body at the entrance to hers, he looked into her eyes as he eased himself inside her. Jesse raised her hips up to meet him, aching for him to be completely inside. They moved together, looking in one another's eyes, their pace growing faster and faster until Jesse exploded into what felt like a million pieces. She half moaned, half laughed at the feeling of the orgasm, the joy of the experience having nearly been forgotten. Her flushed face and smile pushed Levi beyond the limits of his composure. Now that she had hers, he wanted his. He pushed and bucked against her, her legs still wrapped tightly around his body. He tangled his hand in her hair, his other hand still pinning hers gently to the bed. He tucked his head into her neck for the final surge and came inside Jesse, holding onto her as if she were an anchor.

They lay entwined together as their pulses slowed. Still inside her but spent, he seemed to cover and curl around her protectively, giving her silent strength and comfort. Levi looked down into her flushed face and chest, heard her breath quicken and felt her readiness and knew he couldn't hold it any longer.

"Jesse, I've missed you," he said as he hardened and entered her again fully, hearing her sharp intake of breath.

God it felt good to be inside her again. Her body wrapped around his in a way that made him feel 18 again. This time, their lovemaking was hard and fast. Knowing there would be time for tenderness later, their hunger for each other was too much to prolong it. Jesse cried out again, silent tears the only outward proof as the flood of feelings, both physical and emotional that she hadn't known in most of her adult life, cascaded through her. Levi was quiet with his, closing his eyes, pulling her so close as her body pulsed around his own. They separated and lay together in the rays of the sunlight, sleepily watching dust speckles float about in the air. They were physically sated, content and more fulfilled than they had been in a very long time.

Jesse and Levi lay together, comfortable in their silence, bodies exhausted and utterly relaxed. After a while, Levi propped himself up on an elbow and looked down at Jesse, smiling.

"You're right. You are pretty fantastic in bed." Then he ducked as she reached out to playfully swat him on the arm.

"So are you, I'm glad some things are the same," She smiled as she stood up and shot him a look with an eyebrow raised as she feigned seductively bending to gather up her clothes. At her expression, he chuckled and waggled his eyebrows at her as he watched her dress.

"We could go again, you know," he started to say as she threw her head back and laughed.

"You're as horny now as you were as a teenager! Put it away, mister. I've got to get back home. Laundry awaits." He stood and dressed while she took her turn to admire him. He really did look good. She wouldn't have guessed his chest would be tanned. He must do the yard work shirtless. That had to be exciting to the biddies that lived in the neighborhood. Jesse could just imagine the neighbor ladies calling their phone chain when he stepped outside to cut the grass. Levi threw his arm around her shoulders as they stepped into the hall and made their way down the staircase.

"I wish you'd stay. I could fix some lunch. I make a mean fried bologna sandwich. I even have Cheetos," he said as he took her hand and started to tug Jesse towards the kitchen. She held firm, pulled him back towards her and gave him a warm, soft kiss.

"Levi, I really need to get home. I'm so glad you were here." And with that, Levi walked her to the door and watched as she drove away. He knew in his heart she came to him as much out of a desire for closeness as an escape from her pain at being without the boys for the very first time. He was more than happy to oblige; she was as warm, funny and lovely as she had been all those years ago. Jesse was even lovelier now, with a substance and intelligence that had only grown with time. He shut the door and ambled back to the kitchen, flicking on a ballgame to watch as he cooked his lunch.

Eleven

As she unlocked the door to her house, Jesse realized she had smiled stupidly the entire drive home. She'd even made it as far as the front door when the realization hit her that the boys were at their Dad's and she had an entire day to kill before she could pick them up. A small part of her kicked herself for not accepting Levi's offer of lunch. They probably could've had a nice afternoon together; however, she was feeling a little unsure of what comes next. They hadn't made a commitment to one another; they weren't dating. On her walk through the house she stopped, wondering if she had just had the equivalent of a one-night stand. Could it be called that if it happened with an old boyfriend in the middle of the day? Shaking her head at her own idiocy, she continued her way to the basement door. Down she went to the laundry area, cussing the fact that her laundry was in the basement. If she got a raise this year she decided she'd have a laundry room built in her master bedroom. There was no reason to have a big bedroom just for her. She'd rather not have to truck it up and down the stairs, carrying clothes for four people.

Jesse made it up to the basement door, muttering to herself about the amount of laundry to be done when she realized something was off. She carefully walked into the living room and saw a man standing in her living room. She gave a little scream and as he turned around to face her, she felt equal parts relieved and angry. Cole Green, her friend from high school had let himself into her house.

"Jesus, Cole you almost gave me a heart attack. What are you doing here?"

"Sorry, Jesse, the door was open. I saw your car was here, but you didn't answer so I figured I'd let myself in and wait," he said as he smiled at her.

"Next time, wait outside. You scared the crap out of me," Jesse said as she made a mental note not only to always lock the door, but to be sure to remind the boys to do the same. She thought she saw a flash of annoyance in Cole's eyes at what she said, but by God this was her house. He shouldn't just walk in no matter how long they've known each other. Letting out a big sigh, she relaxed and crossed the room and threw an awkward one armed hug around Cole. He held her just a bit tighter than she expected, but let her out of the embrace as she gestured for him to sit down on the couch as she sat down in the chair. The tense set of his mouth, or maybe it was his eyes, made her worry for her old friend. He had always been rather quiet, the type you really had to poke and prod to find out what was going on in his mind.

"What's up? I haven't seen you since you helped with the move. What's going on?" Jesse asked as she set the laundry basket down at her feet.

"Nothing much. I was just wondering how you were doing, if you were getting settled in," he explained as he looked around the living room. "The place looks nice. You sure didn't waste any time getting it decorated. Looks comfortable." Cole stretched one long arm out across the back of the couch and crossed ankle over the knee of the other. Jesse had forgotten just how big he was. He didn't seem to have changed much over the last twenty years. Long and tall, at least 6'5", Cole had light brown, thick hair, and eyes that she could never decide if they were blue or green. She always thought his eyes looked like the color of the water in Cancun, Mexico. She had been there once on a family vacation in high school and never dreamed that was the most exotic place she'd ever get to travel. Cole had apparently kept up with the lifting schedule that he had back in high school, because his black t-shirt was stretched tight over big shoulders and a broad chest. Jesse decided the age fairy clearly didn't visit everyone in equal measures.

"It didn't take long at all after you all did the heavy lifting. I'm crap at carrying heavy furniture, but I can hang shelves and picture frames with the best of them," she said as she lifted her arms in a mock bicep display. At that, Jesse realized she was wearing only her tank top and pajama shorts. She had showered after coming home from Levi's, piled her hair high on top of her head and put on her pajamas, set to relax, watch T.V. and fold laundry for the rest of the night. She crossed her arms over her chest as she saw Cole's gaze linger there. The silence grew awkward for Jesse while Cole looked pretty comfortable on the couch. In the back of her mind Jesse was reminding herself how much laundry and housework she had to get done. If she was really honest, she just preferred to be alone for her first big pity party. After it seemed like Cole really didn't have much else to say, she stood up and walked a few steps towards the door.

"Well, it was nice to see you, but I'd better get back at it. The boys go through clothes like you wouldn't believe and those football pads are stinking up my laundry room." At that she took a few more steps towards the door. At mention of the boys, Cole looked around as if he just noticed for the first time that the kids weren't home.

"That's right, where are the kids?" he asked as he got to his feet. Jesse wasn't sure why, but made a snap decision not to mention that the boys were away. She couldn't put her finger on it, but she felt uncomfortable admitting to anyone that she'd be home alone for the night. It was probably just weird feelings from walking into the room to find a man in her house unexpectedly. Tough as she was, Jesse wasn't very comfortable sleeping alone in the big house so instead of telling the truth, she lied.

"Mom picked them up to run errands. They're picking up some snacks. You remember what it's like with teenagers, it's impossible to keep enough food in the house," and she took the remaining few steps to the door. "I need to get this first load folded and put away before they come back in. They're big now, but it's still easier to get housework and laundry done when they aren't in the room."

Jesse smiled as she held open the door for Cole. He followed her forward and stopped right in the doorway as she held her arm outstretched to keep it open. He smiled down at her and she realized for the first time just how handsome Cole was. He practically towered over her and he was so much more muscular than she remembered him as a teenager.

"I'm glad you're back, Jess. I've missed you." At that, Cole unfolded his sunglasses from the neck of his t-shirt and put them on as he walked down the steps to his motorcycle parked in the driveway. Jesse stepped back inside and threw the deadbolt on the door. She quickly checked the back door, and even the basement door, then went straight to the kitchen where she cast a quick glance at the clock to be sure it was technically afternoon, but not really anywhere near five o'clock. She hesitated about a second, then reached for the wineglass. *What the hell did it really matter?* she thought to herself as she poured a large glass of Reisling. It had been a strange day. She crossed the house and parked herself on the floor, prepared to watch a romantic comedy, and lose herself in the mundane and preciously mindless job of doing loads of laundry and drinking white wine.

Twelve

Sunday morning dawned bright and sunny, with a breeze that cooled off the sweltering August heat. Jesse woke late, feeling only momentarily guilty for missing church. She and the boys had done pretty well on church attendance since moving back home. Without Drake around to criticize and sneer at her while she fussed to get herself and the boys ready for church, it really wasn't much of a hassle. When she had been married, he would always find a way to make her feel guilty or ignorant for insisting on taking the boys to church. She couldn't count the times he had told her to just let the boys sleep, there was no reason to waste their time listening to a bunch of hypocrites pat themselves on the back and act like they weren't just as screwed up as everyone else. Jesse refused to budge on that issue. She and the boys may have rolled into church late and frazzled, but they had almost always made it on Sunday mornings. Jesse knew she was far from perfect, but she did know that she loved God and could at least give him an hour when he carried her through the entire week.

She rolled over and stretched in bed and felt a delicious kind of muscle soreness and blushed as she quickly realized why. Jesse got up and made her bed as she always did, first thing, and then she padded down the stairs on the way to the coffee maker. Once she got to the kitchen, she threw away the empty wine bottle sitting on the counter and made a mental note to not drink an entire bottle each time the boys were visiting Drake or she'd end up with a big belly and puffy face like her Aunt Martha. Aunt Martha had been a sweet soul overall, but everyone in the family knew not to call her after 5:30 at night because by then she'd be well into her cups. With that memory, Jesse laughed to herself as she took her full coffee cup into the living room and turned on the news.

The Laundry Beast had been tamed the day before, but Jesse looked around and saw the house needed a good scrubbing. After that, she'd have time enough to get groceries before leaving to pick up the boys. Thinking about groceries made her remember that odd visit with Cole. Jesse quickly looked to the door and felt relieved when she saw it was still locked. She had been so unnerved about that visit that she had been a little afraid of having bad dreams. As it happens, a bottle of wine will make a person sleep right through the night. Jesse had actually slept better than she had in a good year. There were no sounds in the night, no listening to hear which boy got up to go to the bathroom, if they flushed, if they washed hands. Although they were big, she was still constantly on them to wash their hands. She smiled to herself thinking of the things she seemed to harp on just because it was her motherly right to do so.

The rest of the day went by in a blur as Jesse prepared to drive to pick up the boys. By the time she left, she felt an odd mix of accomplishment and silliness. She felt good about having time to get the housework and laundry done, the meals planned and groceries purchased, but she also felt an incredible bone deep sense of loneliness without the boys at hand. Jesse also felt more than a little pissed at herself for taking such preparation with picking out her outfit and doing her makeup and hair as she got ready to pick up the boys. She didn't know if it was more because she didn't want to see Drake without looking her best, or if it was because she was halfway expecting to meet the Whore for the first time. She knew she'd have to start thinking of her as Rachel rather than "the Whore". She certainly didn't want to slip and call her that in front of the boys. She just wasn't quite sure she was ready to be mature yet.

Jesse put gas in her Suburban and pointed herself north, ready to go get her boys. To relax, she threw on the Bob Schneider station on Pandora and rolled down the windows. To heck with her hairstyle, she needed this time to unwind and to push away the negative feelings that she didn't want her boys to see in her eyes. Plus, there was a gas station right by Drake's apartment, she could stop there and assess the damage.

The weather was beautiful, the traffic was light and the drive flew by. Before she knew it, she was stopping in at the station to top off the tank, take a quick break, and then head to Drake's. Her hands were shaky as she guided the Suburban into his driveway. She had just barely turned the key in the ignition when the boys piled out the door, bags in hand. One, two, three boys, Drake and... Jesse realized she was waiting for Rachel to come out onto the porch as well. She let out a big breath and got out of the car, popping the hatch so the boys could load up. They quickly walked over with relieved smiles on their faces. Jesse couldn't get her hands on them fast enough. Ryan got to her first, and Jesse's eyes didn't miss the fact that he fought his way from the back of the line to get to her. Thankfully, the bigger boys stepped aside; they must've sensed how badly he needed a hug. She hugged Ryan hard, then pulled back to look in his eyes. She saw him blink back the tears he had been holding and she knew it was going to be a quiet ride home. She couldn't wait to get him alone and just hold and love on him. Damn it, the distance hurt. It hurt badly enough to make Jesse second guess if she did the right thing moving so far away, even if it was only an hour and a half. Would it have been easier on them if she had stayed in the same city, miserable and far from where her heart called her to be?

Luke was next, giving a halfhearted one armed hug, showing every bit of his awkward 13 years. He wanted to hug her as hard as Ryan had, she could see it in his quickly averted eyes. She held on as much as he allowed, then let him go so he could throw his bag in the back of the SUV. Michael was last, and gave her a hug so hard her shoulder popped.

"Hey, Mom. I'm starving," he smiled as he threw his bag in the vehicle and assumed his spot in the passenger seat. At that, Jesse saw that Drake wasn't going to walk over to her like a gentleman. What an ass. She walked to the porch and said, "Well, how did it go?"

"How did it go? How do you think? You didn't call on Friday night to check that we made it and Ryan cried like a baby over that. I'm not going to let you turn my boys into a bunch of sissies," he sneered at her. No matter how many times it happened, Jesse could never stop herself from flinching at his unnecessary hatefulness.

"I'm sorry to hear that. I'm sure you offered to let him use your phone to call me, right?" she asked, noticing that Drake looked quickly to the side. That jerk. He probably didn't offer just so he could hurl this at her feet the minute he saw her.

"Oh, of course you didn't. You're such a dick," she said low and turned on her heel to walk towards the car. She plastered a fake smile on her face as she walked back to the SUV, though the wideness of Michael's eyes showed her that she hadn't been as quiet as she thought she had.

When she buckled in he whispered, "Mom that was awesome," quietly enough for the boys in the back not to hear, and for Drake not to be able to read his lips she was sure.

"Boys, I need you to be 100% certain that you have everything you need packed. I'm talking retainers, socks, homework, t-shirts. I don't want so much as a pair of underwear left there that we have to come back for, ok?" As she looked each of her boys in the eye, she asked, "Are we good to go?" They each nodded or mumbled yes.

She turned back around and noticed Drake was still standing rooted to the spot on the porch as she backed out which gave her more than a small thrill. She had never given into the desire to spar with him when he spit ugly words at her. Calling him a name was probably the most fun she'd had in years. She wasn't going to give into the ugliness, but taking him by surprise just once tickled her to no end.

With each mile Jesse put between the vehicle and Drake, she felt the mood lighten. By the time they were home, the boys had mellowed out and she felt considerably better as well. It was good to be back home and back to normal. It was astounding to feel herself absorb the ugliness that comes from being around Drake. He was like a storm cloud or a black hole sucking the love and light from everything around him. Having the freedom to simply drive away from him was like magic. No more sitting up at night, waiting until he would no doubt be asleep before she would walk back to the bedroom. No more going to bed early on nights when he came home late so she wouldn't have to talk with him. That nightmare was over. Pulling into her own driveway in her own town with her own boys felt amazing. It was so much better than living in that emotionally warped prison.

After the boys had unpacked, Jesse took turns going to each of their rooms, giving them a chance to share or not share whatever they wanted about the weekend. She only probed as far as to be sure they got their homework done. She sat on Michael's bed and listened to his funny stories about what his friends texted him about when he was 'so bored at Dad's place.' In Luke's room, he was content to talk about the science project they were going to be doing in the lab the upcoming week, and whether or not he'd get the partner he wanted. Lastly, she went into Ryan's room and laid down on his bed, snuggling him like she did when he was smaller. He didn't have as much to say as the other boys, and she knew his little heart was hurting. If she felt overwhelmed when around Drake, she could only imagine how he felt after having a break from Drake for so many weeks. She pulled him a little closer, reached over and flicked off the bedside lamp and held Ryan close until he drifted to sleep. She kissed his little head, seeing him not as the big 11 year old that he was, but as the toddler it seemed like he was just yesterday. Once he was completely out, she got up and went to her bed where she pulled out her journal.

She hadn't written in weeks, but a line had come to her on the drive home. She visualized a woman who had gathered up her own courage and set herself free. It was a version of herself, but younger, a bit more independent. Grabbing her blue pen, she flipped to the next open page, and wrote what came to her.

Me and the Sea

A little in awe at my own courage, I took my first step on the white sandy beach. I hadn't been on solid land for even an hour, and there I was, the sea spread before me, sun sinking into shades of rose and orange. I did it. My toes wiggled into the soft powder and a slow smile spread over my face, to Hell with whatever anyone watching me thought.

Finally the urge to get my feet wet overcame my need to stand and soak it in, so off I went down to the area of the beach where the water firms the sand. Down dropped my sandals, down dropped my bag. Forward I walked feeling the hard-packed sand meet the cold water, foaming at the edges, washing over the tiny cracked shells that had poked the feet of everyone before me.

Up to my ankles, up to my shins, the water felt so cold and good that I threw my head back and laughed. I probably seemed a little nutty, but I was a little nutty. Relief emanated from me as tears of thankfulness for my strength streaked quickly down my face. I fought them back though; if I started that up, it might be a while before I stopped, and today was about me.

Not my trials, my sacrifices, my internal battles waging in my mind for weeks and months and years. Just me. Just me and the sun on my shoulders, the sound of the waves, the wind in my hair, and the shock of cold water rushing in waves at my legs. I had forgotten just how much I liked me.

Jesse read the passage a few times and could even smell the tang of the sea air. She could feel the breeze caressing the arms and hair of the woman, standing there taking in the ocean and feeling so very proud of herself and confident in her choice. She decided she loved the entry and put away her journal, now at a much better, calmer place so that she could say her prayers of thankfulness to God for bringing her boys safely home. Writing always seemed to help relax Jesse. Simply putting the words on paper to get them out of her mind left her feeling peaceful and relaxed.

Thirteen

Monday brought its own typical set of challenges. The boys were grumbling and none too excited to jump out of bed and scramble to get ready. Being just a few weeks into the school year, the new was quickly wearing off, and Jesse was starting to realize she was going to have to talk to Drake about moving the pickup time up a bit. The boys were dragging, her nerves were frazzled and she realized she was going to move up her wake-up time as well. She needed at least one solid hour of peace and preparation in the morning before the boys were running around, arguing and fighting over the upstairs bathroom.

"Mom, Michael put on so much cologne I can't even breathe in here!" Luke bellowed from the upstairs followed by a grunt that Jesse could only assume was the result of a shove.

"Shut up, Luke, at least I care how I smell," Michael sneered as he stepped around his brother on his way to get dressed. Jesse thumped her way up the stairs, reaching into the bathroom to flick on the vent. She gave Luke a hug and a smile and leaned in close to his ear.

"You smell just fine, honey. You do a good job taking care of that, unlike some of your friends," she said, pinching her nose and grimacing. She succeeded in getting at least a halfhearted smile out of Luke. She gave him one more squeeze and took joy in the roll of his eyes and the slight smile. Thirteen was such a strange age. Such a hormone addled mix of little boy and little man.

She walked into Ryan's bedroom and sat down on the bed and smoothed back his hair. Her littlest man had already dressed himself, brushed his teeth and put on his shoes. She noticed how he had scootched down to the middle of his bed so that his feet dangled off the edge. For a little guy he'd always been pretty particular with cleanliness. She was glad at least one of her three had taken after her in that way.

"They are so dumb when they fight like that, Mom," he said as he looked up at her.

Jesse gave him a reassuring pat and worried a little over his sensitivity to his brothers' bickering. She vowed to carve out a little more time this week for some one on one with Ryan.

"I know, buddy; that's just how it is sometimes with brothers and even sisters. Aunt

Anna and I used to have some doozies. I remember one time we didn't talk for a whole week after arguing over who got to use a curling iron one day before school. Grandma Eadie was so sick of listening to us squabble that she took the curling iron away and neither one of us got to use it for an entire week." Jesse let out a bark of laughter at the memory and at the bored expression on Ryan's face. "You don't understand son, this was in the 1990's; big hair was the thing back then. Anna's hair was flat as a pancake that week, and I couldn't achieve my mile high bangs without that curling iron. No amount of Rave hairspray was going to fix that mess." She got up and looked at Ryan, "Come on, big fella. Go downstairs with me and you can eat breakfast while these yo-yos are finishing up getting ready." He obligingly followed her down the stairs, and gobbled down his French toast in peace.

The days flew by in a mix of conference calls, football practices, pickups and drop offs. Morning scuffles aside, the boys seemed to all be doing well. Michael had even broken the teenager code by thanking Jesse for not letting him get carried away with school shopping. The local boys didn't really seem to wear more than t-shirts and jeans; a button down shirt was considered dressing up. The girls, much to his delight, wore significantly less. Jesse said a silent thank you prayer to God that she'd been given boys to raise instead of girls.

The first football game of the season was Friday night, and on Saturday, a little week-long carnival would be open at the Fairgrounds. When there's not much to do in the way of entertainment, people have to make the best of what they have, and the fair had always been a pretty great time when she was a kid. Jesse had promised the boys she'd take them on Saturday afternoon for dinner and rides. The days were still plenty long and they had some errands to get done that day. She would take Luke and Ryan, and Michael, of course, would be going separately and would probably grace them with a hello should they cross paths.

Halfway through the week Jesse decided she had put it off long enough and called Drake. She decided to do it in the middle of the workday, hoping if she caught him in the office, he'd be less of a jerk with witnesses around. The phone rang three times and she was preparing to leave a voicemail when he answered and took her a little off guard.

"Drake Williams," he answered and immediately made her blood boil. First, she'd be in his phone address book, he didn't have to answer like he was answering for a stranger and second, who is so self-important that they answer with their name instead of hello. What an arrogant pig.

"Hey, Drake. Do you have a few minutes? I need to talk to you about something," she said into the phone, trying not to let her irritation show. It was so weird to move from having been so intimate with someone, to being torn up with worry over a simple phone call.

"Jesus Christ, Jesse, I do have a job to do here. What do you want?" he blustered. So much for her theory about him being civil during the workday.

"The kids are hard to get up on Mondays after getting home so late on Sundays. I'd like to change the pickup time to six o'clock on Sundays rather than seven o'clock," she practically spat into the phone.

He let out a big sigh and said, "Whatever Jesse, just don't call me during the day any more. We aren't married any longer. You're an annoyance," and with that he hung up.

Tears welled in her eyes as she put down her phone. How could he be so cold? He wanted out of the marriage as badly as she did when it finally ended, but they had made three precious children together. Why did he have to be such a hateful, cold, arrogant piece of crap? She put her head in her hands and gave into the cry she'd been needing to have for a long time. She had decided not to give into these bitter and sad feelings before she even ended the marriage. She felt deep in her heart that she had wasted enough of her energy on those feelings while they were together, but damn it, sometimes it just hurt.

After a few minutes, she got up, washed her face, thanked God that she worked from home where nobody could see her and got back to business calling clients. After the first call she thought she heard someone at the front door, but it hadn't been a very loud knock. Jesse thought maybe it was the elderly woman who lived down the street. Miss Suzie liked to drop by occasionally for a little visit; it was usually a welcome break in the day. Jesse didn't see anyone at the peephole, so she threw the door open. On the welcome mat was a red rose. Just one, no tag or card attached. Jesse stepped further out on the porch, looking from left to right, but she didn't see a person or a car out of place. She picked the rose up, shut and locked the door behind her, and put it in a bud vase in the kitchen. She couldn't imagine who would give her a rose except for Levi, but that wasn't really his style. In all the time they dated, he only bought her flowers for dances, and that was because she broke down and asked. Back then he had the audacity to take a manly, logical approach to flowers. They died, and therefore they were a waste of money. Jesse realized even back then that he had a pretty good point, but still there was something sexy about being given flowers. Jesse liked flowers so much that she planted bulbs all over her yard so that she could have cut flowers all through the blooming season. She carried the rose up to her desk and sat it there, all lusty red and fragrant. She couldn't help but smile stupidly at it wondering if this was Levi's attempt at romancing her again. She hadn't heard from him since she left his house and was busy trying to pretend that it didn't hurt her feelings just a little.

Later that night, while the boys were upstairs working on homework, she was putting dishes in the dishwasher. She had just pushed the button to start the machine when her phone rang. She was a little disappointed to see it wasn't Levi calling but she pushed that feeling down. Just because she had gone over to his house uninvited for some exquisite sex didn't mean he was going to start doting on her. Just because he probably left a beautiful rose on her doorstep wasn't a sign that he was going to attempt to woo her. What a damned disappointment. She buried her crummy feelings, clicked on her phone and put a smile into her voice as she answered the call of her best friend.

"Hello?" she answered, and was met with the typical 90 to nothing conversational style of Megan O'Malley, her best friend since college.

"Hey Jess, how are you? How's the house? How are the boys? I'm so sorry I haven't been able to call; there was no reception where we were in Alaska!" she blustered, one question right after another. Jesse had long since gotten used to the bombardment of questions and was an expert at keeping up with Megan's rapid fire style of communication.

"Megan, I'm so happy to hear from you! The house is great, comfortable and chock full of boys. The boys are adjusting well, they've got one visit down and so far none of them have mentioned having met the whore, so that's nice." At that, Megan let loose a very unladylike snort. "All in all we're settled in nicely. Tell me all about your trip to the wilderness!"

And then she was off. Megan told her all about the salmon fishing, whale watching, hiking and overall glory that was her honeymoon trip to Alaska with Ivan, her Russian born hunk of a man. Ivan was what Jesse thought of as a stereotypical Russian right out of the movies, which was big, strong and bullheaded. At least the movies had been her only exposure to Russian men until Megan's wedding. The wedding was a virtual buffet of testosterone, showcasing the Russian population of St. Louis at its finest. Had she not been there with her kids, Jesse might have been interested in getting to know at least one of them a little bit better. She was long overdue for some fun, after all. Megan's husband, Ivan, was tall, dark headed, heavily muscled and had an accent that could melt the clothes right off your body.

"We're back in St. Louis now, and I have a mountain of laundry that I can barely see over. I'm headed to the grocery store next to stock up, then I've got a date with the washing machine." Jesse and Megan talked a little about what was up next for the week. Jesse almost decided to tell Megan about what happened with Levi, but there was a part of her that wanted to keep that secret for a while longer. She wasn't ready to share that just yet, let alone analyze it to death at warp speed.

The conversation wound down after an hour when Jesse realized she needed to check on the boys. She promised to call the following weekend and ended the call by telling Megan that her ears were tired, their signature end to their long winded phone calls.

Fourteen

Jesse felt a little drained by the end of the week, but rallied her strength. The next night there would be both a JV and Varsity football game, so she had to get the kids in bed at a decent enough time so that they'd have some energy left over for the weekend.

With fun plans ahead, the workday flew. Before she knew it, she had the kids home, fed, cleaned up and ready to go back out. Michael had to be at the field an hour before his game, so a buddy was picking him up. Jesse felt so proud, she was ready to burst at the sight of him in his uniform and pads. When his friend Mark picked him up, she horrified him by having them stand in front of the pretty oak tree while she took a few pictures. No sooner did she hassle him with one last kiss were the boys jumping in the cab of the tiny Chevy truck. Mark fired up the engine and Pantera's Walk roared out of the speakers. Jesse made a mental note to horrify Michael later by telling him that she used to listen to that before games with Levi and the boys.

After cleaning up the dishes it was time to put on the purple and white and gather with the rest of the town to cheer on the boys. There was just something nearly magical about attending high school football games. Every time Jesse climbed into the bleachers, the excited feeling of the crowd soaked into her, right down to her bones. In an instant, she could be transported over twenty years back to her own high school days. When enough time passed, it was easy to pretend it was all great fun, after all. She remembered cheering on the track, her back to the football players. Most of the girls were clueless about the rules of the game except for the cheerleaders who had older brothers that played. There was one mom in particular the girls zoned in on to know which cheer to yell. The mom would stand up and scream, "First and ten!" and the captain would holler out the name of the sideline cheer that was up next. To this day, Jesse had no idea what 'first and ten' meant, but the memory still brought a smile to her lips. Here she was, getting to be an official Football Mom. Looking around the crowd Jesse could see so many familiar faces that were present even back in her high school days. She smiled fondly at those she knew, saying hello here and there as she found her seat in the bleachers. She patted arms, gave hugs and made several comments to people she grew up with who had either relocated back home as she had, or had never left the town. So many had decided to make their home in the same town they grew up in, a testament to the overall goodness of the town.

Thankfully, the game went off without a hitch. Michael had just a small amount of time on the field, but boy did Jesse's heart swell to see him out there. Even Luke and Ryan seemed a little in awe at their big brother, a rare occurrence indeed. Jesse hollered and cheered along with the fairly sparse crowd, noticing how it filled up as the evening went on. Mostly parents and friends came for the JV games, but nearly the whole town came to watch the Varsity play. Jesse gave the younger boys money to go buy popcorn and sodas at the concession stand to break up the monotony of sitting in the bleachers. Along the side of the field she could see kids playing, running wildly, and throwing their own footballs. She made a mental note to let the boys bring a ball if they wanted for the next game so they could play too. After the Varsity victory, Jesse ushered Luke and Ryan to the car while texting Michael a reminder of his curfew. He might be a big football player now, but he still had rules and knew better than to test them when it came to curfew. Jesse remembered her parents saying, "Nothing good happens after midnight," and how it used to make her blood boil. Now that she was a parent, she knew her parents hadn't been old fashioned, they had been wise.

Fifteen

Late Saturday afternoon, Jesse, Luke and Ryan walked up to the grandstand at the fair, the air buzzing electric all around them. With so little else to do in the way of entertainment, most of the town turned out for the county fair every year, and this was no exception. The smells of carnival treats like popcorn, funnel cakes and various fried monstrosities wafted in the air as Jesse noted that it seemed most of the people at the game seemed to be at the fair as well. There were little children darting in between the crowds, chased by tired looking mothers and men grouped together near the beer carts, laughing and telling stories.

As they made their way toward the food tent across the fairgrounds, Jesse's stomach dropped as she saw Levi standing with a group of friends. Her heart gave an unexpected twinge at seeing him after not getting so much as a phone call, his alleged rose be damned. As one of the men moved aside, Jesse realized that standing next to Levi was an absolutely beautiful woman. Her arm was slung around his waist, her head leaned into his shoulder. When Jesse saw her turn her face up to whisper something in Levi's ear, so intimately snuggled against him in front of his friends, she felt her heart clench as if someone had reached right into her chest and squeezed it.

Suddenly, she felt so incredibly out of place. There she stood in six-year-old jeans and in a shirt she considered new, purchased from the clearance rack. Whatever extra money she had went into clothes for the boys who were growing like weeds. How in the world was she supposed to compete with the likes of that...that... girl? Jesse sucked in a breath of surprise so sharp that Ryan stopped walking and pulled at her hand.

"What, Mom? What's wrong?"

"Nothing honey. I just..." and she realized she didn't even have the words. "Nothing, Ryan. Let's to grab a bite to eat," she said as she forced herself to physically relax her stance, her gait and what no doubt was the scowl on her face.

Jesus, whoever she was, she was stunning in her soft camel colored sweater with dark brown leggings and high dark brown leather boots. Her red-brown, straight satiny hair literally gleamed in the late afternoon sun. Jesse couldn't help but hate her on sight. Levi's arm was loosely draped around her shoulder and they looked so cozy Jesse could have bent over and thrown up there in the gravel. Seeing them together caused an absolute avalanche of insecurity to nearly tumble Jesse down. She knew she couldn't give in to the weak, sad feelings because her boys were beside and behind her. She took a few more steps and walked right past Levi and that girl, shapely and perky in all the right places. Jesse noticed as she walked around them, daring a glance at the girl's face that she was absolutely lovely and that she was very young.

Jesse's gut twisted, going over her own insecurities and flaws with a fine tooth comb. No matter how she shook it, the redhead trumped her at every turn. She was young, firm and, damn it to Hell, genuinely sweet looking. Whomever she was, she was probably the perfect person to start over with. She didn't even look old enough to have any baggage trailing behind her, certainly not the kind that Jesse had. She gave a quick mental shake of her head at that thought. She would never consider her boys baggage, but the scars from the failed marriage felt a little like a backpack full of lead sometimes. Even though she damned herself for getting so wrapped up in what was apparently just sex to Levi, Jesse felt her eyes well up with tears as she showed the kids where they could go to get some food. They were, at this point, oblivious to their mother, having given over to the strong aromatic pull of corn dogs and funnel cakes.

Despite her good sense, Jesse risked one more glance at Levi as she walked away, and their eyes connected. She saw a flicker of panic cross his face as he dropped his arm from the lovely girl. Jesse didn't smile or change expression. She couldn't. She was absolutely terrified that her hurt would show if she attempted a smile. She quickly dropped her eyes back to her boys. Levi hadn't earned a dirty look or any judgment on her behalf. They had been in love once. They made love last week, after years of being apart. It was one of the greatest moments in her life. The sex had been perfect, full of strength, tenderness, and what had felt to her like a surge of making up for lost time. She and Levi had been away from each other for a lot of years. Of course, after his wife had passed he would have met someone. Maybe the redhead was the person that filled a need for him, a companion, a friend and undoubtedly a lover. Jesse couldn't really begrudge him that.

She felt completely alone standing in line with her boys around her, arguing over what to order for dinner. It hit her then with force that she was being a hypocrite. On one hand, she was nowhere near ready to dive into any sort of relationship, but on the other she had thought last week's lovemaking would have meant something. She and Levi hadn't voiced any declarations that day, but her heart had certainly made one.

After several hours and at least fifty dollars later, Jesse finished unloading her vehicle full of exhausted sons, and directed them all to their beds. Hugs and kisses were administered lovingly, as well as nighttime prayers said over them. No matter what life threw at her, her sons were her anchors.

She walked into her bedroom, stripped down, and avoided the mirror. She couldn't bear to see the hurt in her own eyes. As she dressed in her pajamas, she played the scene over in her mind. Levi with his lovely young thing, the flash of shock in his eyes when he saw her there. Jesse went into the bathroom to sweep her hair up into a bun, brush her teeth, and wash her face. She sent a quick text to Michael to see that he had made it to the friend's house where he was staying overnight. He was quick to reply that all was well, and she said a mental prayer that he was safe and sound. It was harder than she ever dreamed to hand over independence to her sons. She preferred when they were little and tucked in their own beds where she could guard them and check that they were fine. She had to constantly remind herself that her own parents had done the same, and every set of parents before them. Letting go in bits and pieces was just part of the job.

Finally downstairs with tea in hand, she pulled her legs up under her on the couch and got out her journal. Pouring her heart onto the pages of a book had been a constant in her life, through all the twists and turns. Jesse figured that journaling was much more affordable than therapy, and as long as nobody found it, less humiliating than spilling out her hurts, wants and wishes in front of another person. She picked up her blue ink pen, slowly closed and opened her eyes, then wrote.

When I went to greet you I saw a
flash there in your eyes
Was it 'here we go again?' Dread?
My heart crushed in surprise.
It started me thinking of this war
inside my head
Is this not a second chance, but
Delusion instead?
It wouldn't be the first time that I
misread the cues
Flashing back under the stars,
tangled limbs, tongues and you
Right now I am mired in
uncertainty and confusion

Do I stay put, stay safe, or jump
straight into Delusion?

Jesse read and reread that and even she had the sense to feel embarrassed for herself. She closed her eyes, threw her head back and spit the word "idiot" out in a hateful whisper. She reached down for her pen and dumped the rest of her feelings out on the paper in front of her. Maybe once it was out, she could get some relief from the pressure that had been bearing down on her all evening. She felt like a tick that was about to burst.

Oh that fool, she chased him down and
followed him all over town.
Yelling I love you with hands and eyes, that
stupid girl was so surprised!
He doesn't want what he can get, offered
up with no regret.
No stars should shine bright in your eyes,
you have to hide, have to disguise!
Silly girl, the time has passed, let it go with
all the rest.
There's no promise, no lovesick spell, no
passion to make you scream and yell.
Bury it now with half a smile, it would hurt
less than wondering why.

Put it to bed, accept what is true. Lay it down now girl, he doesn't want you.

After she finished her writing, she reread it a few times, decided it reflected the strange place her heart was at right now. She blew out a big breath and closed her journal. Jesse walked to the bedroom, flicking lights off along the way and hid the journal in her nightstand under the family Bible. She turned off the lamp, tucked the covers up under her chin and closed her eyes on that night at the carnival.

Sixteen

The alarm clock on Sunday morning always seemed a bit more jarring than any other day of the week. Jesse groaned as she rolled over to shut up the alarm and couldn't help but think with a smirk that it was the devil himself urging her to stay under the covers. At least she'd have a leg up on somebody today. She wrapped up in her fuzzy robe and tap-tapped gently on the doors of her sons bedrooms, hearing the *snick* sound of the doors as she opened them to let some of the noise of the day in to help wake them up.

Thankfully, she had the foresight to lay out church clothes the night before. Sunday morning was the one time a week the boys didn't seem to care what it was they wore as long as they could put it on at the last minute. Jesse was thankful that her church had taken the 'just get them in the door' approach to ministering to big kids and teens. They all crowded together in the balcony anyway to escape the watchful stares of tired mothers and the elderly folks. Jesse knew good and well that the elders of the church weren't really scowling at the jeans and t-shirts the kids typically wore, that most likely they were reaching back into their memories of when they attended the old beautiful church, turned out in suits, dresses, hats and shined shoes. Many of them even took the time to pat mothers on the hand and tell them it's good to have the kids present. One lady that Jesse remembered back from her own childhood at the church had leaned in and said, "The pull of the world is strong, and even if they are out raising Cain on Saturday night, at least they're in the pew on Sunday."

Typically, she sat on the back right pew on Sunday mornings, still adjusting to the awkwardness of being there without a spouse. At least when she was married she had the ring on her finger to show she wasn't physically alone. Spiritually, Drake had neglected her for years. Jesse was so thankful to have her faith and her sons. She found her spot on the pew, and said her hellos to the usual folks that sat around her spot. As she dug for her checkbook in her purse, she felt like someone was staring. Jesse looked up into the sea colored eyes and dimpled smile of Cole. He grinned as he gestured quickly around to the packed sanctuary.

"It looks like a full house, care if I sit by you?" he said in an almost bashful tone. Jesse smiled right back at him and stood to gather her purse and look quickly up to the balcony into the irritated glare of her oldest son.

"Let me just scoot my stuff over a bit. It's Communion Sunday; the place is usually packed." She moved down a few spaces, putting a comfortable and respectable distance between herself and Cole. She felt a little embarrassed over the fact that she was pretty certain she had blushed. He smiled over at her once more, then tuned his eyes toward the Pastor who had begun the process of welcoming the congregation and starting the announcements.

The hour moved by in a blur of prayer, standing up, sitting down, singing and reflection. Jesse had always found church to be a restoring time, once the boys had grown big enough to go sit with the rest of the kids. She was thankful they behaved and even more thankful that she could get an hour to herself to reflect and pay attention. There was something very special about being back in the church she had attended as a child. The Pastor ended her sermon and prayed aloud over the bowed heads of her congregation as she walked back to the vestibule of the church, ready to shake hands with her flock on their way out of the door. During dismissal, the Pastor was quick and efficient; she knew it was a race to the death for the area churches to see who could get to the handful of local restaurants first.

As the people filed out the door, Cole stood and stepped out of the pew into the aisle so that Jesse could slide on out. As she turned to face the back door to get in line with the press of the congregation, Cole stepped up closely behind her. He wasn't touching her body with his, but he was standing so close she could feel the heat of him. Maybe it was the rejection from the previous night or the strange thrill of an unexpected hormone rush in an inappropriate place, but she couldn't quite stop the shiver than ran up her back. She shut her eyes tight against the bloom of a blush on her cheek when she heard a quiet laugh escape him. With her hair swept up in a clip, she felt his breath on the back of her neck. Fighting another shiver, she focused only on getting out of the door. Mechanically, she shook the hand of the Pastor and didn't turn around again until she was outside the church. Cole gave her shoulder a squeeze as he walked past and said quietly, "Have a good day, Jesse." And at that, he walked around the corner of the beautiful, big church and was gone. Jesse felt more than a little like an idiot and stood straight-faced waiting for her gaggle of children to file down from the balcony. When they did, Michael made a bee-line for her.

"What the heck was that guy doing sitting by you, Mom?"

"Honey, that was Cole that helped us move, remember him?" Michael squinched up his face in an unappealing grimace.

"Easy there kiddo, I've known him for years. Anyway, he got in the church late and preferred to sit by someone he knew versus smooshing in next to a stranger," she explained while trying to keep her smile as bland as possible. She dug in her purse for her keys and turned, heading straight for her vehicle. By the time she got in the Suburban she felt she was acting a bit more normal. With her mind occupied with the feeling of Cole's breath on her neck, she barely even noticed the particularly vicious brand of bickering that always seems to follow when siblings attend church.

By Wednesday of the following week, Jesse had felt herself in The Zone at work. She had hammered out several plans for two exceptionally difficult clients, and had been busy presenting the options to them by phone. She put her headset down, stood up and decided to go outside for some fresh air. Jesse grabbed her phone and watering can on the way out the door, smiling at the fact that no matter how big her boys grew, she never went anywhere without her phone. Someone might need their mama and she'd be ready. She walked around the side of the house and started plucking weeds out of the red begonia bunches. For a few minutes Jesse lost herself, enjoying the mindlessness of the relaxing task until her phone buzzed in her jeans pocket.

She didn't recognize the number and said a silent prayer that it wasn't a client who had gotten her mobile number from a coworker.

"Hello, this is Jesse," she said just to be sure. She didn't even bother masking her surprise when she heard a deep voice on the other end.

"Hey Jesse." With a jerk, Jesse turned immediately to the driveway, half expecting Cole to materialize before her, big shoulders and all. Nobody was there except for the mailman who waved a brisk hello on his quick clipped walk up the sidewalk.

"Oh, hey Cole. How are you?" she asked, hoping she sounded casual. She felt a little frisson of excitement run up her back at the sound of his voice.

"Not much, I wanted to say hello and see if you'd like to go to dinner this Saturday, if you don't have plans," Cole said, his words so calm and

relaxed. And why shouldn't they be, Jesse sc
to herself. They were adults. Adults go on dates, surely. Jesse did a quick recall of her schedule, remembering the boys would be at Drake's for the weekend following the football game on Friday night. She felt like there was a vibrating softball bouncing around in her stomach, but as her mind went to Levi and how he certainly hadn't called asking for a date, why should she wait around on him? He was probably playing naked patti-cake with that gorgeous redhead in his free time.

She drew in a deep breath and figured what the hell. "Sure, Cole. That sounds like fun."

"Good. How about we go to Rose's Patio, down by the river?"

"What? Is that place still open? I can't believe that!" Jesse grinned with the flood of memories that washed over her at the mention of the restaurant. That little waterfront restaurant had been the to go-to place for all Homecoming and Prom pre-dance dates.

"Yeah, it's still pretty great, but maybe not as fancy as it seemed years ago. You don't have to wear any sequins or anything," and at that they both laughed. There was something sacred to be said for sequins and beaded gowns in the 90s. If it didn't weigh 15 pounds on its own, it wasn't a suitable prom dress back then. They talked for a few more minutes, finalizing plans. Cole would pick her up at 6 on Saturday night. She hung up the phone and put a dirt streaked hand to her stomach. She whistled a quick peal and smiled. She was actually going on a date. She hadn't been on a date since before she had been married.

Once the baby came, she and Drake had settled into the all too common rut of child raising. Several couples that she knew had continued going on dates and vacations, little overnight trips here and there in the name of preserving their relationship. Jesse chalked at least some of the relationship failure up to not making enough effort to keep the spark in the early years. The rest of it she chalked up to Drake being a pompous ass.

Seventeen

Drake had driven down for the Friday night football game and Jesse felt his presence like a hot poker there behind her in the stands, two rows up and bearing down on her with his weighty, hateful gaze. Luke and Ryan chose to sit with her to watch the game since they were going to be with Drake the rest of the weekend, which had gone over like a lead balloon. Drake was beyond infuriated that his children didn't want to sit with him. All Jesse could think was *is it any wonder*? The way he blustered and barked at the slightest difference in reality and what he wanted from it, he prickled just like a porcupine. Of course, the kids had chosen to sit with her. She had their bags all packed and ready for the hand off after the game. Michael had been highly annoyed not to get to go out with his friends, but as it was, that was their custody arrangement. The JV team took a beating, and Jesse couldn't help but feel thankful that Michael had very little time in the game. The less he was in, the less he could make an error, and the less Drake could spit and fuss about it all weekend long. As it was, at least if he was going to complain it was because of the injustice of Michael not getting appropriate playing time. Jesse was so miserable by the end of the game that she was thankful it was over. She made a promise to herself not to let Drake ruin the next one for her. She knew she was going to blink and Michael's high school days would be over. She would be damned if she would go through the rigors of divorcing him, only to let him continue to have a hold on her.

The hand off went reasonably well. She got the boys and their bags loaded up into Drake's car as he checked emails on his phone, happy to have been at the game, but now resenting the hell out of the drive back to his apartment. Despite Drake's exasperated sighs on how much time it was taking her, Jesse kissed each boy and reminded them to do their homework, love each other, and to be ready when she picked them up on Sunday. She put on a brave face and even made it all the way out of the parking lot before she crumbled. She cried big, hot tears that dripped down so fast she didn't even bother wiping at them.

Jesse pulled up to the house, locked the doors and bypassed the bottle of wine in the fridge in favor of changing into her pajamas. She tidied up, amazed at how quickly three boys can demolish a house, and made a few notes of errands to run in the morning. Her heart was broken with handing over the boys to Drake, but she knew it had to be done. They were safe with him, and once he was away from Jesse, he chilled out considerably according to Michael. She knew that if he got out of line with the kids that she would find out, and that there were probably measures that could be taken. She gave her head a hard shake as if to clear the hateful thoughts right out of her mind and made her way up the stairs. She flicked the hallway light off, then turned and thought better of it, a little light might make her feel less anxious.

She decided not allow herself to cry any more tonight. She had to accept that this is how things would be from now on, she had to be an adult about it. Tomorrow would be a new day, she thought as she pulled the soft, cool covers up around her ears. She had to get the groceries for the week, take the sacks of outgrown boy clothes to the Salvation Army, and then she planned to reward herself with a massage and pedicure. She had a date to prepare for, she might as well relax before the big night. Jesse covered up, reached into her bedside table, and pulled out her favorite lavender essential oil and applied a drop on each wrist, enjoying the scent as she closed her eyes on the day. She had just drifted to that delicious stage of not quite asleep, not quite awake when her phone rang.

With her heart in her throat, she jerked the phone off its charger cord, fear welling up that there was a problem with her boys. Thankfully, she saw that it wasn't Drake's phone number or an unknown number, but Levi's instead. Her stomach lurched as she hit the answer button.

"Levi? Is everything ok?" she realized it was only 10:30 PM, but she was always fearful of late night phone calls with the potentially bad news they seemed to bring.

"Yeah, Jesse, shit. Sorry. I didn't realize how late it was," he said into the phone, his words a little slurred.

Jesse wrinkled her brow at this; she knew Levi well enough to know he didn't usually overdo on alcohol. He was an 'all things in moderation' type of man and always had been.

"What's going on, Levi?" she asked, feeling a little edge of bitterness sink into her words as she visualized the beautiful redhead with him at the carnival as well, totaling up the days that had passed since they last talked. Why didn't he call after the carnival? Was this relationship all in her head?

"I hadn't talked to you in a while and wondered what you were up to."

"At 10:30 at night, Levi? I'm in bed," she frowned into the phone. What the hell did he think she was up to that late on a Friday night?

"Mmm, you in a bed. That's nice to think about. You want me to come over?" he said sexily into the phone. At that, Jesse resisted the urge to throw the phone against the wall. So this is what he thought of her?

Jesse nearly growled and answered, "Is that what this is? You think you're going to call me for a late night booty call? What do you think I am? Another one of your whores?" her hands were shaking with anger.

"Jesse? What the hell are you talking about? I don't have any whores!" Levi slurred at her.

"What happened, Levi? Did the little red head dump you? Is that why you're drunk and making late night phone calls?" At that, Jesse heard the pettiness in her own voice and just wanted this call to be over. There was no way she was going to get back to her lavender scented la-la land after this damned phone call. So much for a peaceful night's sleep.

"Jesse, I just called because I miss you. It's been a few weeks and I was thinking about you. Can I come over?" at her sharp intake of breath he quickly added, "Just to talk! Just to talk, Jesse. I swear," and then the silence hung in the air. She looked at the phone for a minute, like it was an alien thing she'd never seen. She sat there for a minute feeling so very alone. She missed him. She wanted him. She was so angry at him, she could pinch his head off, but underneath it all, she wanted to hit rewind and feel him against her.

Jesse put the phone back up to her ear and felt all the energy drain out of herself. Barely above a whisper, she said, "Levi, it's late and I'm tired. Drake took the boys after the game tonight, and I am always exhausted after dealing with him. We'll have to pick this back up another time. I just can't do this tonight," and then she hit the button to end the call, laying the phone on the night stand. She laid her head against the pillow, eyes wide open and stared at the ceiling until she finally drifted into a dreamless sleep.

Eighteen

Saturday morning was a blur of errand running, coffee sipping, and ultimately, relaxing after a nice lunch at her favorite cafe. Jesse had been to restaurants alone when traveling for work and it never really bothered her. She'd often bring a book to read as she waited for her food, enjoying the solitude and ability to eat food while it was hot, without the interruption of often gross commentary by her boys. They had a special knack for waiting until her mouth was full to share the most disgusting detail of the day. There was something a little different, though, about eating alone in a restaurant in her hometown. Here she couldn't go anywhere without running into someone she knew and the cafe was no exception. She wanted to grow a thicker skin though, she knew she had to get used to this lifestyle, and by God, she wasn't going to let any gossips or looks of pity force her into another drive-through lunch.

Jesse walked into the cafe, placed her order at the counter and turned to find her seat, nearly bumping into the large enhanced bosom of her high school class homecoming queen, still very much in possession of her cronies. Jesse stared into the breasts and lipstick smiles of three blond beauties, the Mean Girls. Internally thinking, *Of course. Of course they are right here.* Jesse bit back the words and instead smiled and said, "Hi girls. Wow, you three haven't changed a bit."

Deep, smug satisfaction seemed to roll right off them as Laura Williamson, the queen bee of the group, said, "Well hi, Jesse. Bless your heart, we heard you had moved back home to live with your parents. How are you doing, hon?" At that Jesse nearly gagged. There was something about being called hon, honey, babe or dear by someone her own age or younger that absolutely turned her stomach.

"No, actually I bought a home in town and am all settled in. It is nice to be back after being gone so many years." Jesse realized that she threw the last bit in as a passive-aggressive insult, however she doubted the Big Titty Trio would have enough sense to realize the barb was directed their way. Those three had never even realized there was a world outside of their hometown. As she caught the second in command, Camille, giving Jesse's clothes a poorly concealed once-over, she nearly sighed with relief when her order number was called. Jordan, the most dim of the three, a situation little improved with time, smiled at Jesse and said, "You're welcome to come sit with us, honey," as she tilted her head, better to emphasize her cascading weave as it spilled in a waterfall of glossiness down her shoulder. "Thanks Jordan, but I'm just going to eat and run. I have some things to get done today," she said as she carried her plate to her table. She chose one in front of one of the light filled windows, hoping a little Vitamin D would perk her up a bit. Jesse was a little disappointed in herself immediately for the tidal wave of hateful thoughts that had filled her at the sight of those women. *What was she*, she thought to herself, *sixteen again?* She didn't have to give two shits anymore if those girls approved of her outfit, her living situation or her marital status, for Pete's sake. And as far as the women with their big boobs, false nails and hair went, more power to them. They really did look amazing. Jesse put the kibosh on the small feelings that started to chip away at her as she ate. She fought back the negative thoughts about her own style, her poof of curly hair and her unpolished nails.

Her next stop was for a massage, then a manicure and pedicure. She'd relax a bit and enjoy being pampered, and finally let herself focus on her date. She had been blocking those feelings out so far that morning. Jesse couldn't remember the last date she'd been on before Drake and felt like a nervous wreck about the whole thing. She thought she knew what she was going to wear, but so far had changed her mind about five times. Jesse finished her meal and drove to the spa where she quickly relaxed so much she thought she felt her spirit leave her body.

By the time Jesse got home, she had enough time to do a quick run-through of the house to be sure everything was in its place. She poured a glass of chilled white wine and munched on a handful of crackers, willing her nerves to calm down. She felt a chill run down her spine at the excitement of a date with Cole. For a minute, her mind flitted to the strange call with Levi and all the unspoken words she knew would bubble up in time, but she tamped that right back down. Tonight was about something new and exciting.

Jesse checked her appearance in the full length mirror in the hallway for the tenth time in as many minutes. She felt like a teenager again. She remembered a nasty trick her mother used to pull when she was anxiously awaiting a date to arrive. If her date was due to pick her up at seven o'clock, her mom would yell, "Jesse, are you ready? It's seven o'clock!" at least ten minutes early, and it never failed to scare her. Eadie had a wicked sense of humor and loved a good scare. It spoke a lot about how gullible Jesse used to be by the fact that she fell for it every time.

Tonight Jesse had chosen to wear a dress she bought a few years ago when she and Drake were supposed to go out for their anniversary dinner. This was right before she had made up her mind that the marriage just couldn't be fixed. She had gone all out for this anniversary, making reservations at the nice little Italian restaurant that Drake favored. She purchased a lovely dark green wrap dress, loving how the color made her hazel eyes change to a pretty olive green color. It complimented her dark brown hair nicely as well, if she did say so herself. Jesse had even purchased a new necklace that had a delicate fringe of beading. At the lowest point the beads grazed her cleavage, of which showed more than it ever did in normal daily life. She had wanted that evening to be special, and to try and get back the spark she thought surely had been in Drake's eyes at some point in their relationship. Jesse had also bought a very sexy set of black lace bra and panties. That much hadn't been so much of a splurge, she always tried to wear matching lingerie, something about it made her feel so grown up and sexy. That had been a habit straight from her teens. She'd sneak into the lingerie store at the mall and purchase a matching bra and panty set with the money she had earned working her random summer jobs. The concession stand at the little league ballgames had won her many a hot summer night, making Levi's eyes pop out of his head. Ugh. She wasn't going to let him sneak into any more thoughts tonight, she decided. As she perched on the bed to slip on her nude colored heels, she remembered how the anniversary date had flopped. She had reminded Drake that their anniversary was on Friday night, and that she had made special plans to have her parents come to watch the boys overnight. Yet again, he let her down. She remembered the butterflies she felt getting ready for that date, more the nervous, anxious feelings versus the excitement she felt tonight. Jesse didn't even have to close her eyes to see again how Drake blustered in from the garage, barely bothering to speak to Eadie and Walt who had corralled the boys in the living room, fussing over what type of pizza to order for dinner. Drake did take notice of Jesse's appearance, when she smiled and said happy anniversary to him, he stopped where he stood, looked her up and down and said, "Jesus, Jesse. How much did that thing cost?" and then walked straight into his office. Jesse turned to look at Eadie, embarrassed of Drake's behavior and ashamed for her parents to see what a rat bastard he really could be. Drake hadn't surfaced from his office that night, and after a half hour of waiting for him, hoping he'd emerge ready to go on their date; she went back up to her room where she hung up her dress and shoes and she hadn't touched them since.

Jesse thanked God that those days were behind her now. She had just come down the stairs when the doorbell rang. She opened it to find Cole smiling, flowers in hand. She smiled up at him and stepped back to hold the door open. "Those are beautiful, come on in," she said as he handed her the little bouquet of sunflowers. He stopped her as she started to turn to walk to the kitchen to find a vase for the flowers and with a hand on her elbow to still her, he looked at her appreciatively.

"Jesse, you look beautiful," he said as he looked at her again. Jesse felt a small twinge of unease, but she wasn't sure exactly why. It almost seemed like she saw a flicker of something change in his eyes, and then change back again like it never happened. She took a step back and said,

"Thank you. I'm just going to put these in some water. I'll be right back." It had to be nerves about the date. My God it had been decades since she'd been on a date, even longer since she had spent time around Cole. Back then he had been just a friend, another one of the guys. She returned with the vase and set it on the sideboard in the hall. It looked lovely there, bright and yellow-orange.

"Sunflowers have always been my favorite," she said, reaching behind him to grab her jacket.

"I remember. You used to wear the sunflower perfume. Do you still?" he asked as he took her hand, raising her wrist to his nose, inhaling as his lips grazed her skin. "No, not tonight. A rose scent tonight," he said, lowering her arm, putting her hand in his to lead her out the door. Jesse didn't know whether she was weirded out by what just happened or totally turned on. She decided she was going to have to break out the vibrator a little more often. She was a nervous, horny mess. They walked outside and Jesse stopped and stared. A Harley Davidson was parked in her driveway. She looked back to Cole who had sort of a sheepish grin on his face. "I didn't know you'd be wearing a dress," he said as he pulled a face. Well, that was awkward.

"Well, I certainly can't get on that thing very easily tonight," she said, holding out the hem of her skirt.

"Damn, Jesse, sorry. I didn't think that one through," he said as she dug in her clutch for the keys to her SUV.

"Put that thing behind the gate to the fence, would you? It would be my luck for it to get stolen sitting out tonight," she said as she unlocked and held open the gate. Cole stretched his leg over the bike, firing it up to a delicious rumble. Jesse looked up to see a neighbor peeking through the curtains, no doubt trying to figure out what the ruckus was. Despite the kids yelling and hollering when they were outside, her neighborhood was pretty quiet. She gave the old man a little finger wave hoping the entire population of the Baptist Church in town wouldn't know about her going on a date with a motorcycle riding fella. Cole stood beside her, closing the gate and looking ten feet tall. He wore a V-neck black sweater that really looked good with his hard muscles underneath. Dark jeans, nice black shoes and of course those eyes. He held out his hand for the keys and walked her to the passenger side of the door. Jesse wasn't much for letting anyone else drive her vehicle, but figured it was the least he could do since he showed up for a date on a freaking motorcycle. She said a silent prayer of thank you for the fact that she had cleaned out the Suburban today, ridding it of the scent of boy. She had a 'no trash in the truck' rule, and for the most part, the boys followed it, throwing away wrappers and any other mess they made while in the car, but there was something to be said for the sheer magnitude of boy smell. Thankfully, she had left the windows cracked a bit, mingled with a heavy dose of air freshener, and overall, it smelled clean.

Cole made conversation easily on the drive to the restaurant, through the wooded hills along the way. They talked about what they'd been up to since high school. Cole had gone into the military, not having the money for college or a solid sense of what he wanted to do with his future. He had served in the Marines, ending his eight year service career with the G.I. Bill, which allowed him to go college. He went to the local university for a degree in Forestry. He worked for the Forest and Conservation Department, and loved it.

"I spend a lot of time in the deep woods. I feel so free there. It's quiet and remote. I bought some land out past Josiah's Pointe about five years ago and had a cabin built," he said with a smile, briefly looking over at her.

"Jeez, that's way out there!" Jesse said with a shiver. She hadn't minded the occasional camp out, but she felt a certain level of attraction to the safety of street lights and neighbors that could hear her if she stepped out the front door and yelled for help. There would be nothing but starlight and creepy crawlies that far out in the country.

“It is. I love it. The moon looks huge out there. On a super moon night, it would take your breath away,” Cole said, staring out at the highway. The night was already falling around them. Jesse had always loved this time of year, even though she was a Spring Season girl at heart. She had always loved the idea of snuggling up in front of a fire with all the romantic potential. They arrived at the restaurant, and Jesse couldn’t believe how little it had changed.

“It’s just the same. I fully expect a limousine full of bejeweled teenagers to drive up, ready for the big dance,” she laughed, taking Cole’s hand as he handed back her keys. The stars were bright and there was a slight chill in the air. Cole held the door open for her, and as she walked through the door, she practically stepped back in time. They were seated and served fairly quickly. Cole ordered a bottle of pinot noir and they dined on an interesting arrangement of courses far removed from the chicken fingers and steak they had all ordered back in the day, dripping with dangle earrings and shoulder pads made of gold beading. Big hair was the order of the day back then, and in that regard, not much had changed, Jesse thought as she reached up and smoothed her hair back behind her ear.

“You look the same, you know,” Cole said as he grinned over his glass as if he could read her mind. She noticed for the first time that he had beautiful hands. Maybe the wine was getting to her, she thought as she mentally retraced her steps to ensure she had drunk just the one glass at home while she waited for him.

“Yeah right, Cole! Three boys later...” she laughed, “but I’ll thank you all the same,” Jesse said, taking another spoonful of velvety squash soup.

“Believe me, I remember,” Cole answered. “I remember the first time I saw you, before I even moved to town,” he said, looking down at his plate of grilled skirt steak and peaches. Popping a bite into his mouth, she realized she was waiting intently to hear what he said. “Before we moved here, we came to check out the town and I came to a game. There you were, cheering in that skirt. My God, I had some dreams over those long legs,” he laughed and Jesse felt herself blushing.

“Ok, ok,” she said, waving away the eyebrows he wiggled at her, laughing despite the blush. “I didn’t know that you knew me before you moved. What was that, our sophomore year?” Jesse asked, belatedly embarrassed that her memories of him weren’t as clear as his memories of her.

"Yeah, sophomore year," he answered, spearing another bite of his food, "no wonder you don't remember, you only had eyes for a certain guy back then," Cole said with a smirky sideways glance. Jesse felt a little like he was baiting her. She wasn't about to bring up Levi on a date with Cole, she had better manners than that. She tried to steer the conversation to more neutral territory, mentioning a project she was working on that dealt with a client who had headquarters not too far from where they were dining. She figured talking about how glad she was to be home, living at a slower pace, around friendly people was a safer topic than the one Cole had brought up. They chatted throughout the rest of dinner, sharing a piece of cheesecake at the end of the meal. Jesse was delightedly stuffed and had a slight buzz from the delicious wine they had enjoyed.

Cole took the keys and drove back to her house, a companionable silence filling the car. Just before they hit the city limits, Cole put his hand on Jesse's knee. Her heart nearly leapt out of her chest at that, and their eyes connected briefly as he looked at her, then back to the road. By the time they pulled up in her driveway, Jesse had officially ended the internal argument about being a consenting adult, that a woman had needs as well as a man, and really it was nobody's damned business what she decided to do with her sex life. She had nearly worked herself into a frenzy when her nerves attacked as she opened the Suburban door and took Cole's hand as he walked her up the stairs. As she unlocked the door, he stood to the side, watching her intently to see if she was going to invite him in. Jesse opened the door and took his hand. She tossed her jacket on the chair and Cole followed her inside, shutting the door with his foot as he reached out and put his hands on her. One big hand was behind her neck, tilting back her head where his lips touched hers, at once both soft and hard. He put his arm around her, holding her closely, molding her to his body. My God, she thought, the man had muscles on his muscles. Then she noticed what else was hard and pressing against her. It seems the old wives' tale about the big hands and big feet had some merit.

Cole pulled back from her and Jesse felt the lack of him like a cold breeze against her body. He kept ahold of her hand, leading her to the couch. He sat down in the middle, back-lit from the moonlight filtering in from the big window behind him. He looked incredibly mysterious there, sea colored eyes searching her face, dark hair curling softly, just begging for her fingers to touch it. He gave her a little tug and she settled there, straddling him there on the couch. Before she could lose her inhibition he kissed her again, hard and hot, his lips nearly bruising hers. His hands worked at the deep neckline of her wrap dress, pulling the sides down around her breasts, pushing against the restraint of the thin black lace. Cole groaned and kissed her hard again, thumbs rubbing her body against the lace, fingers cupping the weight of her breasts, pushing up to free them from the suggestion of a bra. He looked down at her body, lowering his head to one breast, touching her with his hot tongue. Jesse rolled her head back, taking in the sensation with the moonlight spilling down on her body. She looked back down as Cole rucked her skirt up around her hips, sliding his hand down, palming the lace covering her center. Jesse gasped as he traced one finger down the length of her panties, then coming back up the front to the edge of the barely-there lingerie. He pushed them aside and let his finger follow the same path. He felt her velvety softness and made a noise low in his throat, almost a growl as he took her lips again, his fingers finding the wetness of her, more than ready for him. He circled her, feeling her body response to his touch. She moved her hips against him as he rocked her, touching that flat little miracle place at a pressure and speed that had her heart racing, her head thrown back as she came against him. He took advantage of his freed mouth to put it against the breast he hadn't tasted yet. She melted against him and realized she heard something outside. She was trying to still her heartbeat enough to listen, the rush of release flooding her senses when someone knocked hard on the door.

"What the hell?" Jesse asked as she looked at Cole, scrambling off him, righting her dress as her heart pounded in her chest. Cole stood, adjusting his pants, no doubt trying to ease that incredible erection. He crossed in front of Jesse to the door, looked back once to be sure she was covered, and opened the door to a very surprised Levi.

Levi stood there for a second, absolutely stunned to see Cole answer Jesse's door. He took in Cole's messy hair and red mouth and looked past Cole to see Jesse with her curls rumpled as well as her dress.

"I'll be damned, Jesse," Levi said, giving her a wilting look. He looked back to Cole with an expression that was equal parts disbelief and disgust. "Cole? I can't believe this, man," Levi said, turning to walk down the steps. He stopped and faced Cole again. "You know what? I can believe it. Damn it, Cole." Levi turned and walked back to his truck, flicked on his lights and drove away.

Jesse was floored. She felt a little guilty, then realized she had nothing to feel guilty about. Did this mean that Levi expected her to wait on the sidelines till he tired with the redhead and whomever else he had going on the side? She had done nothing wrong. Cole shut the door and looked back at her, watching the emotions change on her face as she filtered through her feelings on what had just happened. Despite herself, her hands shook a bit and she felt angry and unsure what it was she had to feel angry about. Cole walked over to her, kissed her forehead and said, "I'm going to go." He pulled back to look at her, his hand still resting on her shoulder. She nodded up at him and took a big breath.

"I'm sorry about that, Cole. He doesn't just drop by. We aren't together," she said, then stopped. She didn't necessarily owe him an explanation, but felt like she needed to say something.

"It's ok. You alright?" he asked, eyebrows up and looking intently at her face.

"I'm fine. Just surprised," she said, putting her hand on his arm as he crossed to the door. "I had fun tonight," she said lamely, then laughed out loud. "That seems like a damned strange thing to say. I don't know what to say, really," she said, grimacing up at Cole who chuckled to himself.

“I know. It’s a little weird. I had fun too,” he said, stepping out of the door. “I’ll call you soon,” he said, pulling his motorcycle keys out of his jacket pocket. “Next time I’ll park in the driveway. And drive the truck,” he said as an afterthought, and they both laughed quietly at the general awful end of an otherwise wonderful evening.

“Right. Maybe you can pee on the porch railing so the other animals stay away from your territory!” she laughed, catching the awkwardness of the statement as it left her lips. She didn’t belong to him or anyone, but she had enjoyed the night nonetheless. Especially the part on the couch. She still felt a little weak in the knees. Jesse shut the door, flicking on the porch light as she heard Cole open the gate and start up the bike. He rolled it into the driveway, got on and the engine rumbled to life. Cole threw up his hand as he drove away into the night.

Nineteen

Jesse paced around the backyard on Sunday morning wearing her fluffy pink robe and rain boots, steaming mug of coffee in her hand. For the life of her, she couldn't figure out what she was going to do about Levi's surprise visit. She glanced at the phone gripped in her other hand, still too early to call her sister Anna. Anna was in Colorado, an hour behind. She could call Megan, but once she divulged that she'd slept with Levi and nearly with Cole, Megan would never shut up about it. The congratulations for finally getting some sexual gratification would eat up all the problem solving time. Megan was a very sexual person; she and Ivan were a match made in heaven. They practically vibrated with energy. The way they looked at each other was something to see; Jesse hoped they'd keep that fire. It was enviable to see healthy passion.

She looked down at her phone again knowing if she called Anna she'd wake her up. Anna and Travis were late sleepers, soaking in all the joyful abandon that comes with life without little kids. Sometimes, Jesse wondered if they would ever have their own after they married. Anna loved kids, but she definitely got her fix and sometimes fill with her Kindergarten class. Nah. She wouldn't wake up Anna. Better to brace herself for the deluge and call Megan. After just one ring, Megan answered, "Hey Jess! It's early, is everything ok?"

"Yeah. No. Well, yes. Everyone is healthy and fine; I just have a situation I wanted to run past you," Jesse said, closing her eyes and stopping halfway across the path she had been walking in the fenced backyard. "Before I tell you this, you have to promise to hear me out before you pounce, ok? I have to figure this one out before I go pick up the boys today," Jesse halfway expected a sarcastic comment or a false tone of offense but instead, Megan chuckled.

"Oh God, this is going to be good," she said, her smile apparent in her voice.

Jesse sighed and said, "Parts of it are. Parts of it are really good," she said, mentally flashing between making love with Levi in the softly filtered sunlight, and straddling Cole in the moonlight. She shook her head to clear the vision and launched into a quick recap of her situation, pausing for the occasional hoots of laughter and "Oh my God's" that Megan couldn't keep to herself. When Jesse got to the part about Cole on the couch last night, Megan crowed, "My God, I always thought he was so sexy!" then yelped as Ivan walked past, delivering a loud smack to her bottom. The new groom wasn't thrilled to hear his bride gushing about another man. Jesse didn't have to think very hard to imagine that big man with his severe glare. Ivan could put up a big front, but she knew Megan would have him naked on the kitchen table as soon as they hung up the phone.

When Jesse got to the part about Levi hammering on the door and stomping off, her hands were shaking. She didn't know if it was anger or nerves, but it was bad enough that she put her coffee cup down and sat on the porch swing.

"I can't even really tell you how I feel, Meg. I'm pissed about the attempted booty call, if they're even called that anymore, even though I know he was drunk, which in itself is weird!" she said to Megan's noises of confirmation. "I even wanted to talk with him and would've called him today to find out what was going on," she left off, not really sure what to say next. She stood again, looking up into the bright sun. "I can't believe he showed up last night. He knew I was pissed at him. I've never seen a look on his face like I saw last night. Never. He looked furious at me and I guess, betrayed by Cole," she said into the phone, her voice drifting off a bit at the end.

"Yeah, but God, Jess, just because you dated in high school and fooled around doesn't make you his," Megan said. Even as she heard the sensible words, Jesse knew it wasn't really true. Sure, high school was a long time ago. A lifetime ago. What they had together back then was more than just a puppy love situation. What they were together, even full of teenage angst and cocky confidence, was the stuff that dreams are made of. They had been the real deal. She tried not to let herself think about it often. She knew she screwed up when she married Drake, even though she'd never take it back. Without that asshole, she'd have never had her boys. Listening to Megan prattle on in the phone with only half an ear, she realized that she still really loved Levi. She didn't know what this business was with Levi and the hot little redhead, and she knew Cole was a delicious, welcome distraction, but was that all? She didn't want to go down that rabbit hole with Levi only to have it blow up in her face. It wasn't just her heart and soul she had to guard, she couldn't have another failed relationship in front of her boys. They deserved an awful lot of security and protection right now, especially with whatever they might encounter at their father's house with his hussy girlfriend.

"I can't decide if I want to call Levi, or let him stew over whatever it is that he's got going on right now," she said, gathering up her cup and walking into the house. Jesse knew even as she spoke the words against the tide of opinion flowing at her from Megan's side of the conversation that she wouldn't call Levi. Whatever it was he had going on, he needed to deal with it before they talked again. She wanted to call him, but it seemed like a smarter move to wait him out. She made all the right comments into the phone, sidestepping the "promise you won't call him" commands issued by Megan and ended the call. Jesse laid out her clothes for the trip to pick up the boys on her bed and went into the bathroom. She turned on the shower water and stripped, staring into the bathroom mirror. Absentmindedly, she cupped her breasts in her hands as she thought back to the absurdity of the events of the last few days. Jesse felt pretty confident naked, but decided with all this excitement, it might be a good idea to pick up some classes at the gym. She had been nearly naked with Cole on the verge of something very big, she giggled to herself at the pun, and then the equivalent of a bucket of cold water had doused her with Levi's knock at the door. Jesse stepped into the shower, suspended her troubled thoughts, and enjoyed the hot water beating down on her skin.

She luxuriated in the shower knowing it would be a full two weeks before she could spend this much time on herself again. The boys were big, but someone always needed something the minute she got in the shower. That much hadn't changed since they were little. She used a conditioning mask on her hair, shaved her legs, used the good body scrub she seemed to save for special occasions and took her time. When she emerged from the bathroom pink, clean, and smelling like the ocean, she stopped, her newfound peace and tranquility vanished. She grabbed the towel from the floor, covering her body quickly. Something was wrong. Jesse threw on her robe, picked up her phone and the bat she always kept 'just in case' under the edge of her bed when she saw it. There was a single sunflower from her bouquet in a bud vase sitting on top of her dresser. Jesse felt a white hot swirl of panic envelop her. Someone had been in the house while she was in the shower. She shut and locked the bedroom door, dressed as quickly as she could while dialing her phone. Levi answered on the first ring, his hello a gruff sound in her ear. She blinked at the phone, shocked at herself. She meant to choose her dad's number from the recent call list, but she hit Levi's instead. Jesse took a deep breath trying to not sound like a maniac.

Whoever had been in her house was probably gone by now. It almost had to be Cole, who else would fiddle with the sunflowers? She peeked out her window at the empty driveway and tried to remember if she had locked the back door. Did he think an unlocked door was an invitation to come on in? It wasn't! This had happened twice now! Jesse closed her eyes, mentally willing herself to sound calm.

"I wanted to call you after last night, to see what in the world is going on, Levi," Jesse said as she opened her door, bat in hand, peeking into the hallway. Empty.

"I came over last night to apologize for the phone call the night before," he said, his anger leaving him at the sound of her voice. Jesse anxiously went from room to room, checking closets, feeling more secure and less alone with Levi with her on the phone. She wasn't really sure what to say. She wasn't going to apologize for going on a date, or for doing anything else she had been doing, though she was certain he had jumped to some pretty accurate conclusions.

"What was wrong Friday night, Levi? That's not like you," she said walking down the stairs, looking around from room to room. So far, the place was empty. Her stomach was starting to relax a little until she realized she still had to check the basement.

"Jess, I'm sorry about the call. My mom kept the kids overnight, they had a big sleepover there with my sister's kids. I stayed home, drank some beer, and had a pity party," he said, sighing into the phone. Jesse had moved into the kitchen, quickly locking the back door she had left unlocked before her shower. As she reached for the bat that she had planned on taking with her into the basement, she saw a note and pen on the counter.

I ran by to check on you, you seemed pretty shook up last night. I'd be happy to join you in that shower next time. Lock your doors, silly woman.

- C

Jesse felt herself deflate and settle into the kitchen chair. At least she knew who had been in the house. She mentally kicked her own rear, she was really going to have to get better at locking the doors. She realized that Levi had paused, he seemed to be waiting for her to say something.

"Levi, I wasn't mad that you called, or even that you called a little tipsy. Hell, I'm not even mad you called wanting sex!" she said, her voice getting a little louder and higher than she intended. She took a deep breath and quieted her voice a little. "But it made me feel trashy to think you'd just call up and place an order for a piece that late at night. I didn't like that feeling," she said, closing her eyes and rubbing between her eyes. She was going to have to make more coffee.

"Come on. I don't think you're trashy, Jess. You know that. It was crass of me. I was lonely. I was lonely for you." At that she started to scoff, thinking back to the little redhead she saw him with at the carnival. Before she could ask him about her he said, "When you came over to the house that time, I wanted it so badly. I had been hoping we'd get another chance at us, Jess," he said pausing, willing her to say something. When she didn't, he continued, "I didn't want to push you. My God, you just got out of that mess with Drake," he said. Blood was roaring in Jesse's ears. She couldn't believe he'd just said that. She felt her heart lurch right up into her throat. Part of her wanted to yell "ME TOO!" but my God, wasn't it too much too soon?

She gave herself a minute, begging the right words to come out. "Levi, it would be a lie to say I didn't feel the same way. There's a connection between us that's hard to ignore," Jesse said, her eyes searched the ceiling as she tried to figure out what to say next. "There always has been."

She hadn't talked freely about her feelings with a man in a long, long time. She was used to having to guard herself at every turn with Drake. That had been awful and sad, but this was also uncomfortable.

"You are right about me needing a little space. We've had a hell of an adjustment. All of us have," she said, almost as an afterthought. Levi had overcome a lot in the last few years, raising those precious kids on his own. "It's not just us in this, or in any decisions we make."

"I know. Things are so much harder than they used to be," he said, his voice softening a little. "I try not to dwell on those days, but it's hard not to, you know what I mean?"

"God, yes," Jesse said, shaking her head at the audacious list of things she'd change if she could. "I spend too much time going over choices I would have made differently, had I dreamed what would happen in my life," she said, starting up the stairs. She had to get going soon to pick up the boys. "But," she sighed and stopped halfway up the stairs. "There's nothing I can do about it now other than not make any more idiotic choices," she said, continuing back up the stairs. "We've both got a lot going on right now, but I'd like it if we talked more."

"Me too, Jesse. I have to ask, even though I shouldn't. Are you and Cole together?" he asked, notably calm she thought.

"Not really. We went out to dinner," she answered, her Methodist upbringing reminding her that she'd been riding Cole like a cowgirl there on the couch after one dinner date. *Not a whore*, she argued to herself! A grown woman who needed some good sex. She was due after that drought she'd called a marriage.

Levi knew better than to challenge her about the date having just been a dinner date, but he had to ask, "Are you going to see him again?" This nearly flabbergasted Jesse.

Her temper spiked and she asked hotly, "I haven't decided within the last twelve hours, Levi. Are you still seeing the redhead?" She'd been dressing while they were talking, switching him to speaker as she pulled on her jeans and sweater, slipping on socks and shoes. She noticed he didn't answer right away.

"Her name is Shannon. We dated a bit over the last year," Levi said. Jesse sat down on the bed. Shannon. It would be a beautiful name to go with that red hair. Damn it.

"You don't have to get too much into it with me, Levi. It's not really any of my business," *like Cole wasn't any of his business*, she thought but didn't say. Jesse stood and walked down the stairs, doubling back through the house to check that the back door was locked before pulling a bottle of water out of the fridge. She grabbed her purse and keys and locked the front door behind her, remembering to flick on the porch light so that the place would be lit up when she returned with the boys. The days were shorter and the house was pretty dark at night, despite the street light that washed the neighbor's house in its yellow-orange glow in the evenings.

"I let her know that we needed some time apart right now," he said in a way that made her feel annoyed. To Jesse, the 'right now' part made it sound like he was going to keep her hanging after he saw if this thing with Jesse would pan out or not. She needed to get off the phone and wasn't going to pick that scab right before ending the call.

"Listen, Levi," she said, standing beside the driver's door, "I'm about to go get the boys, so I've got to go. Maybe we can talk soon," she said, wondering to herself just where this thing was going to end. Five kids between them, they'd have a lot to sort out to bring this together. It made her head hurt just thinking about it when she factored Drake and his snide comments into the equation.

"Ok, yeah. Have a safe trip and we can talk later this week. I'll give you a call," he said, then quickly added, "Not late at night," then laughed a quick, sharp laugh. Jesse couldn't help herself as she laughed into the phone.

"Bye, Levi."

"Bye, Jess," he said, disconnecting the call. She sat in the Suburban, fired up the engine and sat there, resting her head against the wheel for just a minute. *What a weird freaking weekend* she thought, as she backed out of the driveway. Jesse planned to gas up and suck down an energy drink before working up the energy and patience required to act like a sane person when she called Cole. It took her a full hour to calm down enough to dial his number.

While she had been determined to remain calm when she talked to him, at the sound of his voice, the temper she thought she had smothered down burst forth and flared right up again. "What the hell, Buddy? Do you think it's ok to just walk right in a person's house? You scared the shit out of me!" Well, there went any chance at a calm, adult conversation.

"What? I thought you'd be happy that I came over to check on you," Cole answered, the surprise evident in his voice.

"Call. Knock. Ring the doorbell. That's what people do," she said, absolutely seething with anger. "Walking in unannounced? That's what people do right before they get shot or hit over the head. Or that's what they do if they are criminals!" she yelled into the air, thankful that using the speaker option meant she didn't have to drive and hold a phone with her shaking hands. "I'm serious, Cole. That's a creepy thing to do to a single woman. I don't like it," she said, realizing that she just unloaded a lot more than her annoyance and fear at him walking in uninvited. All the frustration of the weekend had just exploded out of her, now she just felt weak.

"Are you done now?" he asked, his voice low and calm.

She wasn't sure how she felt about that particular answer. Was he being patronizing like Drake had been or was he giving her a chance to actually talk?

"I think so," she said, feeling the rage in her fill up her body. Her hands were shaking so badly that she checked her rear-view mirror to be sure there was nobody close behind her and she pulled over on the side of the road. All of the emotion that she had been holding in over Drake and worrying over the boys, the change involved in the move, the weird up and down with Levi, it all welled up and poured out her eyes. Jesse rarely let herself break down, but here it was, the feelings she had been shoving down, down, down, coming out all at once.

"Jesse?" Cole asked, the concern and sadness in the sound of his voice didn't help. God forbid someone be nice to her right now.

"Cole, I can't keep it in anymore. I've pulled over, I'm safe, but I have got to get off the phone," she said, her voice wiggling and wavering to her own ears. "This is humiliating."

"Jesse, please don't be upset. Is this just about me putting the flower on your dresser? I promise I won't walk in anymore, I didn't think much about it. My doors are rarely locked," he said into the phone. She answered with a sniff, frantically searching her purse for her stash of tissues.

"It's that plus a lot of other things I've been holding in. I am plenty pissed about you walking in, but there's just so much more. I'm going to get off of here, Cole."

"Don't. Stay on the phone with me. I'm out at a job site right now sitting in my truck, I can talk for a bit longer. I've got a sister, Jesse. I've talked with an upset woman before, trust me," and before she could protest he started telling her about his day, cleverly not mentioning the creepy part where he had been in her house while she was in the shower. Jesse felt a little eased by the low, rumbling sound of his voice while he talked about the details of his morning, the client he'd gone to see. She had stopped shaking, closed her eyes and just listened to his voice. It was a nice voice, deep and with an accent a little different than her own. Cole had lived in Tennessee before moving to her town in high school. There were certain words that really showcased that Southern drawl. Before long, she noticed her tears had dried and she felt calmer. He had just finished telling her about his phone call with his sister to tell a funny story about her kid's latest attempts to catch the Tooth Fairy in action when she realized she had laughed along with him.

"Better now, Jess?" he asked. She could hear the smile in his voice and answered with one of her own.

"Yes, thank you. I don't often lose my temper like that, Cole. When I do, I do it in style, I guess," she said, feeling just a little embarrassed about the force of her rant, however warranted. "I do really want you not to just walk in though; that creeps me out. Ok?"

“Of course. Like I said, I didn’t really even think about it. I’m sorry that I scared you,” Cole answered, Jesse felt relieved to have that over with, however dramatic it had been. She checked her mirror and pulled back out on the highway, ready to get back on her way to get the boys.

“So tell me about Drake and how all that is going,” he said, surprising her. She had been ready to end the call, but figured what the hell, she had a long drive and he apparently had the time. She knew she didn’t want to get too much into the specifics; it wasn’t really anyone’s business, but she started talking and realized how nice it felt to talk about Drake without constant interruption and commentary. When she talked about different situations with Megan or Anna, they were so busy with their suggestions and “how dare he” that she felt like she never really got her story out. Cole listened with the customary “uh huhs” and listening sounds so she’d know he was still there. She told him about how when they were married, he made her feel small. She shared how he judged the boys and made harsh cutting remarks; however, he still had a right to see them. She felt like he was an ass, but not necessarily one so awful that it was harmful for the boys to be with him. Jesse hoped that when she wasn’t around that Drake would ease up a bit; maybe she had been the catalyst that made him act so terrible around the kids. She wasn't blaming herself by any stretch, but maybe she made him uneasy so he acted out. Before she knew it, she had even told Cole about Drake's affair and how it hadn't even really hurt her feelings since they had stopped sleeping together years before. She had felt like she had died a little bit in her marriage and being away from Drake, living life on her own with her boys, was restoring her.

"He's still with Rachel, the woman he cheated on me with," Jesse said, involuntarily wrinkling her nose in distaste. "It doesn't bug me at all. At least he's occupied," she said, "except that I know Drake will spring her on the boys. They aren't at all thrilled with the idea of having to be nice to her," Jesse shared. Cole laughed softly and Jesse remembered that his mother had moved her family to their town with a new husband in tow. Cole had never talked about it much, but Jesse remembered him and his sister Carrie not being home a lot. She had wondered if there were problems with the step-dad back then, but figured if Cole wanted to talk about it that he would have. Now she wondered if that had been the right approach.

"That can be awkward for everyone," Cole said. "It's hard enough making a marriage work,

I'd imagine, let alone combining families with kids," he said, his voice trailing off a bit. "Jesse, I'm sorry Drake was and is such an asshole to you and the kids. You deserve so much better in this life than that guy. You did the right thing getting yourself and the boys out of there," he said, and she felt a little lump well up in her throat.

"Thanks, Cole. And thanks for the conversation. I'd better let you get back to work."

"Anytime, Jesse. I mean that," he said, and she felt like he really did mean it.

"Ok, thanks. Bye," she said, and clicked the button ending the call. With one more hour to go, Jesse pulled up the Pandora app on her phone and tuned it to the Iron and Wine station, cracking the window to let a little brisk air in and relaxed to the very eclectic combination of music intended to relax her spirit. She wanted to be calm and happy when she picked up her boys. She couldn't wait to get them home and get back to normal.

Twenty

Jesse pulled up to Drake's house and the boys came spilling out of the front door. They had all their gear packed up and met her with hugs once she turned off the car. Drake stood on the porch, once again not helping load their stuff at all. Jesse threw up her hand and said hello, turning back to pop the back of the Suburban, so she didn't have to see that he didn't answer her hello or wave. *What a dick*, she thought to herself, but put a smile on her face when she turned back to the boys.

They seemed content; Michael gave her a squeeze and settled into the front seat talking nonstop about his score on the basketball game from their trip to the adult sized arcade that Drake had apparently taken them to over the weekend. Jesse felt a little bit of bitterness swell up at that. She had taken them once when Ryan was big enough to behave and had gotten a rear-chewing that she still remembered from Drake about the expense of the outing. She looked back in the rear-view mirror to see Ryan contentedly looking down at his book and Luke glaring out the window.

"Luke, you doing ok back there, buddy?" she asked, tensing with worry. He was always so pensive, that poor baby.

"Fine. I just didn't like going to that place with her there," Luke said, his lip curling up into a sneer, his eyes meeting hers briefly in the rear-view mirror.

"Who, honey?" she asked, even though she knew what he was about to say.

Just then, Ryan piped up and answered, "Rachel, Dad's friend," then looked back down at his book. Jesse felt both Michael and Luke's eyes on her, watching her response.

"Ah. Well, at least you got to go somewhere fun," she answered, proud of herself for not saying what she really felt, something more along the lines of *Jesus Christ, can't your Dad just spend time with you alone the few days he has with you a month?* She felt rather than saw Michael relax a bit beside her, Luke just looked back out the window. The rest of the drive was relatively quiet, the boys asleep by the halfway point of their trip. Jesse refused to let herself dwell on the outing. She knew she'd get the details from the boys as they were ready to tell about it. Instead, she worked to keep herself from thinking about her calls with

Levi and Cole. Sometimes she wished her mind had an off switch. Maybe she'd start doing her yoga DVDs again. That was about the only time she could get herself to be completely quiet.

The week ticked by quickly as it often did. The boys were comfortable in their routine, off to school, then to practice for Michael, dinner, homework for all of them, then showers and bed. Jesse found routines to be more comforting than mundane and took pleasure in the little things, like seeing their faces around the dinner table. Work was going well for her; she'd just found out she may have a trip to Florida coming up soon. She generally disliked traveling for work, but if she had to go, Miami wasn't a bad place to land. Especially in the winter.

Michael had handed Jesse an updated football schedule with a time change to the next out of town game. She cringed a little when she saw the note. She'd have to call and let Drake know, as he had planned to meet them to watch Michael play, then take the boys for his next visit. Once the boys had settled in their rooms to work on homework, she poured a glass of red wine and took a healthy swallow, bracing herself for the call. Jesse was relaxing a bit, thinking she'd get to leave a voice mail rather than speak directly to Drake.

She hated that the sound of his voice made her stomach turn.

"Hello" he barked into the phone.

"Hey Drake, there's been a change to Michael's schedule..." she was saying as he cut her off.

"Damn it, Jesse I can't talk right now. The police are at my house, I don't have time for this," he seethed into the phone.

"What? Drake what's wrong?" she asked? Shock settled in her stomach like a stone.

"Somebody killed Rachel's damned cat and brought it to my porch with a note saying 'Straighten up or you might be next.' I can't talk right now." He said and hung up on her. Jesse held the phone away from her face, staring at it like it was a foreign object.

Someone killed Rachel's cat? Jesus, that was creepy. The note Drake mentioned made her visibly shudder and she sat down on the couch draining the glass of wine. She felt a flush creep into her face and laid her head back against the couch, looking up at the ceiling. When her phone rang, still in her hand, she jumped like she'd been shot.

"Hello?" she answered, a little frantic sounding even to her own ears.

"Hey Jess. What are you up to?" Levi asked, "Have a minute to talk?" Jesse was still stunned by her call with Drake.

"You are never going to believe this," she said, telling Levi about the conversation with Drake.

"Dang, Jess. That's flat out scary!" Levi said, his voice as filled with amusement at the thought of someone rattling Drake. "The poor cat. Good Lord," he murmured under his breath. "The scariest part is the note though, huh? I wonder what the police are going to do about that?" he said.

"I have no idea. I can't even guess. I can't even watch those crime shows on TV; they scare me too much," she said. "I'm not going to tell the boys about this one; they'd be too upset," Jesse said. She was having a hard time processing that someone had actually threatened Drake bad enough to rattle him. She heard one of the boys open their door so she switched to a safer topic of conversation, asking about Levi's kids. "Enough of the creepy stuff, the kids are coming down. How are your babies?" she asked.

"Oh, they're doing pretty good. Hannah lost another tooth last night and James is fit to be tied over it. His aren't coming out at the same rate and he's feeling neglected. I'm going to admit something. I've been a little passive aggressive with this Tooth Fairy thing - I guess that's what you'd call it." He laughed as he told her about how when one would lose a tooth, the Tooth Fairy would give the child two dollars, which one twin would always share with the other. It delighted the one to share with the other, and pacified the one who didn't lose a tooth.

"Wow, the rate at your house is a little higher than it was at mine. My boys would be jealous!" she laughed, "I miss those days sometimes," Jesse shared. "I think I rushed my way through a lot of it and wish I could do it over," she said.

"I know what you mean," he said. "I'm not sure doing it this way is the right thing to do. One kid gets a treat when they didn't really do anything for it, and the other feels obligated to share. I suppose they won't be ruined by it. I guess I just have another year or two if I'm lucky before they figure it all out anyway," he said laughing. "I still remember when I found out the truth about Santa Claus. That was one of the greatest disappointments of my life," he said, and Jesse couldn't help but laugh.

"I hear you. I was ten when I figured that one out. I got up for a glass of water and there sat Mom at the dining room table, Barbie dolls in boxes and eyes as big as saucers. I was crushed until I realized, who cares, at least I was getting a new Barbie!" Jesse said. "I didn't take it as a betrayal of trust, or any of the big-feeling theories people are pushing on each other nowadays," she said, and he laughed in answer.

"I hear you. I had no idea there were so many different schools of thought on parenting and especially discipline," Levi said. "I got a little overwhelmed by it all right after the accident while I was tearing through the books on grief," he said, his voice getting quiet.

"I can't even imagine, Levi. I can't even imagine," she answered, shaking her head in wonder. He had come through the experience of Emma's death, not even properly allowed time to grieve it on his own. He was a father first, man second, she guessed. No, she knew.

Michael came thundering down the stairs, pantomiming something that Jesse assumed was Michael eating a chicken leg or something and jerked open the door of the refrigerator so hard that the bottles on the door rattled.

"Well, I guess I'd better go. The last feeding frenzy of the night is about to begin. I swear I can't fill them up right now." she said.

"Growing boys, Jess. That's how it is." he said into the phone. "Night."

"Night." she answered, putting down the phone as Luke and Ryan came down the stairs.

"Ok, what's it going to be?" she asked, ready to fill them up and put them to bed. She was exhausted.

Twenty-One

Jesse saw the boys off to school and settled into yet another day of work. Working from home was going really well. She enjoyed the freedom of being away from the office and loved that she could slip downstairs occasionally to toss in a load of laundry. She was learning to make friends with her slow cooker to save time in the evenings and felt assured she wouldn't burn the place down like she had worried when she was working in an office. Sometimes she wondered if there wasn't an anxiety medicine out there in the world with her name on it.

She drained the last of the coffee from her cup and stood up from her chair, stretching her back, already feeling the muscle tightness from her morning exploits with the workout DVD she had done. She passed by the mirror in the hall noting that a shower would be in order. Jesse was dressed in yoga pants, a ratty college t-shirt with her hair piled high in a wild bun on top of her head. She'd have to get that done before picking up Luke and

Ryan from middle school or she'd never hear the end of it. She had just made it to the bottom of the stairs when a loud knock startled her. With a loud yelp. She peeked out the peep hole to see Cole standing on the porch, a devilish smile on his lips. Jesse swung the door open with an eyebrow raised and a hand on her hip.

"You've got a pretty good set of lungs on you, Jess." he said, lifting his hand to his face, his fingers brushing his lips as he tried to hide the laugh.

"You're pretty good at being sneaky, Cole. I think I'll start calling you Creepin' Jesus," she said, stepping back and holding the door open so he could come inside.

"What's up?" she asked, "Don't tell me you have some kind of forest emergency here in town," Jesse smiled up at him. "Can I get you some coffee? I'm still in the process of fueling up," she gestured in the direction of her kitchen with her red and white polka dot mug.

"Nah, I don't touch the stuff. I'm a green tea man, myself. I'll live till I'm one hundred, at least," Cole said, grabbing her hand as she started to turn towards the kitchen. He pulled her back to him, one hand on hers and the other resting low on her back with the familiarity of a man who'd had her purring just a few short days ago. Her hand gripped his strong upper arm and she looked up into his sea colored eyes. No matter how many times she saw them she could never decide if they were blue or green. They were some kind of perfect mix, she decided as she noticed the serious set to his mouth.

"I wanted to see for myself that you were okay, Jess," he said, giving her the feeling he was scanning her brain for the truth. The intensity of his gaze jarred her down to the bone. Cole looked at her like he truly cared. He took the mug from her hand and set it on the table beside the couch. He pulled her tightly against his body and moved his hand up her arm to the back of her neck. With the slight brush of his thumb beneath her jaw, he tilted her lips up to his. Cole kissed her hard, his other hand moving from her lower back down to the curve of her butt. He pushed himself against her, giving her all the proof she would ever need about the effect she had on him. He walked back a few steps until his legs found the couch and with the grace of a dancer that belied his muscled bulk, he both lifted her up and sat down on the couch at the same time, placing her firmly in his lap with legs to either side of him.

Jesse felt like the air was being sucked from her body as the flames of desire licked at her, closing all around. She raised her arms as Cole pulled her shirt up over her head and gasped as he closed his mouth on her neck, the feel of his hot tongue against her skin made her throw her head back as his hands cupped her breasts. He peeled her sports bra up and over her breasts, a low groan escaping his mouth as he brought a breast to his mouth, stopping in his efforts to remove the offending garment. Jesse was on fire as she pulled the bra off, wrapping her hands around his neck, feeling the tickle of his short hair against her fingers. She lowered her head, seeking his lips and finding them firm and hot. He wiggled her off his lap and pulled off her pants before he stood up. He removed his clothes in record time and Jesse felt her eyes go round at the sight of him gloriously naked, all broad shoulders, hard muscle and wanting flesh. Before she could even mutter an appreciative word, he laid her down on the couch, covering her body. He towered above her, balancing the weight of his frame with one hand, seeking out her readiness with the other. She was more than responsive to his touch. Jesse briefly thought to herself how she wished she'd grabbed that shower, then decided to not let anything ruin this absolute flood of pleasure. As if he had read her mind, his lips dipped down to her chest, running his tongue along her breast.

“Salty,” he murmured, looking quickly up at her eyes, “I guess that explains the outfit,” he said, ducking as she reached to give him a smack on the shoulder. Her laugh quickly fizzled to a moan as his lips moved lower down her body, kissing a hot trail down her torso. Jesse suspended all thought as Cole found his mark, fingers and tongue working her body, making her ache for time to stop. Her breath came in shallow pants as she came closer and closer to the edge. Just when she thought she was almost there, he left her only to replace his hands and mouth with his hard, strong body. Jesse felt her back arch and legs wrap around Cole’s hips as he kissed her, pumping into her with a strength and urgency that quickly brought her back to a frenzy. He kissed her hard and watched her with those sea colored eyes as he lightly pinched the tip of her breast. The mix of pleasure and pain of his hands and the perfect rhythm as he pumped into her body, threw Jesse off a cliff of release so incredible she saw nothing, then flashes of light against the back of her eyelids. Her body relaxed against his as he held her legs against him, a few more strong pumps causing him to shudder and curl his head in tightly against hers.

They lay in a sweaty heap on the couch for minutes, the weight of him almost crushing Jesse.

Her own boneless state made her wait to move him. Just one more minute, one more minute, she told herself. Finally, Cole realized his heavy weight lay against her, moving slowly to the floor, his back against the couch, his head hanging low as he worked to stop his pulse from racing. Jesse curled onto her side, her hand resting on his big shoulder. She knew she wore a smile of a cat who'd got the cream, but she hadn't dreamed exactly how transparent she must've been until he looked up at her with a grin that turned into a burst of laughter. As she unabashedly smiled back at him, she realized that she could count on one hand the times in her life that she had heard Cole really laugh, despite his ready grin. The sound of it was warm and husky, the gleam in his eyes lit his face. She knew right then that she'd like to see him laugh more.

Jesse felt herself grow a little self-conscious, lying naked on the couch with the morning sun streaming through her living room window. "What is it with you and this couch?" she asked, raising up and reaching for her t-shirt. She pulled it over her head and stood, hand held out to Cole.

"It's not the couch, Jesse," he said, accepting her hand and raising himself to his feet. Without meaning to, she gave him a look that raked him from top to bottom.

"My God, you're a sexy man," she said with a squeak as he reached down and smacked her bare bottom.

"You aren't so bad yourself, woman," he smiled, a silent chuckle wrinkling his nose.

"Come on, enough sexy-time. You up for a shower?" she said, walking the short distance to the stairs. Just then her office phone rang, shocking her back to reality. "Oh no!" she said, running the rest of the way up the stairs. By the time Cole had made it to the top of the stairs Jesse was standing at her desk, leaning over her laptop frantically checking her calendar reminders, not realizing she was giving a fine show of her rear from his angle.

He quietly dropped the clothes he had gathered from the living room to the floor and stood behind her, his hands cupping her, and his body responding to that hint of cheek peeking out from under her t-shirt. "Again?" she asked, looking over her shoulder at him, eyes wide with surprise. Her mind drifted back to when she and Drake had been first married. They might have had sex twice in a row a few times in their marriage, however never beyond the early years. She hadn't even realized that a man in his 30s could do that. That being said, she had almost forgotten her ability to orgasm with a partner and quickly decided she'd have to throw the times with Drake out the window and start doing her own investigating.

Cole removed his hand from her bottom long enough to slowly click closed the top of Jesse's laptop. He put his hands on her shoulders, and with a long foot, he guided her feet further apart. Jesse's skin prickled with surprise and anticipation as he tightened his grip on one shoulder and the other trailed down her shoulder blade, around her side and down her stomach. He didn't stop until his strong arm was wrapped around her, touching her body while pressing the length of himself against her from behind. All Jesse had to do was arch her back a bit more and she knew he'd be inside her, filling and stretching her. The expectation was almost as good as the sensation thrumming through her at the mercy of his fingertips. He circled her while his other hand held her firmly in place, his breath teasing her ear. "I love the taste of you, Jesse. I love the feel of you against my skin," he said in a low voice, rumbling and hot against her neck. The warmth of his breath against her skin made her shiver and shift just enough to for him to find the access to her body that they both so greatly wanted.

Jesse arched and threw her head back as Cole pushed into her from behind, her body already a little sore from their romp on the couch.

The delicious tenderness left her as the heat began to build and build again. The combination of the pressure and the heat of him against and inside her, the open air of her office and absolute thrill of having sex someplace she never dreamed she'd have it, lit the flame of her inner exhibitionist. She bucked against him as he pushed and pumped into her, this time for just minutes. Jesse was so aroused from what had happened downstairs, she didn't have far to go before she came. When the quaking sensations left her, she slumped a little against her desk. Cole turned her and gathered her up against him. For a minute, he held her there, her arms wrapped around his neck. Her head resting against his chest as her heart pounded. When she looked up at his face, she didn't expect to see his eyes so intensely focused on hers. She gasped in surprise when he picked her up, pulling her against him. She wrapped her legs around his hips as he slowly leaned her body against the office window. Jesse might have found her second release, but from the feel of it, Cole still had a ways to go. Nothing but white sheers hid her from view, should a neighbor happen to glance up at her second story window. She said a silent prayer of thanks that the office faced the back yard but didn't dwell on it for long.

The cold press of the glass raised goosebumps on her body, a sharp contrast to the heat of him as he filled her. His muscles bulged as he held her body in his arms, merely resting her against the surface. Cole rocked against her roughly, cradling her in his hands. Jesse felt bold, watching his face as his body jerked, finishing, then crushing her to him. He held her still for a moment, eyes clenched tightly, his forehead resting against hers. Cole gently lowered her feet to the ground and they stood still for a minute.

Without talking, they walked slowly into her bathroom. Jesse turned on the water and stepped in, Cole close behind her. They didn't even speak as they washed each other and looked into one another's eyes, sharing small smiles of the exhausted and sexually satisfied.

Eventually, the water cooled and the soft spell of intimacy was broken; Cole and Jesse stepped out of the shower. As they dried off, Jesse felt awkwardness creep in and felt a little sad. She hadn't showered with a man since the one she snuck with Levi back in high school. For a minute she frowned as she towel dried her hair, wondering at the absurdity of never having shared such a personal act with Drake. He hadn't been one for nakedness outside of the bored bedroom sex. Come to think of it, Jesse realized she had never made love with Drake on a couch. Shaking her head a little to halt her line of thinking, she looked up at Cole who had been watching her as he dressed. He looked a little rumpled from his clothes lying in a heap on the floor, however he wasn't much the worse for wear. Jesse wrapped her towel around her body and stepped over to Cole.

"That was one hell of a nice surprise, Cole," she said, pressing a kiss to his lips before turning to walk back to her closet. As she pulled out a pair of jeans and her favorite olive green sweater, he sat on the edge of her bed. Jesse threw him a look, then figured at this point, he had seen her in some pretty compromising positions. She decided that if he could make her come to the point of nearly blacking out, if he wanted to watch her dress, she could deal with that. She moved to her dresser, selecting a set of pale pink bra and panties, and mentally thanked God that she owned so many sets of pretty lingerie. It wouldn't have done to pull out a boring beige bra and pair of granny panties at such a time. Not at all. She dressed efficiently, not being overtly sexy, but being mindful of unflattering angles at the same time. When she finished and looked back at Cole, he wore an air of distinctly male satisfaction. Why is it that extremely good sex left her wanting nothing but a nap, while this man seemed like he was ready to go out and chop wood for God's sake? She tilted her head towards the door and smiled at him, and he raised himself up off her bed. She didn't know where this thing was going, but she admitted to herself that she kind of liked the look of him seated there on her bed. Cole was a hard one to crack and she couldn't quite shake the feeling that there was much more to him than what he shared.

They made their way down to her front door, casually touching hands as they went.

"Well, I've got to get back to work," he said, one hand on the doorknob. "I came by to check on you and to let you know that I'm going to a conference down in Southeast Missouri later today," he said, lifting and smoothing her damp hair off of her shoulder. "I'll be back on Sunday. May I call you?" he asked, tilting his head a little to the side, the twinkle in his eye affirming that he too knew it was a little funny to make someone come twice within the space of an hour, then ask politely if he may call in a few days.

"Yes," she nodded, feeling strangely tongue tied. There was a weird mix of innocence and intrigue going on his face, and it made her feel a bit off kilter. "That would be nice," she said, feeling trite and awkward. He put his hand on her jaw, pressing a soft kiss to her lips and treating her to a rare, big smile.

"Okay then," he said, pulling his keys from his pocket and opening the door. He walked out into the brisk morning and Jesse watched from the open door as he climbed into his big truck. The diesel engine thundered to life and she watched him slowly back out of her driveway. Once he was gone, she shut and locked the door and turned and leaned against it. *What in the world? Had that really just happened?* She shook her head in awe as she walked into the kitchen for the cup of coffee that had brought her downstairs in the first place. On her pass back through the living room, she straightened the pillows and looked around for any visual clues that she had just had some of the best sex of her life there in the living room.

"Good Lord," Jesse said aloud to herself. "What am I now, sixteen years old?" she said with a shudder, realizing that her son Michael would be sixteen soon. She was going to have to talk with him again about safe sex and wrapping 'it' up twice. Jesse stopped in her tracks at the bottom of the stairs. Birth control. She and Cole hadn't used a condom.

"SHIT!" she yelled. "Shit, shit, shit, shit, shit, shit!" she said, quickly making a beeline up the stairs and to her desk calendar. She scoured the calendar for the notes on her cycle, a habit her mother had instilled in her since she was a teen. She quickly counted the weeks and realized that she was due to start her period in a few days. In theory, she ought to be fine.

"Idiot," she said to herself as she sat down in her office chair. "That would set a fine example," she said aloud, closing her eyes tight and rubbing between them for a minute as she gathered her wits. She took a reassuring gulp of hot coffee and flicked her laptop open just in time to see she was almost late for a conference call.

Twenty-Two

The house smelled of beef stew and rising bread, and even the bitter cold weather outside hadn't put a damper on Jesse's mood. She was enjoying one of those rare moments of complete satisfaction where her house was clean, and Luke and Ryan had agreeably gone upstairs to do homework before dinner. She leaned over, peeking through the oven window to see if the bread had risen when the front door opened and slammed shut. She frowned and walked into the living room as Michael hung up his coat and kicked off his shoes. When he turned around to face her, Jesse gasped when she saw Michael's black eye and swollen lip.

"What happened, Michael?" she yelled, closing the gap between them quickly. He moved his face away from her reach and tried to squirm away.

"Not now, Mom," he said, turning to go towards the stairs. The younger boys came barreling down the stairs at the racket as Jesse quickly got in front of Michael.

"Don't you tell me 'not now' when I ask you a question, Michael," she said as he stopped and gave her a stern look. "Honey, what happened?" she asked as she gently reached up and touched his face, her eyes softening as she looked him over.

Michael sighed and stared hard at her for a minute before answering. "I'll tell you about it, but not in front of these two," he said, tilting his head at the open mouthed faces of his little brothers.

Jesse halted the flood of "that's not fair," and "does it hurt?" with a sharp glance, and Luke and Ryan knew they weren't going to get anywhere with her at the moment. They sulkily walked up the stairs as Jesse grabbed Michael's hand, leading him to the couch. She sat down then immediately hopped back up, walking into the kitchen and returning with an ice pack. She knew it would do very little for him at this point, but she had to do something.

"Okay, son. Spill," she said, sitting beside him, trying her best to remain calm.

"After school today, I was in the parking lot looking at Jake's new car with a bunch of the guys," Michael said, looking anywhere but at her face. Jesse didn't miss the emphasis on the 'new car' part of the sentence. Though he lived just a few doors down from the high school, he bitterly resented the fact that he wouldn't be getting a car for his 16th birthday, new or otherwise.

"Jake said something about my birthday coming up in a few weeks and asked if I'd be getting a car or truck. I told him nothing this year when Seth Williamson laughed really loud. At this, Jesse winced, remembering Seth was the son of Laura Williamson, the head Mean Girl from her class. She couldn't help but wonder if the little asshole apple didn't fall far from the tree.

"I asked Seth what was so funny, and he said that his mom said that my mom was too busy to worry about buying me a car. I asked him what the hell he meant by that, and he said his mom told him that you were too busy screwing around with Levi Murray to have time to buy me a car. So I hit him," Michael said, finally looking her dead in the eye.

Jesse felt her face getting red and heard the familiar buzzing in her ears that she experienced when she was extremely mad. It was almost like a white-noise type of sound; it must've been something like blood roaring in her ears. She knew Michael had continued talking, but she closed her eyes and held her hand out to him hoping he would just stop talking for a minute while she gathered her senses. She sat like that for at least a full minute on the couch, trying to let the flood of rage subside so that she didn't completely lose her shit in front of her son. She vaguely heard the oven beep and felt Michael get off the couch to pull the bread out of the oven. When she felt like she had control over herself, she opened her eyes to see Michael staring warily at her from the kitchen doorway.

She took a deep breath before speaking, then stood up.

"Michael, I am so sorry that this happened. I'm sorry that you were embarrassed in front of your friends, and I am sorry that you had to punch that little shit-head to shut him up." At that, Michael's eyes bugged out. He could count on one hand the times that he had heard his mother use profanity. "Now, before I go talk to Seth's mother, I want to tell you something." At that Michael put his own hand up like he didn't want to hear it, but just one look in her eyes made him slowly put his hand back down and close his mouth. Jesse continued, "Levi and I dated in high school and were very close. He is one of the best friends I've ever had in my whole life, and I love spending time with him. We are not dating right now. We are not in a relationship right now other than friends, and our utmost priority in this world, both his and mine," and at that point, Jesse realized she was almost flat out yelling, so she took a breath and attempted to lower the volume of her voice. "Our utmost priority in this world is to care for, and make a secure home for our children. I don't know what the future holds for the two of us, if anything. The best I can do is explain what is going on right now," Jesse closed her eyes, drew in a big breath and slowly released it.

"Now. Before I go to Seth's house, please tell me how much damage you did, if anything else was said, and if you were caught fighting by a teacher." Jesse forced herself to fake a sense of calm and sat on the couch, choosing to ignore the fact that Luke and Ryan had inched their way back down the stairs with eyes as round as saucers. They may as well hear this all at the same time to spare Michael from having to repeat the story over and over. She also decided to ignore the innate sense of pride Michael displayed when he told them how he gave Seth a black eye and doubled him over with a punch to the stomach, thereby ending the fight and walking away with Seth lying in the gravel parking lot surrounded by his friends. Jesse said a silent prayer of thank you that they hadn't been caught by a teacher and also that no real damage had been done. Michael had walked away from the parking lot and walked around the neighborhood a while, burning off adrenaline and no doubt agonizing over what Seth had said. Jesse could not imagine belittling another parent in front of her children. Why would someone, even Laura, be that classless?

Long ago when Jesse and Levi dated in high school, she was aware that Laura had a crush on Levi. He had only had eyes for Jesse, and she knew Laura had been envious, but could she possibly have carried that with her all these years? Heck, Laura had done well for herself. She had attended college, making sure everyone knew that her father footed the bill for her to go to a swanky private college in the South. She had graduated majoring in who-knows-what and married well straight out of school. She married the son of a construction giant and lived in an incredible house at the Country Club. Laura was impeccably maintained, amazing hair, nails, boob job, the whole nine yards. And, she had never worked a day in her life. What in God's name did she feel she lacked so badly that she had to belittle Jesse in front of her son?

Jesse served the stew, bread and butter to her wide-eyed and silent boys, and told Michael to watch Luke and Ryan. She went upstairs and dressed in a sweater and jeans, checked that her hair and makeup were adequate, and fired the Suburban up, pointing it in the direction of the

Country Club. As she drove she thought about how beauty could really only be skin deep. Laura was admirably attractive on the outside and apparently a classless, hateful bitch on the inside. Within minutes, Jesse pulled into the brick circle drive in front of Laura's house. She took a deep steadying breath and got out of the SUV, slamming the door a little harder than she intended.

With a shaking hand, she rang the doorbell and stepped back a step. Jesse did her best not to smile when Seth answered the door, one eye ringed with a bruise.

"Seth, get your mother, please," she said to the stunned boy with an "Oh shit" look on his face. He stepped to the side as Laura walked to the door. She reached and locked the glass storm door when she saw it was Jesse on the other side. Jesse shook her head, wondering if that idiot woman thought she was going to charge through the damned door and attack her weave.

"And just what the Hell are you doing here?" Laura asked, indignant as ever. As if it had slipped her mind just whose words had caused this whole predicament.

"Really, Laura?" Jesse said, hands raising in a questioning gesture. "I'm not going to talk about this in front of Seth. I actually prefer to handle adult conversations while NOT in front of my children," she said as Laura hastily took notice that Seth was standing there texting away on his phone, no doubt notifying the whole damned high school that Michael's mom was on his doorstep, madder than a wet hen.

"Seth, go to your room. Leave your phone," Laura said, unlocking the door and stepping onto the porch. "Did you see what your son did to Seth?" she asked, pulling the door closed behind her.

"Yes. Michael has a black eye and busted lip as well," she said, not missing the smirk on Laura's face. "Did Seth tell you what was said to start all of this? What YOU supposedly said that started all of this?"

At that, Laura's eyes bugged out a little. She clearly hadn't expected Jesse to delve into this mess. "Well, he did tell me," she started, interrupted by the look on Jesse's face and the hand held up in the air to shut her up.

"Laura, I'm not sure what your fixation is on my relationship with Levi, be it romantic or otherwise, but whether there even is a relationship to talk about is the business of myself and my family. It's not something to be thrown around in front of kids, especially in the form of ugly, hurtful gossip." Jesse didn't miss the way Laura's eyes narrowed. She was sure Queenie here didn't often get told when to shut up.

"And as far as Seth mocking Michael for not having a car, look around Laura. Take a look at this town beyond this beautiful neighborhood. This town is full of empty store fronts and abject poverty. My boy, from a *'broken home',"* Jesse added air quotes around broken home for Laura's benefit, as she no doubt took a small victory in Jesse's failed marital status, "is not the only kid that isn't being handed a car on his Sweet Sixteen."

The minute Jesse stopped to take a breath, Laura leaned in close.

"Now you listen here, Jesse. This is a free world, and I'll say any damn thing I want to, about anyone I want to, in front of my kid or not. This is my house. My property. Get off it," Laura said, chin lifted high, finger pointed in Jesse's face.

Jesse momentarily wished that she was the type to throw a punch herself right then. There wasn't much in the world she'd like to see more than Laura with a shiner to match her son's.

Jesse threw her hands up in mock surrender.

"Sure thing, Laura. I just want to warn you. The next time Seth spews this trash at school around the other kids, I'm taking it to the principal," Jesse said, loving the way Laura's eyes widened.

The principal was Jesse's cousin, Paul. He was an absolute disciplinary tyrant to the parents and kids, but to Jesse he was Paully, the closest cousin to her in age.

Jesse climbed back into her Suburban and took her time driving back home. She felt better getting that off her chest. She didn't want to go home spewing fire at her kids when her issue was with Laura. When she walked through the door fifteen minutes later, she noted that the boys had finished supper, cleaned up the mess and were upstairs doing their homework. Maybe she needed to flip out more often, she thought, locking the doors and making her way upstairs. Jesse kept her calm while checking on the boys and updating Michael with the general details on how the conversation went over so that he could be prepared for whatever was said the next day at school. This was one day she was happy to put behind her.

Twenty-Three

The call ended, and Jesse clicked the conference line closed. The backyard that she looked out over was covered in snow and frigidly cold despite the bright sunshine. Her supervisor had just given her the travel dates for her trip to Miami. She would leave for a three day trade show the following week. As she picked up her calendar to get a handle on what the kids had going on so that she could call her mother for help with the boys, her mobile phone rang. Her belly felt warm when she saw Levi's name flashing on the screen. She had snapped a funny picture of him with his kids at the BBQ over the summer, assigning it to his contact information, and she smiled to herself every time it popped up when he called.

Her smile must've been evident even in her hello. "Well, hi. You sound like you're in a good mood for a hump day," Levi said, sounding rather perky himself.

"Well, I do love a good hump day," she laughed into the phone at her own coarseness as he apparently choked on his coffee or whatever he was drinking. "I did get some interesting news just now; I'm headed to Miami next week for a three day trade show."

"Miami, huh? Are you going to dance around in a bikini on roller blades at all when you're down there?" he asked, clearly amusing himself.

"Well, I remember seeing that in movies back in the 90's, but I'm not sure that's even still a thing. Come to mention it, I was probably sitting beside you watching those movies!" Jesse said.

"God, we're old, aren't we?" Levi said, letting out a breath. "Is it just me or do the 90's seem just like yesterday? I'm continually surprised that it's been such a long time ago." Jesse didn't want to dampen her current excellent mood with feeling old, so she decided to change the topic.

"Yeah, it's been a while. I'm going over the schedule for next week, then I need to give Mom a call to see if she and Dad can come stay with the kids. What's up?" Jesse asked, thumbing through her calendar and glancing up at the football schedule and the variety of email notices she got daily from the boys' schools.

"I was going to see if you wanted to go on a date," he said, her stomach doing a funny little flip as he waited for her answer.

"Hmm, that would be fun. What have you got in mind?" Jesse asked, casually adding in, "It's a little chilly for fishing."

"Definitely," he said around an audible smile. "Fishing is out. I was thinking more like Friday night, dinner at the new sushi restaurant in town. I haven't been yet, but think it sounds like fun. Do you like sushi?"

Jesse's mind was racing. On one hand she would love to go to dinner, especially sushi, which she loved and hadn't had since moving back home. On the other, the two of them on a dinner date would set tongues to wagging right on the heels of Michael's fight. She decided she had better just be honest than try and keep that one held in.

"Levi, I love it and think that sounds like fun, but I have a little nervousness about it. Here's what's going on," she said, launching into the quick version of Laura Williamson's big mouth and Michael's fight with her son.

Levi listened patiently. She could imagine him with his jaw clenched and fingers drumming on his desk.

"Well, that little bitch hasn't changed much since school, has she?" he said, the annoyance plain in his voice despite his effort to stay calm. "I hate that he had to deal with that," he said, adding "and you" as an afterthought.

Jesse quietly laughed to herself, remembering the look on Laura's face as she told Jesse to get off her property.

"Yes, although he did a pretty good job with it. Seth gave him some shitty looks, but the boys pretty much kept to themselves from what I heard. I did call Paul the night it happened and gave him a heads up about what was going on in case something blew up."

At that Jesse laughed a little bit and said, "He pretty much said the same thing you did about her not changing much since school. He said he'd hang out in the area where the boys had their lockers between classes. I'm sure that helped at least a little bit. I don't think the kids know Paul is Michael's cousin. Hopefully that won't become an issue."

"Yeah, that could be tricky if they pushed the favoritism thing. Hopefully it won't come to that," Levi said, letting out a big breath. "Well, maybe a date in town isn't the best thing just yet. How about we run up the road a bit to Carverton? I heard they've opened up a fancy new restaurant in one of the buildings downtown. I can make reservations if you'd like," he left off, waiting for her answer.

"I think that would be nice, Levi. Michael's game is Saturday morning, so I'm going to get as much time in with the boys as possible before the trip. Can we make it a little late on Friday? Pick me up at 7 o'clock?" she asked, hoping he wouldn't mind the late time. Around the city, people tended to eat dinner later, but she had noticed here that people tended to eat dinner more around five or so. That fit her usual schedule just fine; she preferred to get the boys fed and get through the rigors of homework and spending time together before bed.

"Sure, seven sounds good to me. I'll have a snack after work," he said and she could visualize his dimples in his smile. "Talk to you later, Jess."

"Seven it is. See you then," she said, hanging up the phone. She sat back, closing her eyes and rubbing the seemingly ever-present frown lines between her eyes. She checked her email quickly to make sure there was no dire emergency needing her attention before popping downstairs to run yet another load of laundry through. She'd have to have it all put up before her brain would let her transfer to packing mode for her trip. She had to have one mess put up before making another. It had always driven Drake crazy that she would clean the kitchen before cooking dinner, then clean it again afterward. Jesse hadn't really given a rat's ass; she was the one who did all the cooking and cleaning anyway. The reminder that she never had to really care again about Drake's particulars, made a smile creep up on her face despite the fact that she was doing laundry in a creepy basement.

Twenty-Four

"But Mom, I don't want you to go anywhere tonight," Ryan whined, "It's bad enough Grandma Eadie and Grandpa Walt will be here all week long, now tonight, too?" he said, his baby face reminding her of the early days when he was just a little fella.

"Ryan, I will not have you be rude about Grandma and Grandpa helping out. I'm thankful that they agreed to watch out for you while I'm gone. And, it's three days, not a whole week," Jesse said, her eyes quelling any future argument from Ryan. She walked around the kitchen to the dining room chair where he was sitting, cupping his face in her hands.

"Tonight, I'm just going to dinner. I'll be home and will check on you when I get in," she said, pressing a kiss to his forehead since the other boys weren't in the room. Ryan at least gave her a little leeway and let her cuddle him when the big boys weren't there to tease him.

Ryan rolled his eyes, a perfect mimic of Luke who seemed to be one perpetual eye roll right now. She hadn't been able to pull him out of his funk lately, and had almost made her mind up to call Drake about it, though the thought of that conversation settled on her like a lump of lead. Luke was doing well in school, he was still polite at home, but Jesse had noticed that he hadn't been sketching much lately and he was spending more time alone in his room. She went in each day, and made as much conversation as possible with a sullen 13 year old. She demanded that the boys eat together at the table, much to their dismay. The supper table was the perfect chance to catch up with the boys and continue imprinting that they were in this together. Jesse felt a little guilty going on a dinner date. She hadn't planned on going on a date when the boys were home, but this was just one dinner, and it wasn't as if she was going to bring Levi in for some freaky hot monkey sex afterwards. She felt her cheeks go red at the thought and turned back to the kitchen to get the boys' dinner ready to serve.

"Sweetie, set the table for me, please," she said, spooning the Sloppy Joe meat into a big bowl. She didn't often give in to what she considered junk food, but she supposed she was treating them because she felt guilty for making plans on her night with them.

Ryan rattled past with a stack of plates and napkins to set the table. She walked to the stairwell and hollered up, "Luke, Michael, dinner is ready!" and before she even made it back to the kitchen, she heard the heavy footfalls racing down the stairs. They didn't mess around on Sloppy Joe night.

Luke sat down first, piling the food onto his plate.

"Hey babe," she said, smoothing back his curly hair to kiss him on the forehead. He pulled away a little but smiled up at her.

"Hey, Mom. My homework is already done. Not much this weekend."

"Good buddy, one less thing to worry about then. How did your Spanish test go today?" she asked, dreading his answer. Jesse had taken two years of Spanish in high school, and never had more than a minor grasp on anything beyond counting and remembering the days of the week. She had spent the previous night attempting to go through a study guide with Luke, but even he knew he was largely on his own with that particular subject.

"Not bad, I got a B," he answered, and seemed pleased. If he was comfortable with it, she was thrilled.

"Good job! That was a hard one. I never could conjugate verbs, no matter how hard I tried, it never seemed to stick," she said, thankful to be sitting down with a glass of iced tea while the boys gobbled down the sandwiches, tater tots and green beans. Her plate was of course empty so that she didn't spoil her appetite. She rose to put it back in the cabinet and sat back down, neatly avoiding Michael's slight dirty look. She had told him right after school that she had plans, and Grandma was coming over to watch the younger two. He was leaving to hang out with his friends, so he wouldn't be subjected to the horror of staying home to be babysat by his grandparents on a Friday night.

She had gone into his room while Luke and Ryan were watching TV right after school, knocking on the door before going in.

"Michael, I need to talk to you for a minute," she said, looking around with more than slight irritation at the state of his room. "By the way, if this crap doesn't make it down to the laundry room, I will not wash it," she said, giving him the stink eye.

"I know, I know, I'll do it in a minute," he said, plopping down on the bed. "What's up?" he asked, kicking a sweater under his bed with a toe.

"I'm going to dinner tonight and thought I'd warn you that it's with Levi," she said, noting the way his eyes bugged a little. "Now, I won't hide it if I go on a date, but I don't necessarily plan on running it past you for approval if I'm asked to go on one," she said gently, settling down beside him on the bed. "I'm only giving you the specifics this time because of what that little turd, Seth, said at school the other day. We're going to Carverton to dinner and I'll be home tonight. Grandma and Grandpa will stay until I get home, and I want you to keep your curfew of 11 o'clock, okay Michael?" she said, waiting for him to look up and nod his head.

"Mom, I don't mind if you go out with Levi. I liked him, plus I know you've known him a long time. I just don't want to catch any crap for it at school, you know? That was gross and embarrassing," he said, wrinkling his nose.

"I can't even imagine, Michael. I can't apologize for Laura being uncouth enough to say something like that in front of Seth, and I can't really expect better of Seth, considering, well, you get it," she said, shrugging her shoulders.

Getting up from the bed she ran her fingers through the top of his short, dark hair, scratching him like a pup like she had done a thousand times before. To her delight, he didn't pull away and he even smiled a little.

"You said you're going driving around with Joe and Mike, right?" she said, holding his eye contact, "No drinking, right, Michael?"

"No, Mom. No drinking," he said. She remembered well enough the trouble she got into as a kid that thankfully her parents never found out about. It was enough to terrify her.

She walked back into the room and put her arms around his shoulders.

"I love you, kiddo," she said, smiling down at his handsome face. He was starting to gain muscle she thought, still sometimes surprised that her first son was such a big boy.

"I love you too, Mom," he said as she released him from the hug. It was a nice moment, but boys do have their limits.

"Your birthday will be here before you know it, kiddo. We need to start thinking about plans for your birthday dinner the night I get back. My flight will be in in time for us to have dinner Thursday night. I can shop Sunday before I leave. What do you want to eat?" she asked, mentally tallying the tasks she'd have to do over the weekend in addition to packing and preparing for the trade show.

"Can we just go grab some wings uptown?" he asked. Much relieved, Jesse smiled.

"Yes, that sounds great. And, easier than cooking. Cake and presents here after?"

"Sounds good."

"It's a plan," she said, looking around where she stepped. "Seriously though, get these clothes downstairs before they mold or something, okay, buddy?"

"Yeah, Mom, sure," he said, already piddling around with his phone. God, Jesse missed the world pre-mobile phone.

She walked into her bedroom, checking again that she had figured out what she wanted to wear as she thought about how much mobile phones had changed the lives of her children versus when she was a teenager. She loved the convenience, but God she missed the old days. She actually had to remember numbers and make plans and lists before going to the store or taking a trip. She couldn't just call up her mom for a quick rescue, she had to depend on her own brains. Thinking now how dependent she was on the contact list, she probably only remembered five or so phone numbers, not to mention shopping without a list. Forget about it. She even made out her grocery list by where the items were in the store just to make the trip more efficient.

She ran her fingers along the sleeve of the black dress and heels she had picked out for her date with Levi, regretting in more than one way that Levi had seen her in her new green wrap dress. It was by far her favorite, but Levi would no doubt remember it from when he busted in on her and Cole after their date. The one she had decided to go with tonight was also very pretty. It was a black dress with a lace overlay, lined in a nude fabric in the elbow-length sleeves and bodice. The neckline was a V-neck, though not too showy. The dress had an Empire waste and full skirt that fell just above her knee. Her heels were comfortably high and strappy. One thing Jesse didn't have to worry about any longer is coping with any insecurity issues about height with the men she had been seeing. Levi and Cole were both so deliciously tall and big. Being nearly six feet tall herself, Jesse appreciated a big, strong man. She had planned to wear her hair pinned back at the nape of her neck with a few loose pieces here and there to keep it looking touchable. Jesse had rooted around in her jewelry box and found the perfect dangle-drop earrings and a bangle that sparkled just enough. She had a black beaded clutch laid out on the bed, packed with the essentials. Her stomach did a little flip and she tamped down the excitement, planning to put off getting ready until the boys had eaten dinner. She had already taken her bath and washed her hair, carefully smoothing and moisturizing her body. Even her toenails were freshly painted. Jesse knew her mother and dad would be waiting for her to get back home, so she wasn't going to be staying out late and getting wild by any stretch of the imagination, but she wanted to make Levi's jaw drop.

Jesse talked with the boys while they cleared the table after supper, getting one more assurance from Michael that he'd be on good behavior. She saw the glint in his eye just before he asked her to do the same, then wisely thought better of it. After being dismissed from the table, Michael went upstairs to get ready for the night, and Luke and Ryan agreed to go play video games in the living room as the doorbell rang. Jesse walked to the door, and let in a chattering Eadie and Walt. Eadie was going on about something that happened with her Bridge group, a cluster of women that Jesse had known since she was a little girl. Walt hung up his hat and coat, gathering Eadie's as well then made for the recliner after a brief hug hello to Jesse. He was content to sit and read the paper tucked under his arm rather than listen to the latest gossip from Bridge. Eadie followed Jesse to the kitchen where she accepted the glass of chilled white wine and then seemed to really notice Jesse for the first time since she hit the door.

"Dear, you aren't going to wear that, are you?"

"No, Mama, I just didn't want to serve Sloppy Joes in my dress and heels," she smiled, giving her mother's shoulders a squeeze. "I'll run up and finish getting ready now," she said, grabbing her glass and heading up the stairs.

Jesse smiled to herself at the scene below, Eadie tittering about, hugging and patting on the boys who had slipped into the stupor induced by video games. She settled into the chair to watch the boys play, pulling her knitting needles and yarn from her bag. Eadie was constantly working on one project or another, and made the most beautiful scarves. It looked like someone was getting a blue and green one for Christmas; Jesse hoped it was hers.

She walked past Michael's room and smelled rather than saw that he was nearly ready. Before he and his friends went out, there was a literal fog of cologne that would precede him. It's a wonder the girls didn't drop like flies when they all got together. She couldn't help but smile, thinking back to her day when Cool Water and Polo were the scents du jour. She still felt a little weak kneed when she'd catch a waft of Herrerra Cologne occasionally. She even secretly kept a bottle of Elizabeth Arden Sunflowers that she used most days. She wore it back in high school and college, until she dated Drake. He had hated that scent, so she stopped wearing it. She still loved it because it brought back so many good memories and generally positive feeling of freedom. As she stripped down to her black lace bra and panties, she pulled out the bottle of perfume and dabbed a little behind her ears, décolletage and behind her knees for good measure. She didn't have any plans of Levi's nose getting near her knees, but who really knew what the night had in store for her. She fussed with her hair, pinning back the wild curls into a semblance of order, and slipped on her dress, heels and jewelry, feeling very much a woman. Jesse didn't put a whole lot of stock in fancy clothes and appearances, but it did feel nice to clean up well on occasion. She put on a dab more eye liner and lipstick, and headed down the stairs just as Levi rang the doorbell. Being closest, she answered the door and took immense pleasure from the look on his face.

"Jess, wow. You're stunning," he said in a half whisper, reaching out his hand to take hers, and leaning in to press a kiss to her lips. She pulled back, eyes wide, just as a flurry of noise erupted in the form of a very excited Eadie.

"Jesse, you look beautiful darling!" Eadie exclaimed, smiling broadly as she turned her head to take in Levi with his dark sport coat and pants, and devilishly dimpled smile. "And you, Levi, you handsome thing, get in here. Walt, Walt! Come see the kids," she said as she stepped back so that Levi could enter and shut the door behind him. "Walt, honey, doesn't this bring back memories?" she said, smiling back and forth between the two of them before turning to walk into the kitchen as she asked over her shoulder if she could get Levi anything.

"No ma'am, it's nice to see you two again though," he said, speaking to Eadie and Walt, but looking only at Jesse. She smiled and went into the living room to kiss the boys goodbye as Michael thundered down the stairs, wafting cologne.

"Mom, you look pretty!" Ryan said, smiling up at her from his seat in time for her to give him a quick squeeze and a kiss. "Hi, Levi," he said with a wave to the door.

"Yeah, Mom. Pretty," Luke said, glancing up to Levi. "Hey, Levi," he said, turning his attention back to the game.

"Be good, sweeties. I'll come in and check on you when I get home," she said to the matching dark heads. "And you," she said to Michael, putting her hand on his shoulder, "be careful. Be smart. I love you," she said, Michael smiling in return. This was her mantra to him anytime he went out with friends.

"I will, Mom. You look nice," he said, as a bevy of honks sounded from the driveway. Michael stepped to the door and puffed his chest out a little before delivering a polite yet terse, "Hey, Levi." Jesse couldn't help but feel tickled at Michael's protectiveness. With a glance back, Michael said, "See you guys later," and walked out the door.

"Remember, 11 o'clock!" Jesse called after him. She turned to the boys with a quick wave and another in the direction of the kitchen where Eadie and Walt were trying badly to not appear to watch them like hawks. "Bye, Mom and Dad, thanks again for watching the boys," she said, thankful to see Walt's strong hand on her mother's shoulder. Without it there was a chance Eadie would follow them to Levi's car asking questions about where they are going, how Stan and Myrtle and, of course, the twins were doing, etc. She gave her Dad a thankful smile and turned to leave, as she grabbed her coat from the hook by the door.

Outside on the porch, Levi stopped Jesse to hold her coat as she slipped into it. As she turned to step down to the sidewalk, he put his hand to her elbow causing her to pause. "Jess, I'm not kidding. You are absolutely gorgeous. What a beautiful dress," he said, his fingertip touching the raw edge of the lace bordering her V-neck. His finger barely grazed her collar bone, but she felt her pulse kick up at the contact.

"Thank you," she said, raising an eyebrow at him in answer. He took her arm and together they walked to his truck. He gallantly walked her to her side and held the door for her while she attempted to enter the truck with some iota of grace.

"I guess this thing isn't necessarily built for heels and a dress, huh, Jess?" he said, averting his eyes in fake chivalry.

"True, but I think I'll manage she said, clicking the seatbelt as she smiled at him. He closed the door, got in the truck, and fired up the engine. Jesse had to admit to herself that she was tempted to skip dinner and go straight to his house, but she admonished herself with a shake of her head and focused instead on making conversation for the remainder of the drive.

The moon was bright as Levi and Jesse drove to the restaurant, the trip taking nearly an hour since the deer were so thick.

"I somehow forgot about how many deer there are here," she said, looking out into the darkness. "See? There's one on the right there. No, make that two."

"I see them, thanks," he said. "Not many deer up where you lived?" he asked.

"Not really, I wasn't on the highway much. Maybe that's why I didn't see them," she said. "God, I don't miss that place," she said, looking over at him. "Not just because of the relationship stuff, just because it never really felt like home. Don't get me wrong, I loved the shopping," she said, preening a little and plucking at her skirt as he laughed softly. "But beyond that and the occasional day trips to do fun things with the boys when they got big enough to take places, I don't miss a thing."

"Well, that's good to hear. Home does have its own appeal, doesn't it," he said. After college, Levi had moved back home to start his own body shop and towing business. He was one of those rare breeds who not only knew a trade, but did a good job running his business as well. His reputation for providing honest, excellent service was well known.

"You want to know what I missed the most?" she asked, leaning forward a bit in her seat and looking up through the windshield. "The stars. I never seemed to realize how much I missed them until every trip when it was time to leave," she said, exhaling. "I remember more than once crying my way out of town after a visit with my parents. My boys would be babbling and talking in the backseat, completely oblivious that my heart was breaking," she said, realizing the dark turn the conversation had taken. "Guess that's the job though, right? Protect them from the worst parts," she said, reaching her hand over to pat his knee, remembering his loss and how terrifically hard it must've been to keep his grief from overshadowing the job of raising his children. Levi reached down and squeezed her hand, nodding before putting his back on the wheel.

Thankfully, the song changed to one she loved. Otis Redding, "These Arms of Mine" began to play, causing Jesse to sway automatically and smile over at Levi.

"Oh Levi, I love this one!" she said, closing her eyes and tilting her head back just a little, simply enjoying the music. He looked over at her and grinned, thinking to himself that he could sit and watch her listen to music for hours. She had always been that way, he remembered. He would watch her get lost to Dave Matthews Band, a particular favorite of hers back then. She seemed to feel the music a little deeper than most. He made a mental note to add that one to his playlist on the off chance he'd ever get her alone again for any length of time. Automatically, he pictured her in his bed, flushed and swaying on top of him with her head back and eyes closed, feeling him and taking in the music at the same time. He said a silent prayer of thanks that it was such a dark night and he had a few more minutes to calm down before they were at the restaurant and he embarrassed himself.

They arrived at the restaurant and parked the truck. Levi came around the truck in time to help Jesse down. As she grabbed her clutch from the truck, she looked around.

"This city feels completely different at night than during the day," she said, accepting Levi's arm and walking towards the restaurant. "I was here with the boys a few weeks ago and it felt still very much the same college town. Tonight," she said, looking up into his eyes, "it feels so different. So much different," she said as she shrugged. Something about the music on the drive over had relaxed her, moving her past the general awkwardness of being on a formal date. It even slid her past the walls she had built up after Levi's late night phone call and surprise appearance on her date with Cole. She had decided to put that behind her. If she had learned anything from her divorce, it was to not let the past sully the future.

Jesse immediately loved the restaurant. It was dark and intimate, with sparse tables draped in white linen and a large mahogany bar. It had eclectic decorations with just enough pretention to make a person forget they were in a little college town.

"Levi, this place is great!" she said, sitting down in the leather booth seat.

"It is, isn't it?" he said, picking up the menu. Jesse couldn't help but wonder if Levi had been here before. He hadn't said otherwise, so she'd just have to assume he had been. Ugh. She wondered if he had been here before with that lanky, lovely redhead. She decided to push that out of her mind; this was her night out. She wasn't going to squander it by being petty. Plus, she had just had a few whopping orgasms of her own with a person that was decidedly not Levi, so she decided she couldn't exactly judge.

They ordered two glasses of Syrah and reviewed the items on menu, none of which Jesse had ever tasted. They decided to order a selection of tapas. Jesse let Levi take the helm, smiling to herself that the truck driving, auto body mechanic knew his way around a wine list and a tapas bar. He was a pretty magnificent man.

They talked about their parents and kids as they waited, carefully avoiding the subject of friends, given the latest uncomfortable snafu with Cole. When the salads arrived, they ate in companionable silence. The Brie with fruit compote was so delicious that Jesse nearly moaned. Deep down, she was a foodie. She studied her food as she ate, remarking about how it might have been cooked. Levi knew she was planning to try and reproduce what they were eating. They had Vodka poached shrimp, a cheese and sausage plate, and the best of all, duck with a mustard sauce. The server took their order of pecan pie for desert and refilled their wine glasses.

"Levi, this may be the best dinner I have ever eaten," she said, looking down at their empty dishes in unmasked delight. He couldn't help but think it was nice to see a woman actually eat and enjoy it. He really liked that Jesse didn't play coy or seem to be anything other than the woman he had known for more than half of his lifetime.

He had done a fair bit of dating before marrying Emma. He had even dated a few women, nothing serious, after Emma's passing, but there always seemed to be a game or an angle being played that he didn't feel comfortable with. Refreshing seemed to be an odd word to attach to a person, but that seemed to fit the bill. Being with Jesse, with her lack of airs, was refreshing.

He nodded in answer, "Yes, definitely delicious. We'll have to come back," he said and noticed a funny look in her eye.

Jesse decided that he most definitely had been here before. Fine, she was going to leave that one alone. They were in Carverton for God's sake, how many really nice restaurants could there be?

"Sounds good," she said, leaning back in her seat as the server brought out the pie with two forks.

They shared the pie, Jesse giving up halfway through and laughing at Levi's look of relief at being allowed to eat the rest of it. It was heavenly. He paid the bill, and they walked back to his truck arm in arm. He opened her door, and as she turned to step into the truck, he put his hand on the small of her back. She looked at him and he leaned in, touching her jaw softly. He pressed a kiss to her lips, and she felt that familiar surge that came with kissing Levi. There must be something just plain magical about kissing the person who basically taught you to kiss. Everything from his lips to his tongue was just what Jesse had been wanting. She put her hands on his neck, holding him to her as they kissed like a couple of teenagers in the parking lot of the restaurant. He pulled away as he heard the click of shoes on the sidewalk and smiled at her, giving her his hand as she stepped up into the truck. He shut her door and walked around the truck as she caught her breath. He stood outside his door before getting in, willing his body to cooperate with his mind. There was an electric connection between them.

On the drive home they talked about traveling and where they'd been and where they'd like to go. That topic alone was in-depth enough to see them all the way back to her house. Levi walked her to the door as she pulled her key from her clutch.

"I guess there's no chance of me coming in tonight, huh, Jess?" he said, grinning like a devil.

"Hmm, let's see... what's more off-putting? My geriatric parents on the other side of that door, or my three sons who would no doubt murder you in your sleep if you did," she said, tapping her finger to her chin, faking deep thought.

"Ok, fine. Can we do this again?" he asked, the teasing note gone from his voice. He pulled her to him again, placing a soft kiss on her lips.

"Yes, I would love that," Jesse said, stepping back, letting his hand drop from hers as she unlocked the door. She turned and gave him a small wave as he stepped off the porch, and pulled the door shut behind her. Jesse carefully gathered her wits before tip-toeing to her dozing father in the chair.

"Dad, I'm home," she said, tapping him softly on the arm.

"Huh? Oh hi, honey, did you have a nice time?" he asked, blinking as he gathered his wits about him. "Better wake your mama," he said, raising up out of the chair and going to the couch where she was softly snoring. "Mama. Mama, wake up. Sis is home. We can go home now," he said, Jesse touched by the gentleness in his voice.

Eadie sat up on the couch and smiled up at Jesse, "Kiddo, I want you to call and tell me all about it tomorrow," she said, gathering her purse and coat up in her arms. "The boys were just fine, and Michael was home by 11 o'clock, just like you asked. Not a minute earlier, but not a minute late either," she said, adjusting her coat as Walt helped her into it.

"Thanks so much you two. I appreciate it," she said, waiting until her parents got in their car and pulled out of the driveway before locking the door and turning out the lights. Jesse kicked off her gorgeous heels and quietly made her way up the stairs. She peeked in at each son, making sure their blankets were on, whispering a silent prayer to God in thanks for a nice night and for her many blessings.

Twenty-Five

Saturday morning brought all its familiar chores; dusting, vacuuming, folding laundry, many of which could be farmed out to the boys. Jesse tip-toed out of the house after leaving a little list outside each of their doorways with their respective tasks written down. She wasn't super strict about when they completed it, but she did give them a deadline of 1PM. Her boys usually didn't gripe about the chores unless of course they didn't get them done in time and she started taking away privileges. She figured it was a good character building exercise. They needed to learn to take care of a house; they would eventually fly the coop one day.

Jesse decided on a whim to take the long way to the grocery store and drive by Levi's house. Sure, it was a little bit of a stalker move to do an unnecessary drive by, but she was awash in happy feelings from such a nice evening the night before. As she crested the hill she saw a green Civic parked in front of Levi's house. She slowed down and saw Shannon exit his door, red hair tousling in the breeze. Jesse made it exactly one block before she had to pull over. She looked at the clock in her car, it read 10 AM. She looked at the clock on her phone, sure enough 10 AM.

Levi had dropped her at her door at 11:45 last night. What the hell had he done? Drop Jesse off at the door with a chaste kiss then call Shannon over for some hot and steamy sex? Was she on speed dial? After all, it hadn't been that long ago that Levi had called her up for some late night action only to be denied because she at least had some class, for God's sake! The coffee she had guzzled before leaving the house seemed to turn in her stomach. She felt for a minute like she was going to be sick, but pressed her cool hands to her forehead, rubbing out to her temples. Jesse cracked the window a little and breathed in the cool air, willing her hands not to shake.

After just a few minutes, she had composed herself bodily enough to get back on the road, but she could have easily bitten a nail in two. What are the freaking odds that Jesse would drive by at just the right time, she wondered out loud. As she parked in the grocery store parking lot, she shut the SUV door with a little more enthusiasm than necessarily, startling an elderly lady in the car next to her. She closed her eyes and took a deep breath, hoping to calm the hell down before looking like a maniac in the store. That's all she needed after the rampage at Laura Williamson's front porch. She didn't want to earn the reputation as the Town Psychotic.

Jesse entered the store, rifled through her purse for her list and made her way around the produce section, checking off items as she went. She had made it as far as the dairy department when her cart was nudged by another. She jerked a surprised head around to find Levi smiling down at her. "Hey, Jesse," he said, casual as could be. It took the absolute grace of God above for her to not growl at him.

"Levi," she said coolly, looking back to the yogurt section to dig out the boys' favorite flavors. Levi moved beside her, so close that she could feel the heat of his body.

"Are you going to tell me what the frostiness is about?" he asked, brown eyes boring into hers. She looked right back into his eyes, absolutely terrified that she didn't see anything in his face that betrayed the fact that Shannon had been at his house mere hours after their date. That scared her. Was he that used to lying that he could conceal it so easily?

"I'm not about to do this here, Levi. No way in the world," she said, looking back to the shelf. She could feel the tears pricking at her eyes; she wasn't going to let him have the satisfaction of seeing that.

He didn't move immediately. She felt his eyes on her face, but refused to look back at him. She would have stood in front of that cooler for six hours if she had to as long as she didn't have to look into his lying eyes. After a minute or so, she felt him turn and heard his cart wheeling down the aisle. She faked immense interest in the products on the shelf for a while, taking her sweet time making her choices and moved slowly towards the front of the store. Jesse prayed to God Levi would be gone by the time she got out to her car, but it seemed God might've been a little too busy to grant that particular prayer. She pushed that cart like the hounds of Hell were behind her, lamenting the fact that she had what was probably the furthest parking spot from the entrance of the store. If she had been right up front maybe he wouldn't be standing at the back of her Suburban with his big red truck parked right beside hers. Then again, the more she walked the madder she felt; maybe it was better this way. Fewer witnesses.

"What the hell was that about, Jesse?" he said, moving out of the way just in time as she popped the hatch on the Suburban. She saw the same face she had seen in the store, not even a hint of guilt or guise on him. Jesse felt a hint of insecurity creep in, what if she had misread the situation? She decided to question him instead of delivering the full frontal attack she felt like giving him.

"I drove by your house on the way here today," she said, relieved to see his eyes cloud up a little, thankful that she could still read him after all. "I saw Shannon leaving your house all smiles," Jesse had to look away from his face when she saw him pale a little.

She didn't know which of them was more pathetic. Levi had some kind of hold on her. When she was around him she felt renewed. Alive. How stupid would she feel if he could light her up like a Christmas tree by taking her on a simple date, then go home to screw the brains out of someone else? And what kind of a jerk did that make him? Why did he get to be God's gift to women? What was so special about him? She looked back up at him, hand on her hip, tears threatening to sting at her eyes again. She didn't want him to get to see how much he had hurt her after a few phone calls and a date.

He put his hands in the pockets of his coat and took an almost imperceptible step back from her. "Jesse, when I got home from our date she was waiting at my house," he said, his voice dropping off when he saw Jesse close her eyes and the wrinkle mar her brow, palm facing him. He felt like the air was being sucked out of him when he saw her eyes filled with tears. He didn't know if he had ever felt lower. He started to tell her that he was sorry, but before he could get the words out she spoke.

"I can't," she said, opening her eyes, tears barely held at bay. "I can't listen to it," she said, shaking her head. "I'm just damn glad I happened to drive by today after what I thought was a lovely night together," she said, surprising him when she barked out a sharp, bitter laugh. "Good grief, Levi," she said, slapping him on the arm in what might have been a playful gesture had it been in any other context. "Is every man just a piece of shit? It doesn't give me much hope for my boys. I know you were raised well," she said, looking him hard in the eye.

At that she turned and loaded the last sack of groceries into the back of her SUV. She pushed the cart at him and shut the hatch and walked past him. He stood there stupidly holding her cart as she got in her SUV, backed up and drove away. Jesse didn't look back at him; she just drove out of the lot.

The drive back to her house was a blur. She made it into the house with the first load of groceries, saying a quick prayer of thanks that her boys still seemed to be sleeping. That was a good thing. She needed to have a quick cry before they woke up anyway. She wasn't going to let Levi's antics screw up her day with her boys and no way was she going to let them pay for his mistake by putting her into a pissy mood. Sometimes a good cry could let the tension out. She didn't have much time to waste on him anyway; she had to pack for her trip.

Twenty-Six

It was a little after 11 PM Florida-time when Jesse checked into her hotel room Sunday night. She was exhausted and a little disoriented at the fact that just a few hours ago, she had been in a different state, kissing her boys goodbye and leaving last minute schedule instructions with Eadie and Walt about the next few days to come. Thankfully, she wouldn't be missing any games. Football had wrapped up and basketball games wouldn't start for Michael for another two weeks. Even Ryan had asked to sign up to play basketball with a church league. She couldn't wait to see him decked out in a jersey. He was such an eager, sweet little boy.

Jesse's brow wrinkled a little when she thought of Luke who still wouldn't consider any team sports. She didn't mind that he wasn't necessarily athletic, she just hoped he'd find his niche soon. He seemed lonely, but at least he was talking more than he had. He was hanging out in the living room more than his bedroom for a change, and she'd take it, even if it meant seeing him with a video game controller glued to his hand after homework was done. He had asked to hang out with friends a few times over the last month, and Jesse had been relieved.

She unpacked her clothes and ran a quick iron over the suit pants, blouse and blazer she'd wear during the trade show that started at noon the next day. Jesse pulled out a pair of jeans and a top to wear during setup of the booth. She had a coworker coming in from St. Louis to help with the show, and she was looking forward to some catch-up time. Her coworker, Marie, was a ball of fun. She was a petite little lady with a huge poof of curly dark hair, the kind of curl you just wanted to pull straight and watch it ping back into place. Marie was always ready with a laugh, and had a way of pulling information out of you without even realizing you were giving away the farm. She leaned in close while you talked, her big blue eyes huge and intent, instilling an instant feeling of corroboration. She was the perfect person to plug into a booth for a customer facing trade show. When someone talked to Marie, they felt like they had 100% of her attention. Jesse couldn't wait to catch up with her the next morning.

Tasks done and dead on her feet, Jesse double checked the locks on the balcony and front doors, brushed her teeth, slipped into her pajamas and into bed. As she reached up to turn off the lamp, her phone gave a little buzz. With an ill-mannered curse, Jesse checked her phone.

Missed you while I was away. Did you miss me? - Cole

Despite herself, her belly did a flip at the message. Cole was a breath of fresh air compared to Levi, who could frankly go to Hell at the moment. Jesse didn't want to be rude and not answer. With her luck, Cole would show up in the morning ready to surprise her with wild, hot, chandelier swinging sex and scare the bejesus out of her parents.

Glad you're back, missed you a little. Have a good trip? - Jesse

She kicked herself for starting a conversation when she was dead on her feet; she wanted nothing more than to go to bed. She'd have to keep it short or she'd look like death warmed over in the morning.

A little, huh? Are you flirting with me? You little strumpet. If you were here beside me now I'd spank you for that. - Cole

An involuntary shiver ran through Jesse. She visualized herself lying beside him, curtains open wide against the dark of the hills and the light of the stars, bent over his lap in nothing but a pair of panties, Cole sitting naked on the edge of the bed, big and strong against her with his work roughened hands on her body. One on the middle of her back, the other delivering a smack on her bottom. Jesse shook her head, she'd never even tried that, God knew Drake didn't have an experimental bone in his body when it came to sex. Until this moment, Jesse hadn't even realized she'd been open to trying it. *Come on, Jesse,* she said to herself. *That's too far out there, you dirty perv.*

A bit pervy tonight, are we? - Jesse

You have no idea. It's been a while. I bet I could make you shine in the moonlight. - Cole

Jesse uttered an involuntary groan. *Good grief,* she thought. What was it about this man that made her feel so hot? He certainly had a way with words. And that body, wow. She felt her mouth go dry at the thought of him. She had to calm this down before she ended up awake all night.

Ok, you've got to knock that off or I'll have to get out of bed to take a cold shower. I'm a little long in the tooth for sexting, or whatever this is turning into. I'm a respectable Methodist Woman, you know. - Jesse

One I've fucked on her couch. And in her office. And in my mind, a hundred different ways. - Cole

Oh there he went. The F word. How could one word be so offensive sometimes, so hot others? Jesse was getting horny despite herself, and she didn't have time for that. She needed sleep or she'd be worthless tomorrow. She felt like a teenager who needed to hide a dirty note from her parents.

You've got me there. Or had me there. It was awesome. I have to get to sleep or I'll be a mess tomorrow. I'm in Miami for a few days for a trade show and will be back late Wednesday night. - Jesse

Against her better judgment she followed with another message before he could reply.

Unless he pulls something, the kids will be at Drake's this weekend, want to get together? - Jesse

She held her phone away wondering to herself just what the heck she was doing. She just asked Cole out on a date. She did a quick mental calculation, relieved that this weekend she would neither be on her period or ovulating. Score. *Come on Jesse, you're an adult. What's the big deal?* she thought. *I'm a woman. I like him. He likes me. He's amazing in bed.* She tamped down that respectable Methodist woman remark, rearing its head in ugly reminder that technically she wasn't supposed to be having wild, crazy sex with a man to whom she's not married. It was too late for either moral debate or sexual innuendo. Or both.

I do. Drake's, huh? Is he behaving himself? - Cole

Jesse laughed out loud at that.

He's Drake. About as personable as a skunk. He's hateful and rude to me, but I don't have to worry much about it as long as he's good to the kids. - Jesse

Sounds like he's pretty consistent. Asshole. So, Friday at 7:00? - Cole

Yes, 7:00 it is. - Jesse

I'll pick you up. Pack a bag. - Cole

Jesse's stomach tightened at that. An overnight. Was she ready? She typed the reply and held her finger over the button to send the message, butterflies filling her middle. What did she have to lose? Levi had certainly shit the nest with her, and she knew first hand he wasn't wasting any time seeking pleasure. What's good for the goose is good for the gander, she decided.

Ok. - Jesse

Monday morning came early, Jesse thought. Her sluggish state could have been blamed on the time zone difference or the fact that she laid in bed awake until one in the morning after the sexy text messaging with Cole. He was like a dirty little present at just the right time. She did need to frequently remind herself not to get too far into it though; she had a responsibility to his feelings as well. Levi's antics had been an excellent reminder of what jerks men could be. She had her boys and that was all she needed. Dates and sex and fun were all well and good but she didn't necessarily need any more entanglements in her life right now. Gritty, puffy eyes be damned, Jesse hauled herself out of bed, dressed in her yoga pants, t-shirts and tennis shoes and threw her hair up in a bun. Squinting at herself in the mirror as she brushed her teeth, she mentally patted herself on the back for not hitting snooze. She rarely had a chance to work out at an excellent fitness center, and she was going to make use of it. The resort the trade show was booked in was incredible. Jesse wished the event had been booked when she could have made better use of the beach, but she was going to find a way to get out and sit in the sand for a while before she had to leave. She hadn't been to the ocean many times, but the sound of the waves soothed her soul. She could do with a little soul soothing right about now.

She shut the door on the path her mind was about to take her on and instead turned on the 90's Hip Hop station on her phone, put in her ear-buds and enjoyed feeling the burn of her legs on the treadmill. Jesse was drenched in sweat and surprised at her own mental escape when her alarm sounded to send her back to her room to prepare for the day. Jesse loved all kinds of music, from Pop to the obscure, but there wasn't much that could beat 90's Hip Hop. It was certainly more enjoyable for her to listen to than the crap the artists were pumping out today. The new stuff was so dirty and base that she was totally disinterested. As she showered and dressed, she continued along her little trip down memory lane, thinking of the pool at her friend's house where all the kids would gather and listen to music pumping out of the boom box while some of the boys manned the grill. It never failed, the hamburgers always turned out the shape of baseballs, but there were nothing but great memories of laughter and hormone rushes. Rarely did anyone end a night at those pool parties without getting kissed. Really kissed. The kind that made your heart pound, and spurred nights later on naked at the levy or behind the grain silos on the edge of town.

With one last glance in the mirror, Jesse grabbed her laptop bag, phone and made her way down to the ballroom where the trade show would be held. She walked down the floor and smiled as she saw Marie up on a ladder, trying to hang a banner on the upper decking of the display.

"Here, Hot Potato, let me steady that ladder for you," she said, slapping Marie on the butt. Marie gasped, whirled around nearly knocking herself from her step on the ladder, and hooted with laughter when she saw it was Jesse.

"Jesus Christ, Jesse, I almost screamed!" she admonished as she scurried down the ladder, wrapping Jesse up in a tight squeeze. "We don't want these big city assholes thinking we're a bunch of hillbillies," she said, faking a very stern frown.

"Good to see you, Marie. It's been too long," she said, reaching out to pick up a box of brochures that needed to be laid out on the table top. She had only been to a handful of other trade shows; it felt a little exciting to be doing something out of the norm, even though she hated leaving the boys.

Marie grabbed the box of promotional material and arranged it on the table, sneaking a look at Jesse out of the corner of her eye.

"Oh yeah? Miss me enough to come back to work in the office?" she asked nonchalantly, then snickered at Jesse's automatic grimace.

"God no, Marie. That would put me within arm's reach of Drake and I'd rather eat a booger than be that close to him ever again," she said, causing Marie to choke and sputter on her coffee.

"Keep that up," she said, quirking a brow at the man that had just passed their table, "and they really will think we're hillbillies," she said. Marie stopped shuffling the papers, tucked the laptop bag under the table skirt and grabbed Jesse's sleeve. "Come on, let's go load up on coffee and bagels before the good stuff is gone," she said looking intently at Jesse. "Then you can start talking about how you're really doing."

Jesse put her hand on Marie's shoulder and gave it a squeeze and nodded, turning toward the refreshment table. She was thankful to have a fresh set of ears to talk to. Marie didn't know anything about Levi, and of course nothing about Cole. Jesse wasn't entirely sure how much she wanted to share, not because she feared judgment from Marie, but maybe she hadn't mulled over all of it enough to talk through it in a sensible manner.

They walked away from the refreshment table, Marie holding two bagels and a small coffee and Jesse holding two large coffees and a bagel speared on her little finger. Marie raised her eyebrows at her double fisted caffeine requirements of the morning.

"Long story," Jesse said as they made their way back to their partially finished booth. "I'll tell you as we work." At that, Marie waggled her eyebrows and didn't bother hiding the excitement she felt at what would surely be a juicy story.

Throughout the next few hours, Jesse went through what all had happened over the past several months since they had moved. Marie listened intently, commenting here and there, but more than anything, she let Jesse talk. Jesse hadn't realized how much it helped to go through it without much interruption. By the time she finished the recap, she sat down on her chair looking around at the well setup booth they had put together.

"Wow, Marie. I'm exhausted. I feel like I've just had a therapy session. Buy you a drink after by way of payment?"

"You bet! There's a martini with my name on it somewhere in that bar downstairs," she answered, scooting her chair a bit closer to Jesse's. "Listen, Jess. I've been single for a while now. I can't factor in motherhood because thankfully God withheld children from my disastrous first marriage, but the rest is a bit more relatable." Jesse and Marie started gathering their things as they talked, it was time to go up to their rooms, dress and grab lunch before the start of the trade show. As they walked to the elevator Marie put her hand on Jesse's arm, stopping her midway down the hall.

"Please hear me when I say, do not waste energy feeling guilty over good sex with Cole. As long as you're straight with him about not wanting more in the way of a relationship, you aren't doing any harm. Plus, the sex is good for you. Hormones and whatnot," she said with a wave of her hand. They turned towards the elevator, Jesse not saying anything but mulling over Marie's advice.

As the elevator stopped at Marie's floor, she gave Jesse a quick hug and said, "As far as Levi though, I need some time to think about that one," and gave her friend a smile as she stepped off the elevator. Jesse nodded, she couldn't speak for the big lump that had just filled her throat. When the elevator doors finally shut, she hastily wiped the tears from her eyes. Damn it, Levi she said to herself. Damn it.

The first day of the trade show was a success. A steady trickle of clients came by the booth, happy with the promotional items, and chatting about the product and what they liked about it. Those that had a gripe or suggestion were at least constructive about it. That's why they always staffed the booth with at least two employees. One could greet the clients; one could pull the chatty ones aside to take down notes on suggestions, the odd complaint and contact information for follow-ups. By the end of the day,

Jesse was wiped out. She had quickly grown accustomed to the solitude working from home had given her. When they packed up for the night, she and Marie decided to go back to their rooms to freshen up and change out of work clothes. Jesse had not at all missed dress clothes. She was fine with dressing up for church on Sundays, but her heart belonged to her yoga pants.

Since there were clients and competitors milling around the resort, she couldn't totally relax, but it did feel awfully good to slip on her jeans, ballet flats and her soft pink sweater. It was the only cashmere item she owned, a splurge from last season when she knew she'd soon be out on her own. It had a slight V-neck and was so soft she constantly caught herself running her hand against her sleeve. She had always been one to enjoy textures, even as a little girl. Her mother would trail before her gently touching different items as she went through a department store. Jesse didn't know if it was her natural inclination to do the same or if she had just been emulating her mother. Either way, she was definitely a touchy feely type of woman. Jesse picked up her phone and made a quick call to her mother.

Eadie answered on the first ring, joy prevalent in her voice. She loved being in Grandma-mode and her energy just oozed out of her. She had loved being a mother and took a special kind of joy in serving in that role again when she could. She missed having people to take care of, so getting the chance to watch the boys while Jesse was out of town was right up her alley. Jesse couldn't help but smile at the thought of how her house would look when she got home. She knew everything would be sparkling clean, and she would have no idea where anything was for a while. Eadie was a force to be reckoned with when it came to domesticity, and she had strong ideas on how a house should be organized. To be completely honest, Jesse didn't care if she couldn't find the measuring cup for a while if it meant her kiddos were well cared for. If her laundry was caught up when she got home? Even better. After a quick chat with Eadie and the boys, she felt at ease and was working on catching her second wind for the evening. After Jesse disconnected the call, she threw her curls up into a messy bun and added some dangley silver hoops and made her way down to the restaurant downstairs.

Marie was already waiting for her in a booth toward the back of the restaurant, all the better for swapping stories, Jesse thought to herself. For as long as she had worked with Marie, she had been in awe of how youthful she looked. She was a very petite woman, probably 5'3" to Jesse's 5'10". When they first met, Jesse had learned the instant tall-girl habit of leaning down to talk to shorter friends was definitely not needed with Marie. Her voice would be heard no matter the distance. She had very dark, very springy hair and beautifully light, clear skin. Marie was fit and fashionable and never without heels. Tonight she wore leggings, brown heeled boots and a dark green slouchy sweater. The combination of woodland colors made her look like a forest nymph, something she worked to her own advantage. Marie had been married in her early twenties and quickly learned that her husband had a penchant for drinking heavily and slapping her face. It happened only twice before she decided life was too short, abusers don't change and she wasn't going to live in fear. She moved back in with her parents, filed for a restraining order and a divorce on the same day. It processed quickly and she left her home in Seattle without looking back. When her father passed shortly after, her mother moved to St. Louis to be closer to Marie, and they rewrote their lives the way they wanted. She lived in a town home in a very nice part of St. Louis. Her attractive personality, appearance and uncanny ability to remember details and get people to talk easily translated to a very successful career in sales. Marie's mother lived a few minutes away in a nice

Senior Community where she came and went as she pleased without any of the maintenance she would've had to keep up with had she stayed in the home she shared with her husband in Seattle.

Jesse smiled in approval at the martinis and appetizer tray on the table and took her seat. "Marie, this is perfect. Love the boots; you always look so put together," Jesse said, taking a drink of her martini and closing her eyes in appreciative joy. "God, this is good," she said, putting down her glass and reaching for the carrots and celery, leaving the wings to Marie. She was going to be having wild, toe-curling sex on Friday. She was going to feel her most confident. Ok, maybe a few wings. She wasn't a saint after all.

"Thanks, babe. You look pretty in that color. Pettable even," she said, laughing as Jesse waved her off as she tried to stroke her sweater like she'd pet a cat. One hour and two drinks later, they had recapped the clients they had been working on together and idly gossiped about what they expected was going to happen next with the company and certain coworkers. Finally, Marie felt ready to go in for the kill.

"Now, about Levi," she said, making Jesse flinch. Jesse had made her mind up that she wasn't going to be the one to bring it up, she wasn't even sure she was ready to hear what Marie would say.

Marie never messed with sugarcoating; she was a definite straight talker.

"When you talk about Levi, there's something in your eyes that I've never seen before. Never with Drake and not with this Cole guy who sounds yummy, by the way." At that, Jesse gave an eye roll. She was right though; Cole was definitely yummy in a dangerously sexy kind of way. "It sounds like you love him, but it also sounds like he can't keep it in his pants." Jesse blew out the breath she'd been holding and nodded her head a little. "But," Marie said as Jesse was about to interrupt, "truth be told, it doesn't sound like you're in the 'committed, exclusive relationship' stage just yet." Jesse sat silent, head and heart arguing too much to come up with a reasonable reply. Sure, Jesse was in default love-mode with Levi; she probably always would be. In her mind, they had a perfectly great date and were on the path to something exclusive. Even if they hadn't said the words, that was where her heart automatically went. Maybe it was the serial monogamist in her mind, pre-programmed after so many years of marriage to think that was the next step. Maybe it's because she hadn't done enough dating in college when people were supposed to get that stuff out of their systems.

"Marie, you have a good point. It does turn my stomach that he'd kiss me good night, then go across town and be with Shannon mere minutes after leaving me," she said looking down at her hands on the table. She reached in her purse to check her phone again to make sure she hadn't missed a call or a message from her boys or parents. When she looked back up into Marie's eyes, she shrugged her shoulders. Jesse was used to feeling in control and having a plan. Any sort of turmoil felt uncomfortable to her, mainly because she promised herself she was done with tangled feelings when she left Drake. She had wanted to shut the door on pain, and had pretty much resolved herself to being alone, just to spare herself any unnecessary drama. Then again, she thought she'd be sex-free for the rest of her life with the exception of Mr. Vibrator. It was a big surprise to discover how nice it could feel to be the object of desire again. She just hated the thought of feeling so physically and emotionally high at the end of the date, assuming Levi felt the same, only to go release it with someone else. Unreal.

"The way I figure it, and you can tell me to go screw myself," Marie said, causing a snort of laughter to erupt from Jesse. Alcohol sure loosened the tongue, she thought, trying to remember the last time she had heard Marie talk like that. “As I was saying,” Marie said, giving Jesse the stink eye. “I think Levi needs to build back trust with you; he made a dick move, but I don’t think it’s worth throwing him over for that misstep or whatever you want to call it,” she said, reaching into her purse for her wallet.

“Definitely food for thought,” Jesse agreed. “I hate to even waste time thinking about it. I planned to be done with drama,” she said, digging in her own purse.

“Bullshit, Jess,” she said with a sharp edge to her voice, totally taking Jesse by surprise. “You’re too young to resign yourself to celibacy and loneliness. You’re in your prime now. Didn’t you have health class in high school where the teacher talked about sex drives and peaks for women? I remember thinking ‘ewwww, my sex drive would peak in my 30s?’ That seemed so old at that point, didn’t it?” Jesse was too surprised to do anything beyond nod. Marie continued, “I figured shit would be sagging already by that point,” shaking her head at her own silliness as a kid. “Jesse, look at yourself. You’re gorgeous. You’re fun to be with. Sex with people is way more fun that the all-by-yourself kind, and people are messy. They have baggage, issues, and emotional entanglements,” she said, standing up and gathering her purse. Jesse rose and Marie gave her a hard hug.

Jesse swallowed and looked down at her good friend.

"I know you're right, Marie. I just need a little more time to get there," she said. They walked to the elevator, nodding hello to a gaggle of clients loudly laughing in the lobby. Jesse was thankful for Marie and even for the fact that she pretty much just had her butt chewed. She knew it came from a place of love. She made a mental note to keep the focus of tomorrow's conversations on Marie's life. She didn't want to monopolize the time together with her own issues. They said goodbye in the elevator, and Jesse made quick work of her bath and nighttime routine, rubbing a heavenly smelling lotion onto her hands and feet before pulling up the covers. She flicked off the light and laid down, dead to the world almost as soon as her head hit the pillow.

Twenty-Seven

The next day of the trade show went off without a hitch. Jesse was happy to pepper Marie with questions about her recent travels between visits with clients at the booth. Marie was one of those people that had crazy, random things happen on nearly every trip she took. She told a story about being stuck on a plane, held captive on the runway for six hours during an ice storm that had Jesse laughing so hard that she was in tears. Unfortunately for Marie, she had been seated next to a woman who had forgotten the Xanax she had been prescribed for her fear of flying. By the time the plane actually took off, Marie had gotten the woman sloppy drunk by ordering mini bottles of alcohol from the flight attendant in sheer hope the woman would pass out and shut up.

With the salary she raked in, Marie also traveled for pleasure. She was an exceptionally confident person, and it was an apparent lure for sexy men. No matter where she went, she usually managed to have an erotic encounter with a local.

They made for delicious stories to pass the time between client visits. Jesse hoped the clients took her rosy cheeked glow as a sign of fantastic health rather than a blush of shock from some of the stories Marie had been telling. The ladies ended the day by kicking off their heels and packing away as much of the booth as they could before leaving for the evening. They would do the tear-down of the rest in the morning in more comfortable clothes. They escaped to their rooms to change and for Jesse to check in with her family.

The boys weren't very chatty when she talked with them which led her to believe Grandma was allowing them to have more video game time than she normally allowed. Jesse also learned from Ryan's excited admission that they had ordered pizza from their favorite pizza place and Grandma was making banana splits in the kitchen. That explained why Eadie had gotten off the phone so fast. She didn't want to deal with Jesse's "high handed manner" about limiting unhealthy treats. She was fine with the occasional indulgence; they were kids after all, but she definitely served more broccoli than banana splits herself. When she was getting ready to end the call, she heard a muted scuffle in the background as Michael was apparently stealing the phone from Ryan.

"Hey Mom, I forgot to tell you..."

"Michael, apologize to Ryan. Good grief it sounds like you were trying to kill him," she said, using her mom voice on him.

"Sorry, Ryan," he said quickly, then jumped back into his story. "I forgot to tell you that Dad called. He's in the hospital," Michael said casually, as if he were reporting that he had history homework or something.

"What? Is he okay?" she asked, cringing at the loudness of her voice. She could visualize Michael holding the phone a foot away from his ear.

"Yeah, he's okay, just banged up a little," he said, making her wonder for the thousandth time why it was so hard to get information out of a man.

"Michael, can you tell me more please? What did he say?" she said, taking a calming breath. She wouldn't get anything out of him if she flipped, and she wasn't in any particular hurry to call Drake for the details.

She heard him sigh and stopped herself from snapping. Why was getting the whole story like pulling teeth? She gritted hers and waited for Michael.

"He said he was driving home late from Rachel's house and some asshole, sorry Mom, but that's what he said, in a big black truck nearly drove him off the road. Apparently she lives out in the sticks or something," he said with a chuckle.

Jesse rolled her eyes at that, trying to imagine Drake in his pressed suit pants and immaculate appearance dating someone who lived out in the sticks.

"Anyway, he was on a side road about to pass over one of those narrow little bridges and a big truck got right on his tail with the lights on bright and actually hit Dad's car! Dad hit a guardrail and whacked his head pretty hard. He expected the asshole to..."

"Easy, son."

"Sorry, Mom, that's what he said. But he expected the guy to exchange information, but the guy just kept going. He was able to start the car and drive to the hospital. They were keeping him overnight to watch for a concussion, but he'll get out in the morning.

Suddenly Jesse remembered this was Drake's weekend to have the boys. "Will your Dad be well enough to have you boys this weekend?" she asked, also remembering her date with Cole.

"Yeah, he said he'd have a new car by morning that Rachel would drop off. He'll pick us up at six on Friday."

"Well, that works out well, then," she said, working damned hard to keep the bitterness out of her voice. At least he wasn't her problem to take care of any longer. A six o'clock pickup would give her an hour to slug down a glass of wine, and get changed before Cole picked her up at seven. That was a pretty tight time line; she might need to push Cole off till eight to avoid her worlds colliding. She'd have to figure that one out later. "Okay, Sweetie. Please give the boys a hug for me. I'm going to go to dinner with my friend, Marie, and then going to hit the hay. I can't wait to see you tomorrow," she said into the phone.

"Bye, Mom," he said, and she heard him say in a falsetto voice, "Come here little brothers, Mom wants me to give you smoochies," causing the other two boys to scream and Eadie to holler in from the kitchen. She laughed as she disconnected the call. It sounded like they were all doing fine. She sat down on the edge of the bed and thought about Drake's accident. She could easily imagine there being plenty of people in the world to hate him bad enough to want to run him off the road, but to actually DO it is another thing. That's just nuts. That's the kind of crazy stuff people did in movies but not real life, as far as she knew. Her mind went back to the dead cat incident as she dressed in jeans and a purple sweater and made her way down to the lobby to meet Marie.

She wasn't surprised at all to see her friend being chatted up by a very handsome man. She recognized him as the CFO of one of the companies they did business with. He was a smooth talking son-of-a-gun, and sexy though he may be, she also knew there was no way he was going to make any headway with her friend. Marie might have had a very adventurous life, but she had a firm rule about never mixing business with pleasure. That gave Jesse all the permission she needed to walk up to them and insert herself into the conversation. Mr. CFO looked a little disheartened, but he took the hint. Marie gave her a grateful smile and looped her arm through Jesse's as they went out to get a cab. Tonight, they would be dining at a restaurant right on the water; sushi and martinis, a perfect end to a successful work event.

Twenty-Eight

As much as she had loved the break from reality, Jesse was more than happy to get back home. She arrived a little before midnight on Wednesday and found everyone snug in their beds. Rather than disturb Walt and Eadie from their rest in the guest bedroom, Jesse decided to just let them sleep and checked on each son, then quietly slipped into her own bedroom. She could never stand to sleep with 'travel germs', so she took the world's quickest hot shower. It never failed to surprise her just how refreshed a person could feel after a good, hot scrub. She piled her dirty clothes in the hamper, threw her toiletry bag on the bathroom cabinet, and stored her suitcase away in her closet. There. Nothing left to deal with in the morning. She checked the clock and set her alarm for 6:00 AM. She wanted to take the morning routine back over and give her parents a break. They seemed to get up with the chickens nowadays as it was; she figured they'd get the coffee going, and, knowing her mother, pancakes, bacon and eggs as well. Jesse slipped into bed and pulled the covers up to her chin and whispered a prayer of thanks for her blessings. God had been so very gracious to her. She had her health, her kids, and thankfully, she still had her parents in good health. She knew there were so many people not as fortunate, so she said a quick prayer for them as well.

The next morning she woke up to the smell of coffee made even more delicious by the fact she didn't have to make it herself. There was just something so luxurious about waking to find coffee already made. She brushed her teeth, dressed and patted her hair into place, and made her way down the stairs. Walt was at the table with a newspaper; apparently, he had already been out to the grocery store for the day since Jesse didn't have a paper delivered. He smiled up at her as her mother said, "Hello dear!" and walked over to give her a hug. Nostalgia welled up in Jesse, emotions brimming as she remembered back to her childhood. Her parents had always made home such a nice place to be. Jesse hugged her mother and wiped away the hot tears stinging her eyes.

"Hey Mom," she said, giving her mother one extra squeeze. Eadie pulled back from her, looked at her face, and then pulled her close one more time. A mother's hug must be the absolute best medicine for the human soul. Eadie was never one to shy away from hugs, kisses or the words 'I love you.' Her mother crossed over to the coffee pot and handed Jesse her favorite red mug with white polka dots, then went back to the range to start breakfast. Jesse noticed she had pulled out the griddle, and had a huge slab of bacon ready to fry. She figured the boys must have been eating like kings during the week, and hoped the crash course back to normal wouldn't be too hard on them. She was a master at putting a good dinner on the table, but breakfasts sometimes were a little rushed.

She took her mug and sat down by her dad, quietly reading the paper. Eadie started in with questions about her trip, her friend Marie, was the weather nice, did she have a nice time, etc. Jesse suddenly remembered the Information Extraction sessions disguised as innocent chit chat when she was a teenager. The morning after she went out with her friends, her mother would systematically pull information out of her and her sister Anna by starting off, "Where'd you go? Who'd you see? What'd you say?" and without fail, Jesse would spill the beans without thought. It hadn't dawned on her until Michael got into middle school that by ingraining this habit in Jesse when she was small, it was like taking candy from a baby to find out everything she needed to know about what was going down with Jesse's friends. It was that same day that Jesse herself had started asking the same questions of all three of her kids. Eadie had been a parenting mastermind.

Walt had always had a more laid back approach to parenting. He had pretty much piddled in his workshop, tinkering around with repairing motors on lawn mowers, changing oil in the cars, or more specifically avoiding a house soaked to the rafters in estrogen. Whenever the girls had needed his input, they would catch him in the living room reading the paper or walk out to the shop. Jesse looked over at her Dad and saw in her mind the many times she'd find him alone. He'd always put down the tools or the paper and sit down, patting a chair beside him. He's ask, "What's up, Peanut?" if he was talking to Jesse or "What's up, Sweet Pea?" for Anna. He had nicknamed them as babies and the names had stuck. Even still, though he was a man of few words. If no one else was around, he'd call them by those names. He was a quiet, puzzling, precious man. She sat there drinking in the pleasant domesticity and sense of deja vu when she heard some heavy footfalls on the stairs. She was out of her chair in a flash and at the bottom of the stairs by the time Michael and Luke made it to the bottom.

"Hey boys, so good to hug your necks!" she said, hugging them hard to her. Her boys were so funny. They immediately melted for approximately four seconds before getting squirmy and weird. Male pride and ego is a very strange thing. She shooed them toward the table as Eadie started setting out plates and pouring milk.

"Help your Grandma, boys," she said as she made her way up the stairs. She rounded the turn into Ryan's room just as he was opening his door. He flew into her arms and hugged her tightly, no doubt relieved that the bigger boys weren't upstairs to see and potentially tease him. She sat down on the edge of his bed and patted the space beside her.

"Sit down, Baby," she said, putting her arm around him as he leaned toward her. "How are you, Sweetie?" she asked, noticing that he somehow looked bigger than he had when she left.

"Good, glad you're home though," he said, smiling shyly. "I missed you."

"Ugh, me too, kiddo! It was a little fun to see my friend and talk to some clients, but my favorite place to be by far is home with you fellas. Did Grandma and Grandpa take good care of you?" she asked, already knowing the answer was yes.

"Oh yeah. I'm absolutely full. She cooks and cooks and cooks," he said, eyes wide in his precious face. His dark, curly hair was wild with sleep so she brushed it back off his forehead with her fingers. "And you know I love Grandma, but man, does she drive super slow. The last three days have been the slowest drive to school in the world," he said, shaking his little exasperated head.

"I know, kiddo. She's always been that way," she said with a laugh. "We're very lucky that she was able to come take care of you guys while I was out of town," she said, not comfortable making anything close to a disparaging remark about her mother to the kids. It simply wasn't allowed.

"Well kiddo, go on in and brush your teeth. Grandma's got breakfast on the table and the other two boys are already down there," she said, rising from the bed. "I'm going to get dressed, chug down some coffee and get you to school," she said watching him walk down the stairs. She went into her room, threw on a pair of black leggings, a long knit purple tunic, and her favorite brown sheepskin boots. She was going all-out comfortable today, and if the carpool moms didn't like it, they could go suck an egg.

Jesse threw her hair up in a bun and briefly contemplated bangs while brushing her teeth. She moisturized her face, neck and hands, added a tiny bit of eye liner, mascara and lip gloss, and called it done. She went down the stairs as the boys were gathering their bags. Michael gave her another hug on his way out the door. She handed the SUV keys to Luke, and asked him to warm up the car before sending him and Ryan out the door after they gave Walt and Eadie a quick squeeze.

Eadie walked over to Jesse with a to-go cup of coffee in an insulated travel mug.

"I'll clean up breakfast, dear; then Dad and I will be on our way. We have had such a good time with the boys," she said. Jesse thanked her mother profusely, then gasped with surprise when Eadie grabbed her and gave her a very hard, long hug.

"Jesse you don't know how glad I am to have you home now. Do you realize I wouldn't have been able to have this time with the kids if you weren't here? Dad and I so enjoyed it," she said with tears in her eyes.

"Mom, don't cry or I'll start crying. I really, really appreciate it. I'm glad they were good for you. They are pretty terrific boys," she said, pride welling in her chest.

"Yes, they are, sweetie. Yes, they are," she said, fiddling with the dishtowel in her hands. "Jess, you look so pretty and fresh today. You look like you're 19 years old again," Eadie said, shocking Jesse. Eadie was always dressed to the nines and had probably never worn her hair in a messy bun or left the house without concealer and hair spray in her life. At any rate, she'd take that compliment and save it for a rainy day all the same. Jesse gave Walt a quick kiss on the cheek and went out the door to the SUV.

She dropped the boys off and ran to the grocery store. Her coffee supply was dangerously low after her parents had spent three days at her house. She wondered, as she walked into the store, if their habit of drinking coffee all day long was related to the fact that they seemed to never sleep. Whatever it was seemed to be working for them. They were older, but still full of energy. She was lost in thought trying to mentally compile a shopping list when she felt eyes on her back. She silently prayed it wasn't Levi; she still hadn't fully recovered from the last episode with him at the grocery store. She turned to fake a sudden interest in soups and saw Cole out of the corner of her eye, standing there watching her with a slight smile on his lips. He pushed his cart over to hers, and put his hand on her cart handle. Her back was now to the shelves and he was so close to her that she had to look up to see his eyes. If she had been the claustrophobic type, she would have no doubt had a fit of some kind, having another person eat up so much of her personal space. He looked around, after seeing no other shoppers in the aisle, he dipped his head low and gave her a quick kiss. He pressed his body against hers and Jesse drew in a breath at the hard proof of exactly how happy he was to see her.

Just as quickly, he stepped back, slipping back into a more socially appropriate distance from her. He folded his coat over the handle of his cart, grinning and raising his eyebrows at his own clever camouflage efforts.

"I don't want to scandalize the old ladies," he said, eyes practically sparkling with the kind of pleasure only a man can have over his rather large and obvious endowment.

"Doing some shopping?" she said, leaning over his cart, eager to snoop. He pushed it further up the aisle and looked back over his shoulder at her.

"Yes, and quit being so damned nosey, you'll ruin my surprise," he said with a false serious face.

"Ok, suit yourself," she said, her hands going up to pick up a soup can to check the nutritional information. He walked the short distance back to her cart and put his hand on her lower back.

"Still on for seven tomorrow?" he asked, sea colored eyes intently studying her face.

"Oh! Glad you asked. Drake is supposed to pick the kids up at six o'clock and is usually anal about being on time. If it looks like he's running late for some reason, could we make it 7:15 or 7:30?" she asked, eyebrows raised, shoulders a little shrugged. She didn't want to mess with his plans for what seemed to be some sort of complicated dinner; however, she would rather croak than have Cole and Drake anywhere within a one mile radius of each other.

Cole shrugged his shoulders, "Sure, if it goes off without a hitch, let me know. We can play it by ear. Send me a text afterwards, and I'll pick you up. Just be prepared to come hungry," he said, his eyes seeming to darken. Jesse's temperature surged and she wasn't sure if it was his expression, or his play on words, or just the sheer anticipation of what would happen the next night.

"Will do," she said, a little too chirpy for her own liking. She couldn't fake sultry if her life depended on it. There was something about Cole that nearly unnerved her.

"One more thing. You look hot today, Jess," he said, his hand quickly sliding down to cup her butt. Bring something like that for Saturday morning, would you?" he said, giving her a quick squeeze then walking away. A hot, hulking bottle of pure sex just walking down the grocery store aisle. Her very own hot, hulking bottle of pure sex. She probably stood in that soup aisle staring blindly at the shelf for a good two minutes before she got her legs to cooperate and take her through the rest of the store.

She was a little late by the time she sat down at her desk, but she wasn't that worried about it. As far as her coworkers knew, if they even cared, she had just gotten in from a trade show trip, and had to travel clear down to the middle of nowhere. They didn't have to know she nearly had an orgasm in the soup aisle.

Twenty-Nine

Jesse knew she'd have to lower the standards for the usual birthday celebrations now that she was flying solo, but she still put together a pretty good little party for Michael. She still couldn't believe her baby was sixteen years old.

She had made reservations for the family, plus secretly invited Michael's two closest friends to go eat wings at The Hill, Michael's favorite restaurant, with cake and ice cream to follow at their house. Jesse even hung a Happy Birthday banner in the dining room with streamers on the doorways. She had started that tradition when Michael was two years old, and she'd probably continue it as long as she could stand on a ladder to hang them. Jesse also made birthday pancakes with sprinkles, another family tradition from when the boys were little.

She tip-toed up to Michael's room and knocked, happy when he pulled open the door fully dressed for the day. "Good morning, Baby," she said, giving him a hug so hard that he groaned.

"Moooom," he said, when the length of the hug exceeded every bit of indulgence he had. "Ok, Mom, can't breathe here."

"Sorry, kiddo. Happy birthday," she said, sitting down on the edge of his bed. "Listen, Michael," Jesse said, patting the spot beside her. Michael sat down and she patted his knee. "We've talked about this before, but I wanted to say that I'm sorry we weren't able to get you a car or truck for your birthday," she said, feeling even more disappointed when Michael looked down.

"That's not an option for us right now. However after you get your license today we will figure something out where you can sometimes take the Suburban when I'm not using it. There will, of course, be limitations," she said, frowning a little at his groan. "Come on buddy. It's our family car!" she said, standing up, pulling him up beside her. "I'll do my best, but that's all I'm able to do for now," she said, walking to the hall.

"I know, Mom. I'm not the only one not getting a car on my birthday. But if you decided to get me a brand new Dodge Ram, I'd be happy to go drive it in front of Seth's house just to show off," he said, nose wrinkled up in a sneer.

"Yeah, yeah. I know, kiddo," she said, heading to wake the other boys while Michael made his way into the bathroom. She knew there were worse problems in the world to have than not getting a car when you turn 16; however, she did still remember how excited she was to get one when she was a kid. To date, she had saved up around $2000 and had asked Drake six months ago if he would match it. Michael didn't have to have a fancy car, just a drivable, safe one. Drake had of course hit the fan, saying he wouldn't buy his son some piece of crap car, and he certainly wasn't going to buy him a nice one for Jesse to use to get Michael to run errands.

Sometimes Jesse wondered if Drake had a mental illness that made him so nasty, or if his personality had just kind of rotted over time. She was still waiting for her attorney to get back to her on what could be done about it, if anything. Jesse pulled out her phone and made a note to follow up with that when she had a break in the day. Till then, she had a workday to get through, a driver's license test to chaperone, and celebrating to do with her family.

Thirty

Although the boys were already packed for their visit with Drake even before they left for school, Jesse was incredibly nervous about Drake picking up the kids. She didn't know if it was due to his accident earlier in the week and undoubtedly residual crappy mood, or the fact that she had a date right after he'd be leaving. Though she did detest Drake, she hated the thought that someone had deliberately tried to hurt him. She thought back to the whole dead cat issue from the previous month and a shiver went down her spine. She had called Drake to get more information a few days after that incident. He said the police suggested it was probably someone who was on the losing side of a case. Being forced to pay in a settlement could bring out the nastiest side of people. Jesse thought it was probably likely that everyone that knew Drake hated his arrogant personality. It was more of a surprise that was the first threatening note he'd been left, dead cat aside. That part of it was just horrid.

Jesse went ahead and took her bath before the boys were due home from school, using her lunch hour to get in a workout, then showering, scrubbing and shaving all the appropriate parts. Her skin was soft and smooth, and as she put on her thickest body lotion, she let her mind wander to what would be coming up later in the night. She turned on the Fink station on satellite radio, and let her apprehension and excitement mingle as she went through the motions of getting ready for the evening. Jesse picked through her clothes to find just the right outfit. Apparently, they were eating at Cole's house, and he had made his preferences clear on what he'd like to see her in, come Saturday morning. She pulled out her black leggings and the softest gray sweater tunic she had. She was a firm believer in the rule that leggings were not pants, so any that she wore were paired with something long enough to cover her rump. She packed her soft boots that she had worn the day she apparently tripped Cole's trigger in the store. *Why mess with a good thing?* She asked herself, grinning like an idiot. She picked out a steel gray bra and panty set to go with that outfit, as well as some soft socks in case his cabin was chilly. Now to decide what she would wear for her dinner date at his place. She looked through her closet and finally settled on a deep burgundy blouson sweater. It had a cowl neck that let the top drape a little off her shoulder if she wanted. She paired it with a slightly longer black tank, jeans and black boots. She added some earrings that were shaped similar to a feather in ombre shades of the same hue as her sweater. She dipped into her lingerie trove and pulled out her favorite pink lace bra and panties. Once again, she was thankful for her lingerie addiction. She had never dreamed how handy it would come in someday.

She put her things to the side, throwing in her cosmetics and toiletries in case she ended up showering at Cole's. She'd do a quick touch up before the date after the boys had gone. She didn't want to tip them off that she had a big date planned after they left. As it was, she went ahead and let her hair air-dry and put on a pair of jeans and white t-shirt with her favorite cardigan. She was comfortable and presentable, but she didn't have to be concerned about looking cute for Drake anymore.

After the preparations had been made, Jesse returned to work and jumped when her alarm went off notifying her it was time to pick up the boys already. Thank goodness she had the foresight to make that a recurring alarm. When she was on a roll at work, it was like she went to another planet. She had worked so late for so many years that it was still absurd to her that she would end the workday at 3:00 PM. She might have to spend more late evenings catching up on messages to stay productive, but she wouldn't trade that time with her boys for the world. They would all be in high school in a few years; it didn't hurt anything for her to take the time to pick them up now.

She set a timer to remind herself to put in the meatloaf she had thrown together earlier in the day in time to have it ready for the boys at five. As she climbed in the Suburban she wondered how people had ever lived without a constant reminder buzzing. Was the pace of life that much busier now, or had people become lazy and dependent on devices to manage their time? She mulled that over, and thought of all the ways she had become dependent on alarms and reminders during the entire drive to the middle school. She was still lost in thought as she parked in the pickup lane in front of the school, so much so that she didn't notice Laura Williamson and her two sidekicks stalking over to her driver's side window. Jesse jumped at the loud knock on her window and turned on Laura with a glare that would have speared the hateful smirk off of a weaker person. For a split second, Jesse wondered what exactly would happen if she refused to roll down the window. Quickly, she realized she needed whatever this was to be over by the time the boys got outside, so she gave in and rolled down her window, leveling a bored look at Laura.

She looked at Laura, and Laura and the bimbo twins stared back, apparently waiting to be acknowledged properly. With a sigh, Jesse said, "Yes?" and kept her face neutral waiting for this passive aggressive display to end, hopefully within the next three minutes.

"We are doing some volunteer work for the schools today because so many parents don't do their part," Laura said, attempting apparently and unsuccessfully to hurt Jesse's feelings.

"We heard and thought you should know that Levi has been seen around town with another woman," she said, turning to look at one of the girls flanking each of her sides. "I know you think that you have some kind of...," she said, eyes going wide when Jesse interrupted her. That must not happen much, Jesse thought with joy.

"You mean Shannon? The young redhead?" she said as casually as possible. Clearly she had taken Laura by surprise. The bimbos in the back looked at each other quickly and said nothing.

Laura looked surprised and raised her chin an inch, clearly pissed that Jesse had stolen her thunder. "Yes, I did hear that was her name," she said, flicking a look back at one of the ladies behind her.

"Yes, I know about her. They've been on and off for quite a while now, Laura. I'm surprised you just found out about it," Jesse said, taking no small amount of pleasure in the fact that she was armed with this information.

"Well, after your display the other day at my house I thought you should be aware of what's going on with Levi since you seem to think you have the market cornered when it comes to him," she said in an ugly, hateful way.

"If you remember, Laura, all I said was that our relationship status was our own business and not gossip to be thrown around in front of children," Jesse said, momentary perplexed that a face as technically pretty as Laura's could twist into such an ugly, hateful sneer. "Speaking of children, mine are coming towards the truck now, so at the risk of sounding trite, get the hell away from my Suburban," she said with a smile as peaceful as the Mother Mary.

Laura and the blondes on either side of her drew in a breath that nearly sucked all the oxygen out of the atmosphere. Laura turned on her heel and marched away from the pickup lane, the two dummies with her taking turns looking back at Jesse's vehicle as if she was going to run after them. She unlocked the doors as the boys got to the car.

"What was that about, Mom?" Ryan asked, his eyebrows knitted together in concern. "That lady looked mad."

"Not to worry, Sweetie. She's someone I grew up with," Jesse told him, turning back to face her boys in the backseat. "She's a pretty woman on the outside, but not very nice on the inside. Unfortunately for her, the mask slips sometimes," she said as she pulled out of the pickup lane and headed towards home.

Thirty-One

True to form, Drake was in the driveway honking at exactly six o'clock on the dot. Jesse opened the door, and with a great show of irritation, Drake got out of the car. She noticed with a small, evil measure of delight that he had a goose-egg on his forehead where his head had apparently hit the inside of the car. As soon as she acknowledged the feeling, she repented. That could have been more serious, and she'd have a very sad situation on her hands if the boys were mourning the loss of their father.

"Hi Drake, I'm sorry to hear that you had an accident. Are you well?" she asked, resisting the urge to go down the stairs and take a closer look at the knot on his head.

Jesse was certain she heard Drake mumble something along the lines of "Yeah right, you probably wish I was dead," but he at least had the courtesy to not repeat it as the kids were coming out of the house.

Jesse turned and looked at the boys, "Go back inside please, I want to talk to your father for a minute." At that, three pairs of eyes bugged out at her and they made a beeline back into the house.

"What the hell is this, Jesse? I've got a long drive back home," he said, suddenly looking as tired as he apparently felt. She walked over to the edge of the porch and looked at him.

"Drake, marital ruin aside, I *am* sorry to hear that you were hurt. More importantly, I'm about to let those boys ride in the car with you for over an hour. Can you please have the courtesy to answer a few questions for me?" she asked, keeping the iron out of her voice. Drake nodded, apparently just tired enough to give in and get this part over with. "Do you have a concussion?" she asked, looking at him hard enough that he wondered if she thought she could see for herself by staring.

"No concussion," he answered.

"It's apparently safe for you to be driving; I know you wouldn't have risked it with the boys, otherwise," she said, drawing in a breath and leaning down a bit so that hopefully the boys wouldn't hear her. "Do you or the police have any idea what this was about?" she said, eyes wide, imploring him to give her a straight answer, sparing her the bullshit.

He shook his head before he answered. "No. Nothing. It was so dark out I couldn't say for certain if the truck was black or blue, or even what kind it was. I was pretty shaken up," he said, almost looking human for a moment.

"My God," she said, hating the tears that sprung up in her eyes. Truth be told, she was more afraid that some nut had it out for Drake and here she was getting ready to send the boys with him. "One more question," she said, noting that he had shoved his hands in his pockets, his agitation starting to grow at this barrage of questions to which he had no answers. She knew that made him more frustrated than anything. "Do you have a security system at your house?" she asked, his quick nod all the proof she needed to see that he was afraid.

"Yes, I had it put in yesterday. I'll teach the boys how to use it when we get there," he said, surprising Jesse by walking a few steps closer to where she stood on the porch. "I'm not going to talk about this much with them beyond answering any questions they have. I don't want to scare them to the point they won't come visit, Jess." At that, she flinched. That was probably the first time he had called her Jess instead of Jesse in more than ten years. He never used terms of endearment like 'honey' or 'babe'; however, in the early years, he had called her Jess. After things started to change and morph into something ugly, he had managed to take a simple name like Jesse and say it in a way that suggested that even her name wasn't good enough for him.

She quickly recovered and nodded her head. "Ok then, thank you," she said, turning on the porch to walk to the door. "Come on out, boys. Just had to check with Dad for a minute on something," she said to their curious eyes. "Everything is fine," she said as she passed out hugs and kisses and reminders for homework to be done before she picked them up on Sunday. I'll be there at six, okay Drake?"

"Okay," he said as he walked to the back to help the boys get the bags in the trunk. That was the first time she had seen him help them. She could only pray that maybe this latest scare would make him take stock of what he had. A girl can dream. She stood in front of the door and watched as he shook Michael's hand, clasped Luke on the shoulder and put a quick, uncomfortable arm around Ryan.

She gave a little finger wave to the boys as they backed out of the driveway and hollered "Love you, boys!" She saw Drake wince at that, but she was at her house in her town, and she could do what she darned well pleased. That exchange had put a little spring in her step, which was typically not her experience after the pickup. She picked up her phone and sent a quick message to Cole on her walk to the kitchen.

The chicks have flown the coop! - Jesse, she wrote, chuckling to herself as she poured a moderately large amount of Shiraz into her favorite, fancy, long-stemmed glass. She had a full hour before Cole came to pick her up. She put the phone on Bluetooth, picked up her portable speaker and went into the living room. She quickly picked up a pair of her son's discarded, stinky socks, pitched them into the laundry hamper in the bathroom and sat down in her big comfy chair. She tucked her legs beneath her and sipped her wine as DMB blasted her anxiousness away. She was basically ready except for changing clothes, touching up her makeup and throwing her hair up. It had seemed to have quite an effect on Cole the other day. She closed her eyes and leaned her head back as she remembered how he had touched the curls that had come loose around the nape of her neck in the store. As the goosebumps raised all over her body, she decided to take her wine and her DMB to her bathroom upstairs for a quick rinse and refresher. The steam from a hot bath always made her curls springier and after thinking about it, she loved the feel of Cole's hands in her hair.

Jesse was pleasantly relaxed and had just put the makeup bag into her overnight bag when she heard a knock at the door. She pulled the bag over her shoulder, stole one more last glance in the mirror and made her way down the stairs. Jesse set the bag down and opened the door, butterflies in full force in her stomach. Cole smiled as Jesse stepped back to give him room to enter and walked through the door. He pulled her in close to him, pulling her shoulders slightly back to look at her. "You look happy," he said, giving her a little half smile.

"You have this unnerving way of looking at me like you might know what I'm thinking," she said, smiling up at him.

He leaned in and touched his lips to hers, a warm, soft contrast to the coldness of his face from the chill in the air outside. "I do, do I?" he said, pulling away from her. "Maybe I do," he said, bending down to pick up her bag. "That's a scary thought, huh? Maybe I'm psychic," he said, his sea colored eyes flickering appreciatively down her long frame.

"Hmm," she said, tilting her head one way and then another like she was pondering the great mysteries of the universe. "Maybe that explains it," she said, turning from him to gather up her coat and handing it to his outstretched hands so that he could help her into it.

"Explains what?" he asked, brow wrinkled.

"Two things, really," she said as they stepped outside her door, Jesse turning to lock the house. Looking back at him, she held his gaze, "You never look at me like I'm a puzzle you're trying to figure out. Maybe you already know what I'm thinking," she said as they made their way out to his truck.

He walked around and opened the passenger side door for her and said, "You said two things. What's the other?"

"You always touch me where I want it next," she said, fully aware that the glass of wine she had sipped had nothing to do with that admission. She was done playing careful cat and mouse. She watched his face and saw the color of his eyes deepen from the ocean on a sunny day to the color of the water at sunset. My God, he was an intense man. Whatever was rolling around inside him was certainly stirred up.

He leaned into the cab of the truck and put his hand on her neck, cradling her head like she was the most precious, breakable thing he'd ever held. Cole leaned his face next to hers, his lips a mere inch from hers, and looked hard into her eyes. He kissed her then with a heat and intensity that would've made her knees weak, had she been standing. He issued a low groan that could've been a growl, and she felt her knees instinctively part. Before she even saw him move she felt his hand between her legs, fingers splayed against her lower belly, thumb pressing right on her center. Jesse gasped at the unexpected contact, which encouraged him to press slightly harder. Jesse moved her head forward and down, leaning her forehead against his. Her eyes were shut against the pleasure-pain of it, wanting nothing more than Cole inside her at that moment. He removed his hand and looked hard into her eyes. He backed up, breathing as heavily as she was, and shut the door to the truck. She was beyond turned on and beyond thankful that the night was a dark one.

Jesse watched him move and thought for not the first time that he moved like a hulking jungle cat. He was a spectacularly made man. Cole hauled himself into the cab of the truck and hit reverse, backing slowly into the street. He turned at the school and made his way to the southeast end of town. Jesse felt as if she were holding her breath, willing his home to not be too far away. He reached his hand over and patted her thigh in a familiar and possessive gesture, but not overtly sexual. She jumped like a skittish horse, and Cole laughed despite himself. That made Jesse smile and shake her head at her own jumpiness. Cole turned on the satellite radio and a song from one of her favorite Bob Schneider albums played. Jesse turned to him, surprised. "You're a Bob fan, too?" she asked, surprised and thrilled.

"New fan," he said, glancing over at her quickly before returning his eyes to the road. The deer were thick this time of the year, and they were officially way the hell out in the country. The forest was dense, the road was pretty empty, and the moon shone bright and heavy in the sky.

"You mentioned his music on our date, and I gave it a try. Interesting stuff," he said. They talked for a while about the different albums, the crazy ability for the artist to remember the wild lyrics to so many songs, and his innate ability to sing a song in so many different styles. After driving for nearly thirty minutes, Cole turned off the highway and drove up a very steep and windy hill. Jesse looked around and turned to face Cole. Are we near Eagle Mountain?" she asked, eyes wide.

He laughed and nodded his head. "Yeah, I live right on that ridge. You can see the lights from all the little towns. It's beautiful. Prettier colors in the Spring and Fall, of course," he said, words drifting off as he made another turn, still climbing.

"No kidding," she said, her mind flooding with memories of all the camping trips and road trips she had taken with Levi and the guys and often whatever girls everyone else had been dating. She had even been up here with Cole in the group.

If he *was* a psychic that would have been a bit awkward. Before she could stop herself, she visualized herself naked under the stars with Levi in the bed of his truck, the steady and familiar sounds and whispers coming from different corners of the woods. Everyone desperate to get their jollies in whatever little bit of privacy they could carve out for themselves. The whole thing seemed absurd now, but back then, it hadn't seemed that big of a deal.

While her thoughts drifted, she hadn't realized that they had pulled into his driveway. The crunch of the gravel changed, bringing her out of her trance. She looked up in time to see a beautiful cabin, soft lights highlighting the walkway from the driveway to the wide wrap-around porch. She smiled, proud for Cole and turned to him. He pulled into the garage and parked the truck.

"This is beautiful, Cole! Wow!" she said, feeling for the strap of her bag and reaching for the door handle. He got out of the truck and walked around to her side in time to offer his hand as she stepped out of his truck. He took the bag from her, and put her hand in his after shutting the door. He walked her out of the garage, out onto the sidewalk to take her in the front door of the house. He walked ahead of her and unlocked the door, stepping aside so she could walk in first.

The inside was just as impressive as the outside. The living area, kitchen and dining area were all open, one wall of the living area being made primarily of windows. This was the side of the cabin that looked out over the ridge. There was a big deck that would be perfect for sitting outside and looking out over their little corner of Southern Illinois. There was a wide stone fireplace, a thick rug on the floor before it, along with a brown leather overstuffed couch and chair. Before she could stop herself she looked at Cole and quirked an eyebrow. He laughed and grinned at her.

"A fluffy rug like that right there in front of the fireplace, huh? I've always fantasized about trying that," she said, running her finger along the backside of the couch as she walked into the kitchen area. "There's not a thing out of place here, is there?" she asked, the shock apparent in her voice that some people lived without tornadoes masquerading as children that constantly made messes. That being said, her boys were getting so much better than they used to be. Now it was shoes and dirty clothes that littered the ground rather than toys and other gross discoveries like a banana that had been discarded mid-snack and left to rot somewhere mysterious.

"It's just me here, not a lot to pick up after," he said, coming to stand beside her as she ogled his home. "Go ahead, nose around. I'll open some wine, get the fire going, and get started on supper," he said, kicking his shoes off at the door and walking to the fireplace to get it going. She sat on the bench by the front door and removed her boots. She put them by his shoes near the door and picked up her bag. She walked in sock feet down the hallway that she assumed led to his bedroom. The first room she saw must've been a guest bedroom. It was austere in appearance, outfitted with only the bare necessities of bed, side table, chest of drawers and rug. She saw next a bathroom and an office, all neat as a pin. Earthy browns and greens flowed from room to room in the decor Cole had chosen. The furnishings were well-made and masculine. The last door in the hallway opened into a large bedroom with a wall of windows much like the living room. The moonlight filled the room. Jesse flicked on the light and saw that there were rich moss green curtains that slid on a rod to cover the windows and a fireplace and yet another thick, luxurious rug. Jesse was clearly not the only one with a sex-in-front-of-the-fireplace fantasy going on. Within the bedroom, was another bathroom suite with a large two person steam shower and separate large soaking tub. Cole's home was like a honeymoon suite. She put her bag down on the side of the bed, sheepishly wondering which side was his. She walked to the other side of the king size bed to see an alarm clock on the far side, so maybe her guess would be fine. She went into the bathroom to check herself out before walking back into the kitchen.

Cole had the fire roaring and a nice glass of red wine waiting for her. She thanked him and took the glass, breathing in the bouquet, realizing that whatever this was, it was a higher caliber of wine than she had ever purchased. He smiled at her and came to stand next to her, leaning against the counter.

"I've got the grill heating up; I'll throw the steaks and shrimp on in a few minutes. Would you put together the salad, please?" he asked, gathering the items he had set out on the counter by the door.

"Sure," she said, digging in the fridge for salad fixings. Even his fridge was spotlessly clean.

She was in awe at his well-stocked fridge. It was full of fresh veggies and fruits, almond milk, organic chicken and beef. No wonder he had the body of a god. She pulled out what she liked in a salad, and started rinsing and chopping. The wine was going down very easily, and she noticed for the first time that Amos Lee music was playing. *Oh he's good,* she said out loud to herself.

"What's that?" he asked, ducking in the door and rubbing his hands along his forearms, bared under the pushed up sleeves of his dark blue button down shirt. Jesse grinned at him.

"Well, you weren't supposed to hear that, but I said 'oh, he's good', when I noticed the music along with the roaring fire and the best wine I've ever tasted," she said, as she put her salad fixings in a bowl with a quick toss. She washed her hands at the sink and grabbed a towel as she walked over to him. She put the towel down, and rubbed her warm hands up and down his arms, hoping to warm him a little. He allowed himself to be warmed by her for all of a minute before wrapping her in his arms.

"I'm glad you're here," he said, holding her close. "I've played this out in my mind a few times. I'm not really psychic, you know. I'm curious how it'll go down, if you'll pardon the pun," he said, causing her to throw her head back and laugh.

"Oh yeah? Confident, aren't we?" she said, enjoying the way he flared his nostrils at her like a wild beast.

"Me? Yeah. Big-time," he said with a light slap on her rear as he pulled away. "Throw that on the table if you would, the silverware is in the drawer by the sink. I'm going to get this food off the fire; should be ready in a few minutes," he said, grabbing up the tongs and platter. As he got to the door, he heard the oven timer ding and said, "Would you grab that out of the oven as well, please?" he asked. Jesse nodded in answer.

She wasn't used to being the assistant in the kitchen. She kind of enjoyed it. No pressure. *What had he made?* she wondered, pulling little, nubby, bread crumb-coated bites out of the oven. It smelled delicious. She was transferring it carefully onto a plate as he entered carrying what smelled like steak and shrimp scampi. "Avocado fries," he said to answer her puzzled expression. "I ran across the recipe a few weeks ago and didn't want to try it for just me," he said, plating the steaks and shrimp.

Jesse was in awe at this fast, rich, delicious spread before her. He grabbed the wine bottle off of the counter, and gestured with his eyebrows asking if she'd like more. She nodded, already feeling the mixture of the warmth of the fire, the headiness of the wine and the delicious food smells transport her to a very, very happy place. They sat down and ate, not even talking much except to comment on the deliciousness of the food. Jesse was careful not to overdo it on the food or the wine. She was really, really looking forward to this night, and didn't want to give herself a bellyache on what might just be the most erotic night of her life.

"Cole, this is restaurant-quality delicious," she said, reaching over to pat his forearm on the table. "Color me amazed." The electricity between them was palpable. He nodded, sly smile on his face.

"I'm glad you liked it," he said, standing to clear the table. She rose from her chair, grabbing her dishes as well. They worked companionably to clear the dishes and put away the leftovers. The mess was cleared away in minutes, and Cole flicked off the kitchen lights. He picked up the topped off wine glasses and led Jesse to the big overstuffed couch. "Shall we?" he said, walking back to turn off the lights in the room.

There was no need for lights with the magnificent moonlight streaming in through the windows. The fire crackled, drawing her eye. She stared at it for a minute, losing herself and her nervousness for a moment, simply letting her eyes and ears take in all the different lovely sounds. She took one last sip and placed her glass on the table next to the couch and turned back to see Cole watching her intently.

"You're beautiful, Jess," he said, not moving to touch her.

By reflex, she looked down, feeling a little uncomfortable under the scrutiny, no matter the compliment. "Thank you," she said, looking up at him.

"I saw that," he said, reaching over to touch her jaw. "You are. You always have been. I've always thought so," Cole said, looking at Jesse like she was a treasured thing. She turned towards him then, one leg tucked beneath the other. The need and expectation hung in the air as thick as a fog. She felt anxious and nervous and undeniably alive. She held her hand out to him but rather than him come to her like she expected, he stood and gently pulled her to her feet. He stood in front of her and touched her bracelet. He slowly pulled it off of her arm. Then he touched the bottom of her sweater and when she didn't protest he pulled it off of her moving at a languid pace. He tossed the sweater and tank top on the couch, and unbuttoned her jeans. As he lowered to take them off her feet she placed her hands on his shoulders more for a need to touch him than for balance. He helped her free her feet and stayed in that position, crouched before her, face even with her stomach. He pulled her to him pressing kisses to her skin, dipping lower until he found his destination. He wrapped his hands around her body, arms touching her legs, hands cupping her butt. He pressed his face to her body, inhaling the scent that was only hers. He made a low moaning sound and stood quickly, taking off his shirt as she reached for the button on his jeans. He was naked in seconds, and she was left in her bra and panties.

"I really like this," he said, running his hands along the cups of her bra, fingers barely touching the place where her breasts topped the bra. "But there's something I like even better," he said, slowly moving his hands around the back of her lingerie, expertly removing it without as much as a hesitation. "And these?" he said, hands roaming down to her hips. "These are great. But not as great as what they are hiding," he said, slowly tugging her panties lower, lower until they dropped to the floor. Jesse stepped out of her pile of clothes and stood before him unashamed. Cole put his hands on her shoulders seeming to revel in the feeling of his skin on hers. He took a step forward, guiding her with his hands to take a step back. She felt the thick, soft rug under her feet and watched him sink down onto the floor. He held his hand up to her, she took it and kneeled down beside him.

Jesse felt empowered by the rush of pheromones surging through her body. She leaned forward, placing her hand flat on Cole's chest.

"Lay back, please" she said, loving the look in his eyes at this unexpected turn. She sat beside him, kneeling over him, pretending that gave her some of the power. Jesse leaned down and kissed his lips, one hand roaming through the hair on his head, the other touching his neck, his earlobe, his strong shoulder, and his broad chest. His kiss was just right. Strong, present, taking her in and pressing against her, giving as much as she did. He reached his hands up to feel the smoothness of her skin, hand trailing from her neck to her shoulder and back. His hand followed her spine, softly touching each new area like it was unexplored territory. She trailed her hand down to his hard erection, straining there against his body like a separate thing with a life of its own. She wrapped her hand around him, gently feeling the length of him before deciding on the perfect hold. As she moved her hand up and down slowly, she felt his fingers exploring her body as well.

She let her mouth follow the same path her hand had taken, her breath on his body was enough to still his breathing all together. She touched him with her tongue and heard him moan. She had no sooner taken him into her mouth when she braced herself with her hands, feeling herself being picked up and planted on him in a position she was certain she had hadn't tried in twenty years. She removed him from her mouth for a moment, looking down between her legs at Cole's flat, muscled stomach and chest visible beneath her and gave herself over to the sensations he was causing. He had already started the rhythm he knew she loved. She didn't want to seem like she was slacking on the job, so went back to her task and tried for all she was worth to concentrate. They didn't even last a full minute before he moved her, laying her down on her back on the rug. She saw him pause and grab a condom out of the pocket of his jeans. She was impressed with how quickly he put it on and was there suddenly, looming over her.

Jesse was breathing heavily from sheer desire. It pulsated through her, a throbbing feeling. She doubted she would ever get used to that feeling when a man enters a woman with that very first plunge. Cole eased himself into Jesse, reaching to the side and pulling her leg up around his hip as he entered her fully. She wrapped her other leg around him, taking him inside, moving against him and straining for that perfect, perfect explosion that she knew would happen later. Knowing she was capable of climaxing, and that the problem had never been her own seemed to free her body and mind. Cole braced his upper body on his hands beneath her arms. Her hands moved from his neck to his shoulders, down to his arms. She had the wherewithal about her to decide she could probably orgasm just by feeling his arms alone. Every inch of this man screamed the word *capable.* Whatever it was, he could get the job done well. The fire and friction had them both wet with sweat, bodies slippery and smelling of a very thorough gratification. Cole pushed his body into hers, not an intrusion, just a very pleasurable reminder that she was his and he knew all the right places to press gently to rock her world. She didn't bother trying to stifle the sounds that begged to come out of her mouth. The more noise she made, the more he seemed to push into her. The impact they were making on each other was so mind-numbing that there were no words exchanged. Cole was breathing hard, the hot gusts on her neck and hair only made her feel stronger and sexier. When her orgasm came, it tightened inside her like a vice, squeezing and squeezing every long inch of him as her back arched off the rug, despite his weight pressing her down. She let out a sound that was more like a yell, and he curled his head into her neck as every part of him tightened. A tremor went through Cole and he went suddenly boneless for an instant before rolling off to Jesse's side. When she had regained her senses, she looked up at his face and saw his eyes pressed tight, his breath still coming in loud pants. She rolled on her side facing him. She didn't touch him right away. Truth be told, she didn't even really want to be caressed after she had shattered into a million pieces either. After she had her heart rate under control and could breathe well enough to talk, that was a good time for cuddling, but not before.

Eventually Cole opened his eyes and turned to her. He put his hand on her shoulder and lightly ran it down her arm to her elbow.

"That was so good, Jess," he said, eyes soft and glimmering in the firelight.

She grinned at him in utter agreement, "Yes. Undeniably," she said, placing her hand on his cheek.

"Time for a snack, I think," he said, getting to his feet and holding his hand out to her. Jesse was surprised and decided to go along with whatever he wanted. It had certainly worked out well so far. He made a quick detour to the bathroom to dispose of his condom and wash up. When he opened the door, he was still gloriously naked, lit by the moon on one shoulder and by the firelight on the other.

"If I had any artistic ability, I would paint you like that," she said, only aware of how silly that sounded after the words had escaped her mouth. He smiled down at her and kissed her full on the lips.

"That might be the nicest thing anyone has ever said to me," he said, shaking his head a little in sheer pleasure at her words.

"Wash up if you like, there's a robe on the back of the door that you're welcome to borrow," he said, padding barefoot into the kitchen. She heard him moving things around and running some water. When she got back to the kitchen, absolutely swallowed whole by his robe, she was pleased to hear his low rumble of a laugh.

"For a tall woman, you look tiny in that thing," he said, obviously very comfortable with his own nakedness.

They stood in the kitchen sipping the remainder of the wine and eating strawberries and mango chunks out of a bowl. When they got to the bottom of the bowl, Cole put it in the sink and held out his hand to her again. He walked with her into the bedroom and smiled approvingly that she guessed the correct side to use. He pulled the curtains shut to block out what would surely be blindingly bright morning light, and then seemed to think better of it, leaving one large sliver of moonlight cutting across the bed.

"Hey, I just remembered something," he said, getting into bed and arranging the heavy down blanket.

Jesse did the same, feeling more than a little uncomfortable at the intimacy of sharing his bed. *Ridiculous*, she thought, considering what had just happened in his living room. She pulled the covers up and turned towards him.

"What's that?" she asked, enjoying the way she could see the outline of him in the night.

"When you were in Florida, I think I said something about wanting to make you shine in the moonlight," he said, reaching over to touch her hair, now down and spilling over the pillowcase.

Jesse rolled over on her back and moaned loudly, "Oh my God you're going to wear me out!" flinging her hands above her head as he laughed and pounced on her, throwing off the covers.

"Let's see if I can do it. I bet I can," he said, his legs straddling her hips, his body coming to life before her eyes, as he looked down at her naked in his bed. He let loose another big low laugh and dove at her, burrowing his lips in her neck, his scratchy whiskers scraping against her skin. She wiggled and sighed, loving this playful side of him.

There was more than a large part of her hoping to feel that big, low laugh against another particular part of her body. She was sure if she asked he might just oblige her. And he did. Jesse doubted she'd ever look at the moon in the same way ever again.

Thirty-Two

Sometime during the night Jesse woke up to the sound of rain falling against the roof of the cabin. She hadn't thought much of it; she had been wrapped up in Cole's arms with a fire burning low in the bedroom. She tried to think of the last time she had been so comfortable and satiated, and felt a pang as sharp as a dart pierce her heart when she remembered the last time. She had been that content when she was lying in Levi's bed the day she went to his house. It was incredible to Jesse to think she had had such a fiery and tender exchange with Levi. The memory brought him into the room, an unwelcome specter in Cole's cabin. She burrowed deeper into the covers and closer against Cole to banish Levi. She was quickly lulled back to sleep by the sound of the rain. Hours later she woke to Cole stirring beside her.

She opened one eye and peeked at him, not really surprised to see him watching her. After their late night second round, he had closed the curtains, completely blocking out the light. Jesse was disoriented not knowing the time, so she raised up on one elbow to see over him to check the clock. This brought a very pleasing part of her close up to a very pleasing part of him. His mouth opened in a very smug male smile.

"I believe I will," he said, taking her by surprise when he grabbed her and rolled her on top of him. She couldn't believe he was even able to go again. Jesse would say one good thing for Cole; the man had stamina. She was amazed that he could bring her to the brink before diving over that edge himself. She found herself smiling down as she rolled the condom down over that wondrously large cock. She nearly laughed when she saw his burst of male pride at her pleasure over his body. The previous go-rounds were more than enough to get her body ready for another. He was a very inventive lover. She lowered her body onto his, watching his face as she seated herself fully onto him. Cole's eyes were shut, a frown of concentration marring his handsome face. Jesse watched him carefully as she squeezed her interior muscles, gripping him fully with a very firm contraction. His eyes popped open quickly and he grabbed her hips with a force that would no doubt leave a bruise. Her hands went to his shoulders and she clung to him as he drove her hips into him in a pace she probably wouldn't have set herself. He brought his legs up, changing the angle where he was inside her, rubbing against her in a brand new way. He bucked so hard against her, a moan escaped from her lips matching each pump of his hips. He curled up hard against her as his climax seemed to grip his whole body. She held still for a moment and watched his face as it changed from stern to relaxed. Jesse let out a little yelp as he quickly flipped her over onto her back. He slowly kissed her lips, her breasts, her stomach and made his way down between her legs. Sensing that she was beyond sore after the voracious events of the night and morning, he made love to her with lips and tongue and brought her to a completely different type of orgasm than she had the night before. It was light and sweet instead of a blinding explosion. It was perfection.

After lying together curled in the blankets for another half hour, Jesse knew she had to get moving.

"I have got to get out of this bed or I'll never be able to walk again," she said, moving to a sitting position on the side of the bed, completely undone by the wild night and exciting morning.

"I'm kind of thinking you should stay here forever," he said, standing up and stretching. He looked like a big Viking standing there against the curtains. He pulled them open and Jesse let out a gasp. The woods beyond the window were coated with a thick layer of ice. The porch railings had a hard layer of ice that had to have been at least two inches thick.

"Holy crap, Cole," she said, grabbing the robe from beside the bed and standing beside him. "That's a lot of ice!" Jesse exclaimed, looking around in amazement at the view from his window. "It's beautiful!" she said, smiling up at him as he wrapped his arm around her.

"Isn't it?" he said, grabbing his own robe off the hook on the wall. "That's one of the best perks of living out here. The views are amazing," he said, looking back at her. "I'm going to go make some coffee for you, tea for me," Cole said as he walked towards the kitchen. "Make yourself at home; looks like you might be stuck here with me for a bit," he said, gesturing to the window.

"Okay," she said, gathering her things from her bag. She needed a hot shower to soothe the aching muscles pretty much all over her body. She hadn't realized sleeping over at Cole's was going to be such an athletic event.

She was not at all disappointed by his huge steam shower. She washed everything and then washed it again, enjoying the heat and the pulsing sensation of the water against her body. Jesse helped herself to his body wash and shampoo, nearly moaning with delight at being surrounded by his scent. Eventually, she worried she was going to use all the hot water and she wanted to save some for him. She made her way out of the shower, drying off with fluffy towels, and pilfered in her bag for her comb and curl creme. She had never been able to get ready in a robe and it was too hot for clothes, so she dressed in her gray bra and panties and combed her hair, running her fingers through the long wet strands to add the curl creme. Without it, her hair would be a huge mess of fluffy curls poofing out in all their glory. The gunk she put on her hair at least kept it in some sort of consistent order. She added a touch of eye liner, mascara and lip gloss, opting to keep it simple, since she'd no doubt be in a situation to smudge it fairly soon, based on the last twelve hours. Jesse brushed her teeth and dressed in her leggings and sweater and comfy socks, as he had requested. When she walked back into the main living area he was putting a fruit and yogurt bowl on the table for her with a steaming cup of coffee.

Cole gave her a very pleased look as he raked her with his eyes from head to toe. "You look good enough to eat," he said, stalking towards her. She held up her hands as he advanced on her.

"No way, Sir. This woman needs a rest," Jesse said, sitting down gingerly at the table. He chuckled at that and settled on putting his hands on her shoulders and giving a gentle squeeze.

"Fine, have it your way. My turn in the shower," Cole said, walking down the hall. He looked as good walking away as he did walking towards her, she thought.

After putting her dish in the sink, Jesse went back into the bedroom to check her phone. She sat down on the bed surprised to see a message from her mother from earlier in the morning. She held the phone up and tried to listen to the voice mail. The connection was terrible and the message hadn't recorded clearly. She walked into the living room checking for more signal bars. When she found a good spot, she called her mother, surprised when her call went to voice mail. She was just getting ready to try calling again when Cole walked into the room, dressed in jeans with a sweater that matched the color of his eyes almost exactly.

"That color is beautiful on you!" she said, pleased when he crossed the room and wrapped her in his arms for a quick squeeze, before walking to the fireplace to stoke up the fire. "I missed a call from my mom earlier today and the voice mail didn't record clearly. I got her voice mail when I called back, I'm going to try again real quick," she said. "She usually doesn't call on my weekends without the kids, hoping I'll be able to sleep in," she said, trying to find the spot with the most bars again.

"Sure, take your time," he said, adding more wood to the fire. Just then Jesse's heart caught in her throat as she saw Levi's number pop up as she was hitting send to call her mother. Damn it, she had accidentally answered his call. She had to say something.

"Hello?" she asked, wondering if her voice sounded as weird as she though it did.

"Thank God, Jesse. We couldn't get through to you earlier," Levi said, the relief obvious in his voice. Her mind exploded with alarm, what did he mean?

"What are you talking about, Levi?" she said, seeing Cole's head jerk towards her in surprise. She turned away from him, willing everything to be ok.

"It's Walt, Jesse. He's had a heart attack, honey," he said, his voice low and strong. Jesse's knees went weak at that, she fell back against the chair.

"Is he alive?" she asked, Cole crossing the room to her in two steps. He sat beside her, his hand on her back.

"He is Jess, but it's not looking good. We're at the hospital. You mom called me when she couldn't reach you. I'm sorry, I know it's awkward as Hell, but I hope you don't mind," Levi said into the phone.

Jesse shook her head before she got the words out, "No, no, it's fine. I'm glad you're there for her," she said, eyes huge as she looked at Cole.

"I called Anna, too. She and Travis are on their way in. They'll be here in a few hours," he said, hearing Jesse sigh with relief. "There's something else, Jess," he said, a strange note to his voice. "It's pretty serious, honey. Walt's in and out of it right now and he's on some pretty heavy pain medicine. When I got here and we couldn't reach you, your mom gave me her phone and asked me to call Drake so he could bring the boys home," he said, his uneasiness clear in his voice.

"Oh God. Oh God, it's got to be bad then. Oh God," she said, tears spilling out of her eyes. She stood up and paced around the room, trying to stay towards the window where she had a better signal. Cole had gone into the bedroom and from the small noises she heard coming from the room she guessed he was gathering her things for her.

"He got up early this morning and didn't feel well, your mother said. She was going to make him an appointment when the doctor's office opened, but before then he was having chest pains. She got him to the living room and called an ambulance. That was a few hours ago," Levi said, the sorrow in his voice enough to break her in two. "The boys ought to be here in about an hour."

"Okay. I'll be there as soon as I can. I'm um, I'm not in town, but I'm not too far out," she said, deciding she might as well spill the beans. Levi was going to find out anyway. "I stayed at Cole's last night and it's pretty icy," she said. There was nothing but silence on the other end of the phone. Jess felt a fresh knot rise in her throat and tamped it down. She didn't have time to deal with those feelings. "Levi, thank you for helping Mom," she said. "I'll be there as soon as I can, ok?"

"Drive safe, Jess," he said and disconnected the call. She turned to see Cole standing by the door, her coat in hand. A fresh wave of tears fell from her eyes as she crossed over to him. She grabbed him in a hard hug and felt reassured by the one he gave her back, his hand on her head, resting it against his chest.

"Come on," he said, wrapping her in her coat as he went and closed the glass doors to the fireplace before heading out to the garage. He had one of those automatic car starters, so the engine was running and the cab of the truck was toasty warm by the time they got in. Jesse made a mental note to get one of those for her Suburban. She buckled in and put her face in her hands, so surprised at the turn the morning had taken.

As he backed out of the driveway he put his hand on hers.

"Jess, I'll go as fast as I can safely, but this was a pretty big ice storm," he said, looking back at the white glazed world around them. She nodded in response and said a quick prayer for their safety after first saying one for the safety of the boys.

They rode pretty much the entire way in silence, Jesse trying to keep her fingers still in her lap and repeating the same mantra over and over in her mind. *Please let him be okay. Please let him not be in any pain.* When Jesse thought of what her mother would do without her father, she couldn't hold in the tears. She leaned her head against the window of Cole's truck and sobbed, watching the trees slowly pass by. Cole put his hand on her knee and gave a reassuring squeeze, then put his hand back on the wheel. The roads were incredibly icy, and even though he had the truck in four-wheel drive, the progress was still painfully slow. She closed her eyes against the bright white frightening scenery and prayed for her family.

After an hour, Cole turned into the parking lot of the hospital, and Jesse all but vaulted out of the truck. She had made it exactly five steps out of the truck before she realized Drake had just pulled in on the other side. She heard her boys yell at her as she turned back to get to them. She grabbed Ryan and Luke and gave them a squeeze, looking up at Drake to see his face turning purple with rage.

"It's YOU! It's you, damn it! I know it!" he screamed, stomping around his car towards Cole. Cole stood still, looming over Drake, his lips pressed into a hard white line, fists tight against his sides.

Jesse pushed her boys away and looked at Michael, her eyes huge and expressing without words that he was to, in no way, get involved with whatever was about to happen. She rounded on Drake and looked up at Cole with fury.

"What the hell is this about?" she yelled, turning toward Michael. "Get the boys inside please. I'll be right in," she said, spinning back to Drake and Cole.

"It's him, Jesse! That's the asshole that ran me off the road!" he yelled, spit flying from his lips, his face an alarming shade while he pointed his finger inches away from Cole.

"Don't be stupid, Drake!" she said, looking back at Cole who had a look of malice so unholy, she could do nothing but stare at him. She looked back and forth at them and screamed in frustration. "I do NOT have time for this right now! My Dad is inside dying right now, Drake," she hissed, looking up again at Cole. She shook her head again, looking back to Drake. "It couldn't be him, Drake. He lives down here. Why would he drive up north to drive you off the road?" she asked, shocked beyond measure when Cole spoke.

"Because he's cruel to you, Jesse. He never deserved you or those boys in the first place," he said, his voice low and steady through clenched teeth. "He needs to get off your back before I knock his teeth in," he said as Drake visibly paled.

Drake gathered composure quickly and shifted his hateful glare back to Jesse.

"You picked a great man to whore around with Jesse. I figured you'd be spreading your legs for that son of a bitch, Levi, as soon as you got back down here. I know you never loved me like you loved him, you deceitful bitch. I didn't think you'd go out and pick up some other psychopath!" he said, looking back at Cole just in time to see Cole's fist before it smashed into his mouth. Drake dropped to the ground, blood pouring through the fingers clasped around his mouth. Cole stood above him, fists doubled, visibly daring Drake to get up.

At that, Jesse stood staring stupidly at the pair of them. She gave her head a quick shake.

"I'm sorry," she said, her voice tinny and strange in her own ears. She threw her hands up in total exasperation. "I don't have time for this," she said, shaking her head again in absolute disbelief. Jesse turned and walked toward the hospital, hoping momentarily that the idiots would just kill each other and be done with it. She heard Drake hissing and threatening in his shrieking voice and Cole yelling back at him, but she didn't even look back. She walked in and felt momentarily shocked by the hushed silence of the ER lobby and waiting room, the whoosh of the automatic doors closing on the racket outside. She thought she heard a siren in the background, but she didn't have any attention left to spare for it.

Jesse walked to the desk of the attendant and felt relieved to see it was a familiar face. Jesse thought for an instant how nice it was to be back someplace where she recognized people. She wasn't especially great with names, but she did remember faces. The older woman smiled at her and patted her hand.

"Hi Jesse, he's in room four, dear," she said, her face transparent at the seriousness of the situation. Jesse walked back through the set of double doors and turned to find room four. Her mother sat beside Walt, her form somehow smaller than Jesse had ever realized. Walt looked gray, his color horrible, but he appeared to be resting. The younger boys were sitting in chairs, their eyes wet with tears. Michael stood stoically behind them, an arm on each of their shoulders. She gave him a small smile and nodded in reassurance that whatever had happened in the parking lot was ok. She was completely unsure of that status, but decided not to spare one brain cell on that situation. Levi stood and crossed the crowded room to get to her. He pulled her to him, enveloping her in his arms. He pressed his cheek to the top of her head.

"I'm so glad you're here safe," he said.

Jesse choked on a sob at his words and answered, "Thank you for being here," and hugged him back tightly. He let her go and receded into the corner. The sound of his voice had jarred Eadie out of her trance; she halfway smiled up at Jesse. Jesse crossed to her mother and hugged her gently.

"How is he, Mama?" she asked, fighting to keep the emotion out of her voice.

"Not good, baby. Not good at all," she said, tears streaming down her face. "They're going to move us to a private room as soon as one opens up," she said, her tight expression showing her exasperation at having everyone crammed into a trauma room. Jesse didn't have the heart to tell her mother they normally only allowed two people at a time. It was gracious of the staff to let them all be there next to Walt. Her mother started to crumble, the strain of holding in her fear too much to bear in the arms of her daughter.

Jesse looked up at Levi who put his hand on Michael's shoulder.

"Boys, let's go to the cafeteria and get Eadie some coffee, ok?" he said, gently shepherding them out of the tight space.

"It's ok, Mama, let it out," she said, feeling her mother fighting to keep the sobs in. She heard a raspy noise and looked over to see Walt's eyes on her. Her mother moved quickly to the seat beside his bed and Jesse leaned over him. She kissed Walt on the forehead and looked at him.

"He loves you, Peanut," he said, in voice barely above a whisper. At that, Jesse gave up trying to keep her tears in check and leaned in close to her father. "I need you to be strong for your Mama and Anna. You're going to need help too, though. You're going to need a strong man beside you. Life's hard enough as it is," he said, his voice tapering off. Walt closed his eyes and for a minute Jesse thought he had fallen back asleep. She started to raise up, but saw his eyes flick open again. She pressed her ear closer to him so she could hear him better. "Levi isn't perfect, Peanut, but none of us are. You two belong together." Walt drew in a big breath, Jesse knew it was hard for him to talk. "Fight for it," he said, turning over to look at Eadie who had her hands on his. "I want you to have what we've had," he said giving a smile to Eadie that looked as much a grimace.

Jesse watched then as Walt closed his eyes. He took a deep breath and another as the alarms started going off. Jesse backed out of the way as the nurses took over, and she watched as someone helped her mother up and moved her to the corner of the room. They looked at each other across the flurry of nurses, and knew that her Dad was gone.

Thirty-Three

The next few hours went by in a blur. Jesse was shocked to learn that there was a surprising amount of paperwork that came with death. Anna and her fiancé, Travis, arrived shortly after Walt had passed. Anna was heartbroken that she missed her chance to say goodbye before he died. She was allowed to spend some time in his room, to say goodbye as best she could on her own. Though her heart was broken, Anna jumped right in to assist with Eadie. She and Travis took Eadie home while Jesse stayed to fill out one form after another. She was numb and in a weird state that seemed to be on the verge of a shutdown, but someone had to do this part, and her Dad had plainly told her to be strong for her mother and Anna.

He had also plainly said that she and Levi belonged together. She looked over at Levi in the waiting room with her boys. He had surrendered his phone to the younger boys, so they could take turns playing who knows what game on it. Michael was flipping through an outdated sports magazine while looking up at her every few minutes. Levi sat in a chair, head leaned back against the wall in apparent exhaustion.

After she signed the last form, she pulled out her phone. She had two texts, one from Drake and one from Cole. She didn't have any missed calls from the Police Department, so she assumed they hadn't killed each other in the parking lot. She closed her eyes for a minute against the pounding of the headache that had taken root at her temples.

I told that psycho if he touched me again that I'd have him arrested and he'd rot in jail. I'm serious Jesse. He's nuts. I told him I would sue if he ever came near me again. I'm sorry about Walt, he was a good man. - Drake

I'm sorry about your dad, Jesse. I'm here if you need me but I think it's best if I give you some space. - Cole

Jesse felt for a minute as if this was some cruel time warp into a more technically advanced middle school. *Who sends a sympathy message via text?* She wondered aloud, stunned to the point she was almost amused. At least they weren't in jail or dead, she thought, flinching at the word dead as it passed through her mind. Her dad was gone. It didn't seem possible but yet here she was.

Jesse walked into the waiting room and crossed over to her boys. She gave them each a hug. She looked over at Levi and extended a hand to him as he got up out of the chair. He pulled her into an embrace and just held her for a minute.

"I'm so sorry, Jess. Let's get you guys home." He let her go and looked over at the boys, gesturing with his hand for them to grab their coats. "Come on, fellas. Let's get out of here," he said, as they made their way out of the double doors.

They all piled in his truck and Levi drove them to their house. He walked them to the door and stood there visibly uncomfortable, unsure where he fit in her house. Jesse told the boys she was going to go lie down and asked them to please try and rest in their rooms for a bit. Not surprisingly, they all filed up the stairs. She had some very fine sons, she thought, proud of how well they had behaved in such a terrible situation. She turned back to Levi and said, "I can't say thank you enough, Levi," looking down at the floor, her arms folded across her middle.

"No need, Jesse. You'd have done the same, right?" he said, putting his hands under her elbows, seeking some kind of contact. "Please let me know how I can help. My parents have the kids. I can do whatever you need," he said, his big hand coming to rest against her jaw. His fingers were warm against her neck. She pressed her head into his hand, closing her eyes for a minute. It did feel good to be next to him, to have the overwhelming sense of someone taking care of her. She felt like she had a rock in her stomach wondering how much she could trust him, but damn it, she was tired. And tired of thinking.

"I will let you know, thank you," she said as he took a step back. "I think I'm going to go lie down. The funeral director will call me in a few hours when it's time to make arrangements."

"Okay," he said, turning to go. "Jess," he said, turning back to face her, looking down at her with a funny expression on his face. She stepped towards him, her eyes so heavy she felt like she could fall asleep where she stood. She was shocked when he reached down and kissed her. Really kissed her. It felt like he was branding her, making sure she knew there wasn't room for anyone else's kiss on her lips. "I love you," he said, as the tears she had been trying to hold back spilled down her cheeks. She swallowed hard, hating that her emotions were so close to the surface. "I love you," he said, nodding his head at her like he was trying to break through the fog that was crashing down around her.

Jesse nodded back at him and the heartbreak was so clear on her face that instead of leaving, he turned and shut the door closed behind him. He led her up the stairs, taking her bag and dropping it on her floor. He took off her coat and her shoes and watched her lie across the bed. He tucked a blanket over her and laid down next to her on top of the covers. He turned her to him and held her as she wept for her father. Tears streamed down his eyes as well. Walt had always been good to him and a damned good father to Jesse and Anna. Eventually she drifted off. He held her close as she slept, dozing beside her, very well aware that there were three very protective boys in the house. He had made sure the door was open so that there was no confusion over what was happening. Levi had every intention of being very involved in their future. He wanted to start off at a respectable place with the kids. He knew in his heart that he loved Jesse and hated that he had ever hurt her.

Levi closed his eyes against the memory of when Jesse was extremely angry at the store. He wanted to never again see the rage she had kept barely in check in the parking lot, questioning her prospects of raising good men after his own parents had apparently failed. That comment from her had really stung, but she had a point after all. Levi had been raised to treat women with respect, not to chase after them like a collector of pelts. In his own defense though, he really hadn't been with many women. Jesse had been his first, then a few in college. When he met Emma, there was no one but her for years.

Shannon had fallen into his life during a very lonely time when he was coming to grips with being alone, without a wife and lover for the first time in so long. He had gone on a few dates with other women before he met her, but hadn't felt any level of attraction that justified a second date. Shannon was kind and lovely and so unencumbered with baggage. She was several years younger; no marriages under her belt. He realized with a sick feeling in his stomach that she had probably thought she'd marry him. He felt incredibly stupid that he hadn't considered it.

He had really messed up when he let Shannon in the night of his date with Jesse. He had left Jesse on her porch that night, seeing her safely inside the house. He had been hard as a brick, his erection pressing painfully against his pants. His kids were at their grandparents, he had the house to himself, and had resolved himself to a night of embarrassing masturbation, followed by a shot or two of whiskey, then sleep. When he got home, he saw Shannon sitting comfortably on the rocker on his porch, all familiar and sultry, and all too happy to please. To be truthful, after his date with Jesse and their level of connection, he hadn't even wanted Shannon. He had simply wanted release. He certainly never thought Jesse would find out. Levi knew that Jesse wasn't in a place where she was ready to jump in with both feet like he was. At least that's what he told himself to justify his actions as he walked up to the porch and greeted Shannon, inviting her in. He had had a need and filled it in a generic way.

Levi knew he could put that behind him and not repeat the mistake, if only Jesse would forgive him. There was something that felt so right between them. His stomach turned as he thought of her being at Cole's house overnight. She was fully within her rights. She was an adult and a scorned woman to boot. There was an undeniable feeling of possession when it came to Jesse. She was his. Only his. He'd spend every day showing her if she'd let him.

The house was dark when the jarring ring of the phone woke Levi and Jesse from their rest. She murmured thick voiced answers into the phone as Levi blinked, adjusting his vision to the darkly lit room. He looked at his watch, surprised by the late hour. He needed to get Hannah and James from his parents' house. Levi needed to be close to his kids after such an awful, emotionally charged day. He sat up and watched as Jesse jotted down notes and talked about times as her head cleared.

Jesse hung up the phone and stared down at the little notepad and pen she kept by her bedside table.

Visitation, Monday, 6 PM
Funeral, Tuesday, 10 AM
Graveside Service, immediately following

Three little lines on random stationary didn't seem to do justice to the end of a life of such a good father. She shook her head and pressed her cool fingers to the bottom of her eyes, feeling the puffiness there. She looked over at Levi perched on the side of her bed, eyes locked on hers.

"I've got to go check on the kids and then Mom," she said, reaching back to cover his hand with hers. Jesse thought to herself that Levi looked about as awful as she felt. She couldn't help but wonder how hard death and loss was on him after the death of his wife. She leaned over to him then, pressing her head against him, burrowing her head in his neck and shoulder. She couldn't help but notice how comfortably she fit there.

Jesse took a deep breath and separated from Levi, standing and walking into the bathroom to wash her face and redo her hair. He walked around the room a little, picking up things and putting them down. The door was wide open she noticed, realizing what a potentially awkward situation his lying down with her with the boys in the house actually was. She decided she'd have to work through that one later.

She left the bathroom and smiled at him, reaching her hand out to lead him out of the room. He nodded at her as he started down the stairs, holding his hand up in a gesture that said so much more than goodbye. Jesse went first into Michael's room. He was sacked out completely so she nudged him with her hand on his shoulder.

"Wake up, Baby," she said, smoothing his dark hair that was badly in need of a trim. He'd have to get that done by Monday to be ready for the services. In her mind, Jesse tried to visualize what each son would wear to the services. They had nice clothes that were typically reserved for church. She'd make certain the pants and shirts were pressed by the end of the night. She had a simple black shift she could wear with a cardigan and heels for the visitation. She would look through the rest of her clothes to figure out what she could wear to the funeral and graveside service. At least she wouldn't have to worry with throwing shopping in with the other appointments. She'd have to talk with her mother about their insurance policy and funeral arrangements. She'd have to call the florist immediately to see if she could get the flowers ordered and in on Monday. Thankfully, the nicest shop in town was still owned and operated by a classmate's mother. She wouldn't have to work very hard to find a phone number for the owner.

Michael groggily sat up and blinked at his mother. He looked out at the hallway, and Jesse realized he was looking for Levi.

"Levi went home, honey," she said, bracing herself for some hard questions. Michael flipped on the lamp on his bedside table. "I heard him say that he loved you, Mom," he said, looking at her without the slightest hint of guile or sass.

"He did say that, son," she said, nodding her head just a bit. Jesse's stomach burned at the memory of Michael listening to ugly gossip at school about her and Levi. She looked at him, his eyes clouded and his emotions completely imperceptible. He had gotten that particular expression from Drake.

"Levi and I dated as kids in high school," she said, trying to tip-toe through the conversation, very well aware of how easily grossed out teenagers were when it came to their parents. "He was my first real love," she said, happy to see that Michael didn't grimace at her admission. "We broke up and I met and married your dad, and Levi married Emma. We were all happy for a bit, but then things changed," she said, looking down at her hand where the wedding ring had sat for so many years. She absentmindedly rubbed at her ring finger, still not used to its emptiness.

"Levi will always, always hold a special place in my heart," she said, looking up at Michael's face. "He'd like us to start dating again, spending time together, and we may, but I'm just not sure yet," she said, shrugging her shoulders. "We have some things to talk through first. Because you're the oldest, I'll tell you this, but only you," Jesse said, looking straight into Michael's eyes to be sure he understood her to mean that he was not to share what she was about to say with the other boys.

"He loves me, and I love him, too. I always have, and truthfully, I always will. I'm just going to take my time with this, because I have three other men in my life," she said, smiling as he rolled his eyes at her. "Come on now. It's true. You three are the most important part of my life," she said, answered by Michael's nodding head. "That's all I know. Good enough for now?" she asked, tilting her head, seeing for herself just how much her first baby had matured over the last six months.

"Good enough for now," he said, reaching across the bed for yesterday's left over sweatshirt. Jesse pulled a face wondering how long since that sweatshirt had been washed, but decided she'd work first on the most urgent issues.

"Okay, buddy. I'm going to check on the other boys, then head over to Grandma's. Can you get your socks and shoes on? I might need your help with the others over the next few days. It's going to be alright," she said, pulling her big boy close. "Grandpa loved you so very much," she said, her voice hitching on the past tense.

Jesse made the rounds to each boys' room, surprised to see them all asleep. She woke each one slowly, reminding each of how loved they were, both by her and their Grandpa. She asked them to get ready and meet her downstairs so they could go check on Grandma. On her way down the stairs, Jesse heard her phone buzz and looked down to see the phone number for the flower shop, courtesy of Levi. A quick minute later and she had Mrs. Reynolds on the line. They set up an appointment for Jesse, Eadie and her sister Anna to meet in the morning to choose the flowers for Walt's services. Other than choosing his suit, which her mother had probably taken care of already, there wasn't much to do beyond wait for the hours to pass.

When Jesse pulled into her mother's driveway, she noticed many of the lights were on, and there were a few cars along the street. While Jesse was glad there were people that loved Walt and Eadie so much, she grimaced at the thought of Eadie having to put on a brave face when she no doubt wanted only to lay down in her own bed.

Jesse and the boys filed into the house, smiling and greeting the elderly friends that had assembled. Jesse noticed the counters were already full with casseroles and dishes. The older folks were in overdrive, making certain Eadie wouldn't go hungry, when chances were that she wouldn't touch any of it. At least her boys would dig in, she thought to herself. They could always eat, no matter the mood. The boys went first to Eadie and each gave her a hug, then made a beeline for Anna in the kitchen. She started making plates for the boys while Jesse went to sit beside her mother.

There weren't really words to say; the folks in the house were making polite conversation amongst themselves more than anything. Jesse saw how red her mother's eyes were and how strained her face seemed.

"Want me to get them out of here, Mama?" she asked, leaning in close to whisper.

"Yes, dear. I'm so tired," she said, looking down at the crumpled tissue in her hands. Jesse nodded and stood, deciding to start first with those closest to the door. She smiled as she went, thanking the small groups for coming to check on Eadie, to sincerely say how thankful she was to know her parents had such good friends, and that she appreciated the support. Jesse made a few minutes of conversation with each group before blurting out that her mother needed to rest, then quickly added the times for the services on Monday and Tuesday. Some of the older folks were taken aback at being so politely and forcefully ushered out; however, Jesse's real concern was her mom. The rest would at least have something to talk about over at the diner in the morning over breakfast and coffee. It took nearly 20 minutes to empty the house with as much tact as possible, but she got it done.

Anna had taken Eadie into the bedroom by this time, sitting in the bathroom with her as she washed her face and put on her cold cream. Jesse sat on the edge of the bed and let the tears drip down, felt the burn of her nose, and tried to remember how many times she had lived this particular memory. When she and Anna were little, they followed Eadie around everywhere. She remembered specifically when she told Eadie she was pregnant with Michael how Eadie threw back her head and laughed. "Oh darling, you'll never go to the bathroom alone again!" she hooted, hugging Jesse's neck so tightly. "It's wonderful, Jess. Motherhood is the hardest, most wonderful job in the world," Eadie had said. She had been right.

Travis had a game on in the living room and the boys had all settled in with platefuls of chocolate sheet cake to keep them occupied. The house was locked up tight, only the lights in the back of the house were on, and the phone ringers had been turned off. Jesse felt rather than saw her mother relax as she came out of the bathroom dressed in her pajamas. Eadie didn't have anything to say; she simply kept wiping the tears from her eyes in silence. Jesse knew her mother would work through it and open up when she was ready. Eadie might be one of the warmest people she'd ever seen, but she was also stoic. She'd hold it in as long as she could, then it would seep out in stages. With Eadie settled in her bed, Anna and Jesse both kicked off their shoes and crawled into bed with their mom. Nobody said anything; they simply lay there together. It was enough.

After about half an hour, Anna touched Jesse's hand, a signal to leave the room since Eadie had fallen to sleep. They crept quietly into the sitting room in the front of the house and held each other, crying quietly. After the tears subsided, Jesse talked to Anna about the appointment at the florist and asked about Walt's clothes for the burial. It seemed callous and hateful to talk about such an ugly thing, but the fact was that it had to be prepared, and the sooner they did, the sooner they could stop thinking about it. Once all the details were in place, it was decided that Anna would write the first draft of the obituary. She and Travis would be staying with Eadie as long as they were home so Jesse felt comfortable taking the boys back to her house. It was getting late and they'd all rest better at home.

She laid in bed for over an hour staring up at the ceiling that night, feeling a tremendous pressure on her chest. The whole thing seemed surreal. She took her journal out and wrote down, as fast as she could, every detail of what Walt had said to her. She would write more about his passing later when she had more energy and a bit of distance between the pain and the moment, but for now she wanted to keep every one of his words.

He loves you, Peanut. I want you to have what we've had.

I do too, Dad, she wrote, then closed the book.

Thirty-Four

The appointments with both the florist and funeral director went about as well as could be expected. The pastor of the church came for a quick visit, discussing the preferred hymns and sharing the most peaceful prayer that Jesse had ever experienced. When the church had been assigned a female pastor, the rather traditional congregation had momentarily recoiled in shock. It took only one Sunday to put most of them at ease; the rest weren't ever at ease with anything. The pastor was exceptional and extraordinarily warm and loving. Jesse felt confident that she would continue to check in with Eadie.

The day was a blur of appointments, important emotionally charged decisions, and a flurry of visits from loving neighbors and congregation members who wanted to extend their respects and sympathies. Jesse had to hand it to Eadie, she treated each visitor as a welcome guest and would keep it together during the visits that Anna and Jesse were becoming proficient at ending after no more than ten minute increments.

As she tucked herself into bed that night, she decided it wouldn't hurt to call Cole and thank him for driving her to the hospital. The phone rang several times and she thought she was going to get his voice mail. He surprised her when he answered, his hello out of breath and sounding winded.

"Hey Cole, it's Jesse" she said, her stomach doing a little flip at the sound of him.

"Jesse, how are you?" he asked, his voice full of concern.

"Well, you know, pretty rotten, but we're going to get through it," she said, hoping that was true. "I just wanted to call and thank you for driving me to the hospital. I couldn't have driven even if I had had my own car. I appreciate it," she said, feeling lame and fighting the urge to delve into the 20 questions she had about whatever had happened with Drake.

"Of course, of course," he said. "Jesse, I'm so sorry about what happened. We had such a perfect night and morning together," he said, his words sort of fading. She wasn't the only one who felt awkward.

"We did. It was a wonderful night and morning. I have so many questions about what happened with Drake that I don't really know where to start. I just don't have the energy right now," she said, that being the absolute truth. "I just didn't want to leave it like this without thanking you for your help and kindness. And tenderness," she added, wondering why she had said it. She didn't want to steer the ship back into murky waters with Cole. She was terrified of him.

"When you are ready, ask away," Cole said, his voice steady and sure. "I do want to say this though. I just wanted to scare him a little. I hated hearing how he talked down to you and how he made you feel. It got worse when I'd think about what it must've been like when you lived with him if he could be such a condescending asshole when you weren't living with him," Cole said, talking as calmly as if he were discussing a new project at work.

Jesse shivered a little and knew she had to ask one more question. "Cole, did you kill his girlfriend's cat?" she winced, knowing the answer before she asked the question.

"Well, that was an accident," he said, his voice taking on an embarrassed tone. "I found his address and followed him to her house. When I was leaving, I accidentally ran over the damned cat. It ran out of her driveway right in front of me. I figured it would be wasting an opportunity to shake him up, so I took it to his porch and wrote a note about him being next if he didn't straighten up." Jesse held the phone away from her head, just staring at it for a moment. Unreal. He was so very close to being the perfect package, but he was crazy as a bedbug. As she put the phone back to her ear, she heard him saying, "Jesse? Jesse, are you there?"

"I'm here. Sorry," she said, feeling less afraid of his danger factor, but still completely and utterly freaked out.

"I didn't think you'd find out, obviously," he said, adding it as an afterthought. "I just thought if he knew you had a protector crazy enough to come after him, he'd treat you properly," Cole said, waiting for her to say something. "You deserve so much better."

She exhaled and closed her eyes. "Cole, I think I appreciate the sentiment."

"Okay. Goodnight, Jesse. Take care," he said as he disconnected the call.

Jesse felt such a weird conflicted mix of feelings over Cole. He was danger and sex and discipline. He would have been the perfect man to date in her early twenties. Someone to curl your toes, take on adventures, then safely leave behind in what would be the kind of memories to carry a person through the rest of their boring, responsible life. He did seem to appreciate that he had gone too far with his attacks on Drake. His

'Take care' sounded more like a goodbye than a 'See you soon.' Jesse heaved a big sigh of relief at that. She needed a break from drama. Drake was all the drama she could handle, and she was just now figuring out how to cope with that particular brand of crazy.

Once her head had stopped spinning from her conversation with Cole, Jesse called Levi.

"Can I be there, Jesse?" he asked, "With you and the family?" he said softly. Jesse was stunned. She knew that Levi had taken care of her the day before and he had said some wonderful, comforting things, but that's what she thought it was: comfort and affection. Her heart immediately answered *yes*, but her mind reminded her that she had just spent the night with Cole. She sat for a bit, unsure how to answer. For a minute, she panicked, not knowing what to say. She could hear him repeating her name, checking if she was still there. As she frantically tried to think of what to say, her eyes went to her journal sitting on her nightstand. She heard her father's words saying that Levi loved her, that she was going to need someone to help take care of her while she took care of everyone else. She nodded her head yes before she got the word out.

"Yes," she said, her voice nearly strangled on the tears that welled in her eyes. She couldn't believe there were even more tears to cry. She didn't want to say it, but felt it had to be done.

"There will be talk, Levi. I mean, this is a little more public than having dinner in town," she said, suddenly embarrassed as another realization came to her. "Oh God," she said under her breath, "Unless you mean just as a friend. You have known Dad for most of your life," she said with her eyes closed tight in utter mortification.

"No, Jess," he said in a voice she had heard him use with his kids. "Not as a friend of the family. I want to stand beside you. I want to be with you, Jess. You and your sons, honey." On the last word his voice cracked.

Jesse felt her heart shift, almost like the last piece of the puzzle clicked into place.

"Levi, are you sure? We are a handful. We're a whole package deal," she said, hoping he truly understood the seriousness of what he was proposing.

"I know, Jesse. We are, too," he laughed, his smile audible in his voice. "You want to give this a proper shot, Jess?"

She knew she had to ask one question before agreeing.

"I have to ask one thing. Without the details of which I do not care to know, give me the gist of what happened with Shannon the other night after you dropped me off." Jesse felt a tremendous relief in having said the words aloud. Whatever he said, she prayed to God it would be the truth.

Levi cleared his voice on the other end of the line.

"I was wrong to let her in, Jess. I was so wound up when I left you that night that when I got home and she was there waiting for me, I didn't turn her away." He knew he was treading in deep waters here, but she needed to know the truth. "After Emma, Shannon and I dated on and off. She never met the kids. Looking back now I realize that for me, she was filling a need and for her, well, I never really thought much about what the relationship meant to her. She probably thought we'd end up together, but while she was enjoyable to be with, she wasn't home. She wasn't you," he said.

Before she could speak he continued. "It's always been you, Jess. When you and Drake got married, I bet I stayed drunk for two months. When I met and married Emma, I was able to be happy because I knew you were no longer an option. Emma was as happy as I'd ever get without being with you," he said while Jess listened without drawing a breath. "When you told me you were moving back, I knew this was it. This was my chance. My last chance. Let's try, Jess. Let's make it work," he said, his words coming out in a tumble.

Jesse sat silent for a moment, completely taken aback. "Okay," she said. It was Levi's turn to be stunned.

"Okay?" he asked. "As in, okay, let's give this a try and be together?"

"Yes. Let's try, Levi. We owe ourselves the chance," she said as a feeling of peace washed over her, pushing aside a little of the awful weighted feeling that had been resting on her chest. "I'll talk to the boys tomorrow," she said, thinking she ought to prepare them for her being in a relationship.

"Okay. I'll talk with James and Hannah tomorrow," he said. "I'll be a little late tomorrow to the service. Mom and Dad will want to come pay their respects. When they get home, I'll leave the kids with them and be there as soon as I can. I think they're still a little young to attend. They haven't been to a visitation since losing Emma," he said, to Jesse's total agreement. Those poor kids had been through enough. They ended the call with a shared sense of weightless excitement that can only come from confessing deep feelings. Jesse flicked off her light and fell into a dreamless sleep.

The conversation with the boys went better than expected. Michael had, of course, been confided in the day before about the strange place she and Levi were in. He seemed to like Levi well enough to be comfortable with it. The other boys accepted Jesse's statement that she and Levi cared about each other and would start spending more time together, as well as getting the kids together occasionally. They had had such a nice time earlier in the summer when Levi and the kids had come for dinner that they seemed excited about it. Crossing that conversation off her list right after breakfast left Jesse with time to tend to her mother.

Jesse and Anna continued to run interference for Eadie who was slowly coming to terms with the fact of what had happened was reality and not a horrible nightmare. Jesse worried over what would happen after the service when Anna and Travis would have to go back to work. They would still stay in town the remainder of the week but would have to go back to their own home next Sunday. Her Aunt Ruthie, Eadie's sister, had asked to stay for a few weeks; Jesse was hoping Eadie would agree.

The visitation service was well attended, as many of Walt and Eadie's friends came to say goodbye. The funeral director did a good job of organizing the rather large group of people who came to pay their respects. Jesse kept her tears in check until she saw Stanley and Myrtle, Levi's parents. She hadn't seen them in years, and remembered instantly how much time she had spent in their home. They were such terrific people. Stanley was a tall man, and had what could only be described as an absolutely pleasant demeanor. Even now, as he gave her a hug, he seemed to impart a little of his positivity and peace. Myrtle was a sweet little thing. She took Jesse's face in her hands and told Jesse that she was so sorry for her loss. That was when Jesse lost it, nodding and excusing herself from the receiving line. She grabbed a handful of tissues from the nearest box and stepped out a side door, apparently reserved for smokers. The stench of the smoke stung her lungs, but the air was cold and she was alone. Jesse let her own sadness wash over her, a combination of her own sense of personal loss of this cornerstone of her family, but also such inherent grief for her mother. She and Walt had such a special relationship. She totally understood what a blessing it was for Walt to wish for her what he and Eadie had shared. Sure, they drove each other crazy over typical little things, but they had kept their love alive. Jesse knew firsthand how incredibly hard that could be. She had already failed once. She hoped things with Levi would work out, but she knew there was no guarantee.

Jesse dabbed at her eyes with a tissue as she turned in time to see Levi walking towards her. He gave her a half smile and folded her into his arms when he was close enough to do so.

"Jess, I'm so sorry," he said, knowing exactly how empty those words were to a person who had lost someone. People had to say something. She nodded her head at him as she got herself under control. She looked around him and noticed his truck door just behind them in the parking lot, the door hanging open and two little heads staring out at them. She looked back at Levi who rested his hand on her shoulder.

"Mom figured there would be a big crowd, so to get me to you faster, I'm outside with the kids while they are inside, then we'll switch." Jesse shrugged at that, it seemed like a good plan to her.

"May I go say hello?" she asked, dabbing at her nose with her tissue.

"Sure, come on," he said, taking her hand in his. As she stepped up to the truck, she saw that both Hannah and James gave her a little wave.

"I'm sorry about your Grandpa," James said, flinching at the poke issued by his sister.

"It's her daddy, James," she said, her exasperation very clear in her voice. "I'm sorry about your daddy, Miss Jesse," she said, looking up at her father. "Do we have to call her Miss Jesse if she's your girlfriend, Daddy?" she said, her face all squinched up.

Jesse laughed and smiled up at Levi. "No, Sugar, you can just call me Jesse," she said, reaching her tissue free hand inside the truck to pat each of their little hands. "Thank you for your sweet words." She turned to Levi at that and said, "Well, I'd better get back in there," noticing as she waved goodbye to Hannah and James that Stanley and Myrtle were walking towards the truck.

Myrtle leaned over and gave Jesse a kiss on the cheek as Levi told her he'd be home a little late.

"Ok then, take care of this one," she said, giving Jesse's hand a squeeze.

Levi stood watching to see his parents drive out of the parking lot. He turned and took Jesse's hand.

"Well," he said, looking down at her. "Are we ready to do this?" he said, "To make it official?"

"Ready," she said, feeling a little stronger than she had in days. If she was going to set the gossips' tongues to wagging, she may as well do it while everyone can see what really happened. As they walked into the funeral home, Jesse felt steady again. Levi nodded hello and returned handshakes when offered. They made their way to the receiving line in the front of the room, and Levi shook the hands of their sons. Jesse took her place beside Michael while Levi squeezed in between Jesse and Anna.

People came in for two hours during the visitation, and Jesse couldn't wait to get out of her heels by the end of the night. Levi slid into the front passenger seat of the Suburban and Jesse said a silent prayer of thanks that Michael didn't utter a sharp remark about his seat being stolen. Jesse dropped Levi off at his house, the light glowing from within. He touched her hand and gave it a squeeze, not wanting to rock the boat with the six eyes watching his every move. He said his goodbyes to the boys and shut the door, turning to go up the walk.

Before Jesse could even drive away, Michael said, "I like him, Mom." That would be all the buy-in needed to get Luke and Ryan on board. She smiled back at him, thankful once again to have such good boys.

The funeral and graveside service went as well as the visitation. Jesse held her emotions in check until she saw Megan walk through the doors for the funeral. There was typically nothing somber about Megan, but she truly grieved for her friend. She had practically grown up at Jesse's house, and loved Eadie and Walt like family.

"I'm so glad you came, Meg," Jesse said, hugging her friend tightly.

"I wouldn't miss the service, Jess," she said, "plus I wanted to see this guy," she said, grabbing Levi in a hug. Jesse turned as she felt a shadow looming above her and was wrapped in an enormous hug from Ivan.

"So sorry for your loss, Jesse," he said, his big hand on her shoulder. "And you must be Levi," Ivan said, a tight smile on his face. Jesse hadn't known Ivan long, and hadn't had the chance to be around him face to face much at all, but his expression clearly warned Levi not to do anything to hurt Jesse's feelings.

Not one to typically be outsized by most men, Jesse enjoyed seeing Levi's eyes widen slightly. "Nice to meet you, Ivan," he said, accepting the handshake offered. Megan's eyes twinkled for just a moment, clearly enjoying seeing Levi squirm. She and Ivan turned their attention to Jesse's boys and Eadie, moving their way down the reception line to pay their final respects. Levi looked directly into Jesse's eyes and gave her a wink. *He was certainly a good sport,* she thought.

Eadie made it through all of the services as solid as a rock. Jesse watched her closely, as did Anna. She had told the girls that once this was over with, she was going to turn off the phone, lock the doors and take to her bed for a week. Jesse was a big supporter of just that. People lived at such a frantic pace, she thought grief was always rushed. Eadie had reluctantly agreed to have Aunt Ruthie to come stay, but she had been given the directives that Eadie was going to simply rest. Jesse was relieved to know her mom wouldn't be alone in the house. She was certainly thankful to not have to return to work right away. Jesse had a few more days of leave available to her and would finish out the week helping her mother and trying to get in some much needed time with Anna before she returned to Denver. The boys would be returning to school the following day, so she had three days to take for herself.

Thirty-Five

Jesse had slept restlessly that night, struggling to get comfortable. When she did finally drift off, she kept dreaming that she was waking up, so even though she slept, she didn't feel at all renewed. She made a mental note to buy more lavender oil to diffuse in the air at night, hoping that would help some. She'd have to remember to pick some up for Eadie and Anna as well. She dressed in a tank top, sweatshirt and jeans and ran a comb through her hair, leaving it to fall in curly waves resting on her shoulders. Thankfully, the boys had laid their clothes out the night before, as she was in no mood for any kind of drama. She sipped her coffee and tried to will herself to be the type of mother she wanted to be. Some days it was easier than others she thought. *Some days weren't the day after you buried your Dad, Jesse,* she thought to herself.

Her nose began to sting and her eyes to water, and she brushed the tears away before they could fall. She needed to keep it together as long as it took for her to get the boys off to school, then she could go back to bed and resurface at the end of the day. Jesse stood up to holler up at the boys to please get dressed and was surprised to see them come stomping down the stairs, all dressed.

"Whoa! This is a nice surprise," she said, eyes wide at the sight of them. "I didn't even hear any threats or throttles from upstairs," she said, squeezing them to her as they walked to the table where she had set out a hot bowl of scrambled eggs and toaster waffles.

"We decided we'd take it easy on you today," Luke said, grinning up at her.

"Thanks, baby. I appreciate it. I'll be fine; I just need a few days to myself to go ahead and feel really sad," she said, wanting to reassure them, but still keep it real to them that people have to process loss.

"Is that why you aren't wearing makeup, Mama?" Ryan said, "Because you'd just cry it off?" Jesse let out a sharp bark of laughter at that.

"Pretty much, kiddo. I think I might lie back down after I drop you off. I didn't rest very well last night," she said, astounded to see that Michael had already wolfed down his food. "Good grief, did you chew?" she asked, taking the plate from his hands. "Go ahead, Sweetie. I'll clear it for you," she said, rinsing the dishes before loading them in the dishwasher.

"Thanks. Love you, Mom. Bye, guys," he said, grabbing his backpack and heading out the door. Luke and Ryan finished up as well, tossing the dishes in the sink with a little more enthusiasm than was safe for the dishes. Her mood was already so sour she decided to let that go; she didn't want to have the big one over a stupid plate.

The boys grabbed up their coats and backpacks, and stood at the front door watching her as she rinsed and loaded the dishes in the dishwasher.

"Next up, I'm going to teach you how to load this yourself, the right way. You know, my way," she said, smiling at them. She grabbed her keys and purse and locked the door behind her. The boys talked a little on the ride to the school, but were more or less quiet. Jesse made the boys lean over for a quick kiss on the cheek before they got out of the SUV. She missed the days when they were little and she could grab them up and kiss them hard on the cheek and wish them a wonderful day. She watched as they entered the school and looked in her rear view mirror to see if it was safe to pull out. She saw Laura Williamson stomping towards her Suburban and did something her mother would be horrified to know about. She drove away as Laura was closing in on her SUV. Jesse couldn't even pretend not to have seen Laura. They made eye contact in the mirror. Jesse was just too tired to deal with that hateful woman.

She drove home with the radio off and parked the car in her driveway, clicking the key fob as she went. She unlocked her door, looked around satisfied at the clean state of her home, and kicked off her shoes. Jesse had planned to wash her jeans after this wear anyway, so since the curtains were shut, she peeled off her clothes. She walked downstairs to the laundry area, threw in her clothes and walked back up the stairs naked. It was strangely liberating. With three boys in her house, she was rarely naked. She rounded the corner in the living room and put her foot in front of the stair landing just as a big knock sounded at her door. She threw both hands over her mouth to stifle the scream that nearly slipped out. As quietly as she could, she turned to peek out the peep hole. She closed her eyes in a silent prayer of thanks that it wasn't a delivery man or worse, that horrible Laura Williamson. That would've been something. As she reached for the lock on the door, Levi knocked on the door again, startling her. "Just a minute!" she yelped, opening the door a few inches and peeking out at him from behind the door.

"Well, hello!" she said to his surprised face. He stood there for a second, not quite sure what to do since she hadn't opened the door. Jesse stepped as far back as she could to remain hidden when she swung the door open.

Levi stepped in, took one look at her and hollered, "Wooo hoo!" as he shut the door, locking it with the chain for good measure. There was no great place to put her hands, so she settled with putting one on her hip and the other on the stair banister.

"So, what are you doing, just breezing around here naked as a jaybird?" he asked, gathering her close to him with one hand, and shucking himself out of his coat with the other.

She laughed as he wrapped his coat around her. "Sorry Jess, you uh, you look a bit chilly," he said, unable to tear his eyes from her breasts with their tips pebbled up beneath his coat, still visible from his height advantage. He leaned forward and took a finger to pull the coat out a bit and moaned, closing his eyes for a second.

"Well, I just threw the clothes I was wearing in the washer downstairs and was planning to make a break for my bedroom. But then you knocked as I was right by the door," she said, stepping closer to him, putting her arms around his neck and feeling her horrible mood dissipate as his coat slipped down lower on her back.

"Uh huh," he said, leaning his head down to hers. His hand curved around her bare neck while the other ran along the outside of his coat, molding it to her back.

"Uh huh," she said back, enjoying the feeling of his lips on hers. "Want to come with me?" she asked, enjoying the play on words as she stepped back with one foot on the stairs.

"Uh huh," he said again, kicking off his shoes and already working on the button of his shirt. She turned and led the way up the stairs, looking back at him to see his eyes trained on her legs. At the top of the stairs, she turned and dropped his coat, walking into her bedroom in the gently filtered light from her white curtains. His pants were off before she sat down on the bed. When her rear hit the covers, he was leaning with one knee resting on the bed, his hands coming up to grasp her beneath her arms to lift her up higher on the bed. She fell back against the sheets with her heart pounding so hard she couldn't hear anything else. Levi's body covered hers and his hands traveled up her arms, shoulders and neck to tangle in her hair. He gave her hair the slightest tug and her body responded to the dominance by wantonly opening her legs. He took his hands from her hair and braced himself over her as he kissed her hard on the lips. He was by no means gentle with her mouth, his tongue darting in and out in an invitation for her to push back at him. She lifted her head from the bed to do just that, and he groaned loudly.

One hand braced his weight on the bed while the other moved down to her breast. His lips came down hot on that place, warm against her. Softly, he scraped his teeth against her, her hips lifting in response. Jesse's fingers gripped his shoulders through this sweet torment.

Levi drifted down, kissing a path from her chest to her stomach, sinking further down as he positioned himself between her legs. He put his hands on her ankles, one hand running up each leg until he reached her knees. He looked her in the eye as he pushed her legs apart. Jesse gasped in surprise as his mouth bent to her, his tongue hot and wet against her center. She tried to hold still while he tasted her, knowing he'd be inside her soon. Levi looked back up to her eyes, watching her face as he licked and sucked while he touched her inside with his fingers.

He felt her begin to quiver, and pulled back. He used her wetness to ready himself as he leaned over her. Just as she thought he was going to enter her body, he touched her hip, guiding her to roll over. She raised up on her hands and knees on the bed as she looked at him over her shoulder. Levi ran a finger along her body again, then replaced his finger with his strong length. He put a hand on her hip as he leaned forward and entered her from behind. Jesse's head snapped back and her back bowed as he pushed against her. Levi leaned over her back, tangled his hand in her hair by her scalp and kissed the back of her neck.

As he pushed into her again, and again, he said low and firm, "You are mine. I love you, Jesse. You are mine," he said, pushing into her body. The combination of sensations, hot and soft, hard and wet, pushed her over the edge. He held her in place as she came, the contractions of her body squeezing her muscles and pushing back against him. Levi nearly growled as he released inside her. Jesse felt deliciously boneless and collapsed on the bed. Levi fell beside her, wrapping her up in his arms. Unwilling to let her go for even a minute, he reached down with a foot and grabbed the blanket now at the edge of her bed. He pulled it where he could reach it and spread it over them as she chuckled low against him. Jesse rolled over to face him, still shell shocked by the power of her orgasm.

"What are you doing here anyway, Levi?" she asked, leaning toward him to give him a kiss.

"I wanted to say hi and check on you. I thought right after you got home would be best, so you could sleep the rest of the day. Although, this was better than I imagined. I thought we'd just have a cup of coffee or something," he said, smiling at her.

"Oh yes, this was much better than coffee," she said, feeling a haze begin to fall over her. "But sleep sounds nice," she said, blinking up at him through her sleepy eyes. He put his hand on her jaw and leaned in for one more kiss.

"If you feel yourself sufficiently checked on, I'll go ahead and let myself out, and lock the door behind me," he said, noting that she was already nearly asleep.

"Mmmhmm," she said, with a slight nod of her head.

"Ok, I'm going to go then," he said, stepping into her bathroom to grab her robe. "I'll put your robe on the bed in case you get any more knocks," he said, stepping towards the door as quietly as he could. He let himself out and grinned for pretty much the rest of the day.

When Jesse awoke to the late afternoon sun streaming in through the window, she felt a surge of panic rise up. A quick glance at the clock told her she still had plenty of time before she needed to pick up the boys. She looked down at her bed and saw her robe laying across it, on top of it was a little envelope. She opened up the envelope and pulled out a note and saw something land on the bed. Jesse laughed as she reached down to pick up Levi's class ring, the one she had worn the entire time they dated. She slipped the big ring on her finger and read his note.

The next one will be a diamond. Be mine. Forever.